THE CARETAKER

ALSO BY MARCUS KLIEWER

We Used to Live Here

THE CARETAKER

MARCUS KLIEWER

bantam

TRANSWORLD PUBLISHERS

UK | USA | Canada | Ireland | Australia
India | New Zealand | South Africa

Transworld is part of the Penguin Random House group of companies
whose addresses can be found at global.penguinrandomhouse.com.

Penguin Random House UK, One Embassy Gardens, 8 Viaduct Gardens, London SW11 7BW

penguin.co.uk

First published in Great Britain in 2026 by Bantam
an imprint of Transworld Publishers

001

Copyright © Marcus Kliewer 2026

The moral right of the author has been asserted.

This book is a work of fiction and, except in the case of historical fact,
any resemblance to actual persons, living or dead, is purely coincidental.

Every effort has been made to obtain the necessary permissions with
reference to copyright material, both illustrative and quoted. We apologize
for any omissions in this respect and will be pleased to make the
appropriate acknowledgements in any future edition.

Penguin Random House values and supports copyright. Copyright fuels creativity,
encourages diverse voices, promotes freedom of expression and supports a vibrant culture.
Thank you for purchasing an authorized edition of this book and for respecting intellectual
property laws by not reproducing, scanning or distributing any part of it by any means
without permission. You are supporting authors and enabling Penguin Random House
to continue to publish books for everyone. No part of this book may be used or reproduced
in any manner for the purpose of training artificial intelligence technologies or systems.
In accordance with Article 4(3) of the DSM Directive 2019/790, Penguin Random
House expressly reserves this work from the text and data mining exception.

Interior design by Alexis Minieri

Printed and bound in Great Britain by Clays Ltd, Elcograf S.p.A.

The authorized representative in the EEA is Penguin Random House Ireland,
Morrison Chambers, 32 Nassau Street, Dublin D02 YH68.

A CIP catalogue record for this book is available from the British Library.

ISBNs:
9780857509635 (hb)
9780857509642 (tpb)

Penguin Random House is committed to a sustainable future
for our business, our readers and our planet. This book is made
from Forest Stewardship Council® certified paper.

*For my Aunt Marilyn.
I miss playing board games with you.*

A NOTE FROM THE AUTHOR

This story covers themes and situations related to depression, OCD, grief, and suicide.

You will find no rosy platitudes here. Life can be rough—it's often full of suffering. And it's an awfully lonely thing wanting to stop existing—even more lonely if one fears being shunned for speaking about it. I believe discussing these topics, rather than keeping them buried, does more good than harm.

If you or someone you know is thinking about suicide, please consider visiting www.findahelpline.com.

THE CARETAKER

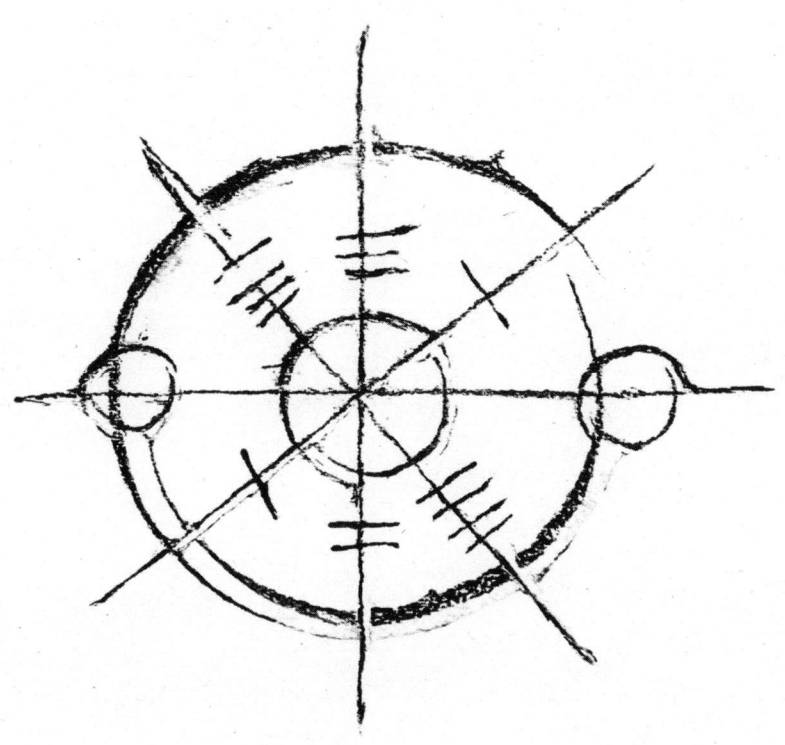

The child cast out of the village will burn it down to feel its warmth.
—Unknown

FOLLOW THE RITES

The trail of muddy footprints led off the front stoop, tracked across the gravel driveway, and disappeared into the darkened woods. David Carnswel had no choice but to follow.

He didn't want to, that much went without saying. He wanted to shut the door, lock the dead bolts, crawl back into bed with his wife of four decades, and doze off to sleep like he'd never heard those three hollow knocks to begin with. But what David *wanted* held no weight. David *needed* to follow those footprints—nothing less than the survival of humanity was at stake.

Careful not to make a sound, he stepped back into his foyer. He pulled on a pair of gum boots and an olive-green rain poncho. He wore nightclothes underneath—sweatpants and a short-sleeve tee—suboptimal attire for the weather. But he couldn't risk rummaging around up in the bedroom for a change of clothes, it might wake his wife. And if Grace woke, she would start asking her questions:

What are you doing up so late?
Was somebody knocking at the door again?

And the one that really got under his skin: *Are you sure you're feeling okay?*

Grace had long suspected David was losing it, that maybe he was in the not-so-early stages of dementia. David had suspected as much himself when the visions first struck. He'd been standing in line at Costco, shopping cart filled to the brim, when a vicious migraine thwacked into his skull like an axe into a cut of dry wood. He'd buckled over, gripping the cart for balance. A flood of nightmare imagery followed, so vivid he could almost hear it, see it playing out on the glossy concrete floors. Hallucinatory aberrations showing precisely what would happen if he failed to return home immediately. Imagery far worse than the darkest depictions of hell. He dry-heaved twice, abandoned his cart, and shoved his way through the crowds. *Get home. Now.*

Soon after, the Rites had been revealed to him in the quiet of his living room. The voice of God didn't boom from the heavens. The clouds didn't part. The Rites simply emerged in his thoughts, self-evident, as if they'd been there all along, as if he'd only forgotten them until now. The Rites he must follow to protect humankind from unspeakable suffering. The Rites that had him tracking down footprints into the dark woods at twelve in the morning.

David scooped up his military-grade flashlight—always left in a tray above the fridge. He padded out onto the stoop and peered down, stubbled chin nearly touching his chest. He flicked on the flashlight—a white circle casting onto the welcome mat between his boots.

Narrowing his eyes, he studied the wet footprints. Sneakers this time. Good omen. Or, at the very least, the lesser of many bad omens. Sometimes it was socks, and on a few occasions, bare feet. David could never predict the behavior of Visitors who opted out of proper footwear. Sneakers, at least, meant who, or whatever, he'd find at the trail's end would be relatively easy to handle. Knock on wood.

He'd taken to calling them "Visitors" as of late, these strangers from the woods. The Visitors came in many forms, and David had names for each and every type. He always named the things that made him uneasy, the things that defied his understanding. He'd once named a spot of melanoma "Frank" before the doctors removed it from his shoulder. Names gave malevolent things a shape, gave them a place in his mind to settle. It was the bumps in the night from the things he could not name that kept him awake.

He looked up from the stoop, and swept the light toward the trees. The footprints led to where they just about always did: one of the many meandering trails that went to the Windfall Inlet. Another good omen. He wouldn't have to hack his way through underbrush and blackberry brambles tonight. He released a weary sigh, his breath fogging into the cold night air, white swirls catching warm light from the living room window.

He softly shut the door behind him, and jangled out his keys. He locked the door and tested the handle. Sometimes, the Visitors tried to double back on him, get inside the house. If they got inside, things would get exponentially more difficult. And he wasn't letting Grace get pulled into this mess—the less she knew, the better.

Stuffing the keys away, he plodded down the stairs. He trudged onto the drive, gum boots crushing wet gravel as he moved alongside the footprints. A dull ache throbbed in his aging knees. During his college years he ran center field lacrosse, but nowadays he could hardly run at all. A salty breeze wafted from the looming woods ahead—the bittersweet stink of rotting trees and the Pacific Ocean.

He lingered at the threshold where the gravel driveway met the tree line—the flashlight's beam cut into the black, glistening off lichen-spattered trunks. The trees were especially drenched through tonight. Droopy and tired-looking, like they'd been dredged up from the bottom of a drained lake.

He started down the trail. The rain had stopped a while ago but drops still fell, stragglers from the branches. The slightest breeze would shake them free, and cause the trees to murmur fragments of a language man could never speak.

And the forest grew more untamed with every step deeper. Trees of different types formed gnarled ranks, enclaves of their own. A huddled clique of birch whispered rumors of the Douglas firs across the path. And the corpse of a fallen oak lay at the feet of the Douglas firs. The once mighty oak had been uprooted in a storm last spring. Now it was a rotting metropolis of bulbous knots, wood-boring beetles, and flesh-colored fungus. David stepped over it.

Three minutes or so down the trail, the night lulled into a tepid stillness, a paused frame in a movie. Quiet too. No birds, no crickets. Yet another good omen. On a wet night in the Oregon Coast wilderness, silence was business as usual. Off-putting if you're not used to it, but David had lived here all his life.

It's when the crickets and the birds were chirping, that's when he knew, without a doubt, he was in for a miserable night. Like nature itself was trying to warn him about whatever he might find at the end of the trail. So he took comfort in the silence. Solace in the lonely sound of his gum boots squelching against the path—

A rustling noise. He swiveled to his left, training his light on the source. An elk, about a stone's toss off the trail, munching away on a wilted aspen sprout. She raised her head unhurriedly. Her eyes reflected back the light's glow, and stared blankly at him. It was a stare that made him feel like just another animal out here, something to be sized up, categorized.

The elk finished chewing, swallowed, then loped off into the woods until she dissolved into the darkness. The muffled thumping of her hooves faded shortly after. It was a rare sight, an elk this far up, this close to the Windfall Inlet. Most of them settled down in the valley, closer to the river. Another slow breeze pushed through the branches above, straggling raindrops pricked against David's hair, seeped down and met his scalp—cold stings blooming into lukewarm blots.

He returned to the task at hand. The path took a sharp turn leftward, but the footprints continued straight on, directly into the woods. Odd. Not unprecedented, but strange enough to make him slow to another stop. Usually the footprints chose one or the other: off the path or on.

He raised the light once more. The underbrush here was sparse. A few spindly patches of devil's club sprouting out from a layered carpet of dead leaves and pine needles. And the trees were politely spaced apart, like introverts at a cocktail party. The footprints were trickier to clock in this terrain, but David barely took another breath before picking up the trail again. A crunched leaf here, a snapped twig there. For him, tracking came just about as natural as walking.

The footprints led in a mostly straight line, veering only to avoid the occasional tree. He noted a familiar boulder—he was nearing the property's edge. He figured it was another five hundred feet or so until he reached the roped-off boundary he'd strung up a few months back.

He should've come upon the Visitor by now. He picked up his pace.

The baritone rumble of the ocean began to hum in the dirt, hum in his bones. And with every step forward the cold grew more shameless, running dead hands against his skin. He grumbled to himself. That's what he got for throwing a rain poncho over top a T-shirt, and—

A white blur darted out from the underbrush straight ahead, moving small and quick along the ground. A rabbit. It shot right by him, making a beeline toward the house—now a glimmering speck between the distant trees.

The rabbits were new this year. Yes, there had always been wild rabbits out here, that mousy brown color, but these new ones, they looked domesticated. Many were chocolate brown, some were calico, a few solid white. The offspring of an abandoned pet, David supposed.

A faint sound leaked out from the shadows which the rabbit had fled. David tilted an ear:

Soft whimpers.

The sound might've sent a chill down most spines, but David only exhaled a sigh of relief. It was just a Weeper. A Visitor type he'd dealt with many times before: calm them down, then lead them back toward the house, away from the property line. As they follow you, don't look back. No matter what you hear, never look back. Soon, the Visitor would vanish into thin air, the sound of their footsteps ceasing. Even still, don't look back, continue to the house. As bizarre as it sounded, this was all but routine by now. Hell, he could practically do it blindfolded.

But in the few times he had failed, the times he was unable to calm the Visitors down, the times they went from whimpering to weeping, or screaming cryptic nonsense—he'd had no choice but to run. Aging knees be damned. Run back home before they could beat him there and make his life even more difficult than it already was.

He marched toward the pitiful sound, wind in his sails, but his confidence quickly gave way to a sinking sense of doubt. The sound of those whimpers, soft and wilting, was terribly, terribly familiar.

It wasn't *him*, was it? It couldn't be *him* . . .

David's legs carried him forward, one foot after the other. He stumbled into a sloped clearing, a jagged gash in the woods barely thirty feet across. At its opposite end, pacing back and forth: the Visitor.

This one wore the typical getup: blue denim jeans and a yellow rain poncho with the hood pulled up. A young man of medium build, face hidden as he stared down at the ground. He didn't react to the glare of David's flashlight, he only murmured to himself, "No, no, no . . ." His voice quivered, already on the verge of breaking into sobs.

David's heart lurched into overdrive. It couldn't be him . . .

David was ten steps into the clearing when his heel snapped a fallen branch. The Visitor whirled to face him, and all at once, David's deepest fear manifested. This Visitor was exactly who David had dreaded it would be, right down to every last detail: the sandy brown hair, the mole on his left cheek, the slight bump on the bridge of his nose. Every detail, save for one:

The eyes.

The Visitor's eyes weren't that familiar dark brown. The dark brown that had paid such close attention when David taught him how to drive, the dark brown that had blinked guiltily when he'd been caught smoking cigarettes behind the backyard shed, the dark brown eyes that could've made David surrender everything—his fortune, his home, his very life—just to look into them one last time and tell the boy how much he meant to him, but . . .

These eyes weren't a dark brown. They were a pale blue, so cold they were almost white.

The Visitor shifted its weight, blinked. "W-what do you want?"

He didn't recognize David. Of course *he* didn't. This wasn't actually him, *it* was only a Visitor, and yet . . .

David cleared his throat and did his best to collect himself. *Calm the Visitor down, don't let things escalate.* "I . . . I'm here to help." David's voice cracked.

The Visitor wiped its nose with the back of a hand, suddenly looking embarrassed, ashamed even. It put on a brave face, and said, "I'm just trying to find the lookout, but I keep getting lost." It gestured behind. "I think it's out that way, but . . . I keep ending up here."

David's gaze shifted to the woods beyond. The property line was visible, that pale, thin rope only forty feet away. "N-no, not that way," David lied. Never allow a Visitor to leave the property while in your presence, by whatever means necessary. One of many things David had learned the hard way.

"All right . . ." The Visitor blinked again. "Where is it then?"

"It's uh, the lookout? It's back here." David nodded over his shoulder, toward the house. "Follow me."

The Visitor remained rooted to the spot. "I'm pretty sure it's this way . . ." The Visitor sniffed again, turned off, and started moving toward the property line, when—

"Wait." David swallowed a lump in his throat.

The Visitor looked back at him. To most, its expression might have appeared neutral, apathetic even. But David could read every crease in the young man's face, read between those lines faster than he could read the words on a page. He could feel, right down to his core, how broken this young man was, unbearably lost and alone. Hopeless. If only David had seen it before, all those years ago, and—

"What?" the Visitor prodded.

"You . . . you don't want to go there . . ."

"So the lookout *is* that way."

". . . Yes," David admitted. "But . . ." *Follow the Rites. Calm them down.* "Whatever you're going through"—David stepped closer—"I'm here to listen. All right?"

The Visitor hesitated, seeming to consider the offer, but again it turned away, and—

"Caleb," the name shot out of David's throat like a cough. It felt strange to say it aloud. He hadn't done so in many years.

The Visitor slowed, and looked over his shoulder, brow furrowed. "How do you know my na—"

"Caleb, please, just . . ." David dared another step closer, doing his best to stay composed, to not fall apart into a sobbing mess. "Stay a bit longer," he said. "Talk to me . . . please. I can listen. Anything. The darkest thoughts, y-you don't have to be alone with them. Okay?"

Caleb looked down . . . no, not Caleb, the *Visitor* looked down, eyes tracing over the wet dirt. He looked up. "Sorry . . . I don't think this is, I need to—"

"There's nothing good for you out that way, do you understand?" David's voice cracked again. "Please, just come with me—if I can't help you, then . . . I'll show you the way back to the lookout, I swear. Just come with me first . . . We'll get out of the cold."

The Visitor considered this in silence, his face still an apathetic mask hiding so much sorrow. He kicked at the ground. With his toe, he absent-mindedly lifted a patch of dead leaves—earthworms writhed and twisted in the muck beneath. "You got a smoke?" He let the patch of dead leaves fall back into place. He wiped his hands on his poncho, first the front of his hands, then the back. "I just . . . I could use a fucking smoke." He shook out his hands and rubbed them together, breathed into clasped palms.

"Yes." David nodded. "Back this way."

"Course it is." The Visitor rolled his eyes, then scratched at his earlobe, the exact same way Caleb used to. "And how'd you know my name?"

"There were others," David lied, "down the trail looking for you, and they said your name was Caleb."

The Visitor studied David for a long beat. "How far for the smoke?"

"They're back in my truck," David lied once more, "ten minutes this way."

The Visitor chuckled bitterly, ground his teeth together. "You better not be a serial killer or something," he said. "I got a switchblade on me." He patted a jean pocket to show.

David shook his head. "My serial killing days are long behind me." He had intended the line as a joke, meant to ease the tension, but immediately felt the urge to clarify: "That was a joke."

"Yeah, I got it. Funny." The Visitor made a shooing motion toward the distant house. "Just . . . lead the way."

David gave a slight nod, turned around, and started forward.

The Visitor's footsteps followed, crunching against dead leaves about ten feet behind.

They walked in a wordless silence. David traced along his own footprints, back toward the main path. He kept bracing for the Visitor to disappear, for those following steps to go quiet like they always did, but—

"So you live out here?" the Visitor asked.

David was startled by the question, damn near almost flinched at the question. The Visitors never spoke during the walk back—well, only once: an old man with a cowboy hat and a missing eyebrow had said: "It's a cold night, ain't it?" David never replied, because the second the question had finished, the sound of the old man's footsteps ceased. So David had kept walking. *Don't look back. Never look back.*

"You live out here?" the Visitor who looked like Caleb repeated.

David considered ignoring him, but . . . maybe for just a little longer, he could pretend he was talking to . . . just a little while longer. "I . . . I do."

The Visitor's footfalls continued crunching against the leaves behind. "For how long?" he asked.

David's light crested the top of a gentle slope and revealed the dirt path ahead. "Coming on seven decades now," he said.

"That's a minute," said the Visitor. ". . . I suppose I've been out here a little longer, though."

David didn't know what to say to that. *Just keep walking. Don't look back.*

The Visitor went on, "You know . . . sometimes I forget who I am, just wake up in these woods, and—"

Instant silence. David froze and tilted an ear without looking back. He listened for the sound of footsteps, the cadence of breathing, but there was only silence. The Visitor had finally vanished. Relief, familiar and overwhelming, fell over David. It was a feeling he would always get after fulfilling a Rite. A calming rush of dopamine. As if, for just the briefest of moments, things had been made right in the world. But this time, the relief quickly turned to sadness—a deep sorrow he had not felt in a long while. A sorrow he'd almost forgotten. The kind of misery that soaks into your blood, tells you to have one more drink, tells you that it might be better to just fall asleep and never wake up, tells you that—

David shook it off, straightened up, and—

"I'm still here, David." The Visitor's voice seeped out from the darkness behind, dead leaves crinkling when it shifted its weight. A twisting lurch formed in David's gut. The tendons in his neck pulled tight, his head began to turn on reflex, but he caught himself, looked straight ahead. *Never look back.*

"I know you don't have cigarettes in the truck." The Visitor still spoke in Caleb's voice but the tone was different now, pitying. Another long and terrible silence crept by. David didn't know what to do. Keep lying? Keep walking? Stay put? He'd never had an encounter like this before.

"I know you blame yourself for what Caleb did," the Visitor said. "I just hope you know that . . ." It paused. "I want you to know that Caleb blamed you too, David. He left this world hating you more than he hated himself."

The words sailed through the air, and crashed into David's psyche like rocks hitting the surface of a frozen pond. The ice fractured, and all the things he feared the most came rushing up. All the things he never allowed to take shape, the things he could not name, the things he would do anything to ignore—drink until he couldn't see, drive until the tank ran empty, follow the Rites, follow the Rites, follow—

The leaves behind crunched with staccato THWACKS and—

Before David could react, the Visitor had pushed him to the ground with a forceful shove. Dull pain shot through David's limbs as he fumbled in the wet dirt, frantic, groping around for his light. Rotting leaves, gnarled roots, and—he grasped the flashlight's cold metallic grip. He raised it, the white circle of light glinting off the Visitor's yellow rain poncho. It was hauling off down the path, straight toward the house.

David's gasp of horror ricocheted around the dark. He lunged to his feet and started running. He ran faster than he'd run in decades, every aching bone in his body screaming at him. *HOME. GET HOME.* His light cast mad shadows as he barreled after the Visitor. Dark shapes began to move in his periphery. More Visitors. Dozens upon dozens. Some tall, some short, some thin, some broad. But all were clad in yellow rain ponchos. And all were running toward the house.

EXCITING OPPORTUNITY:
Caretaker for elderly husband urgently needed.
Three days of work. Competitive pay. Serious applicants ONLY.
If interested, please contact: carnswel54@aol.com

PART I
UNEMPLOYED TRAINWRECK

1
MACY MULLINS

Dad used to catch spiders and let them outside. Spiders were the "good bugs" he once said, they kept the "bad bugs" in line—kept the mosquitoes and the flies from achieving world domination. My childhood self was never quite sure: If spiders were so good, then why the heck did they look so evil?

"Goodness and good looks aren't the same thing, Macy."

I don't know if Dad made that quote up or borrowed it from a Disney movie, but like so many of his little sayings, it never left me. It ran through my mind as I sat in the back corner of the Coastal Connector bus, gnarled trees blurring past my window. A desperate spider clung to the rubber seam outside; an unwilling stowaway to God knows where. The spider kept trying to climb the glass, only for the wind to knock it back down, make it start from scratch. Relatable.

My eyes drifted upward and met my dreary reflection.

A curse upon the miserable fuck who chose fluorescent light for public transit. Its raw sheen was forming a frizzy halo around my curly brown hair. Fluorescent light always made my skin feel itchy—like I'd gone swimming in a slimy bog, then rolled around in fiberglass insulation to dry off. I shuddered, and rested my forehead against the clammy glass—the engine hummed in my skull, a low *vrrrrrr* that blurred into my thoughts.

My eyes flicked back and forth at the endless procession of trees sweeping on by. The final beams of daylight were streaming through their droopy branches. I released a tired sigh, breath fogging onto the glass. I pulled my sleeve over my palm, wiped away the fog, and . . . the spider was gone. Here's to hoping it landed somewhere nice. A spider village: spindly branches, shadowy nooks, all the flies you can eat. Somewhere better than here.

What was I even doing here?

I questioned every life choice, voluntary or not, that had led me to this point: en route to Brooksview Heights for a job interview.

Brooksview was one of those fancy rich coastal neighborhoods tucked safely away from all us poors. Just about the last place I wanted to be going on a Thursday night. But as a college grad saddled with a disturbing amount of debt, I had little say in the matter. None of the places back in town were hiring.

Or at least, they weren't hiring anybody like me.

I couldn't even blame them. I was never built for customer service. Despite all my best efforts to appear happy, likable, and highly employable, people always thought I was mad about something. It felt like I had a big sticker permanently plastered to my forehead, Sharpied scrawl reading: "Fuck off."

I was a mess when it came to landing interviews, and an even bigger mess when it came to landing actual jobs. In the last three months alone my inbox had collected more copy/pasted ChatGPT rejections than I could count:

THE CARETAKER

Dear (Macy Mullins),
It was a pleasure to meet you and learn more about your goals. However, unfortunately, we won't be hiring you for this position, as we discovered candidates whose experience better aligns with our company. We truly value the effort and time you have invested in the application process, and we wish you nothing but the best in your future endeavors.

Regards.

Fuck off.

Soon enough, I turned to Craigslist. Buried among the lawn mowing, the couch moving, the sketchy "looking for a friend ;)" requests—I came across a so-called "Exciting Opportunity."

Caretaker for elderly husband urgently needed.

The bare-bones description had the pull of a fisherman's lure, barbed hook and all. Vaguely ominous. And caretaking didn't even line up with my graphic design "background." I can't say why the ad grabbed my attention, maybe it came down to the same things it always did. Rent, groceries, bills. Just the things that kept me and my sister alive.

Vague as it may have been, this Craigslist posting was the last branch to grab in my twenty-two-year, lifelong plummet to rock bottom. I had shot over a response, pathetic résumé attached, and, to my shock, heard back that very same day:

Hello Macy,
Can you meet for an in-person interview Thursday evening?
7:30 PM, at 5637 Brooksview Heights.

All the best,
Grace

The commute to Brooksview was over an hour and a half by bus, plus another thirty minutes on foot. Long trip, just for an interview. I almost didn't reply, but after another day of zero bites on my other "prospects" I caved.

I sent over a quick "See you then!" and told my younger sister where I was going. God forbid I turned into another Craigslist horror story. Ha.

The bus lurched to a stop. Outside, a flickering streetlamp splashed orange light onto a lonely back-roads bus stop—a crooked shelter flanked by outdated movie ads. Nobody was here. Why did we stop?

I turned my head and peered down the aisle. That cold buzzing light coated everything in its glistening sheen. Black rubber floors, yellow handrails, grimy velvet seats. The bus was all but empty—the herd thinning out with every stop farther from the city. Now, it was down to me, the driver, and one other passenger sitting near the front.

The other passenger's back was turned to me. She wore a neon-blue rain jacket with the hood up, strings of damp red hair dangling out at the sides. Did she pull the stop cord? I waited for her to stand, shuffle away. She didn't budge.

The driver leaned, gripped a hand around a yellow lever, and wrenched it back. The front doors flopped open, and the bus lowered with a wheezing hiss.

My eyes flicked back to the crooked shelter. Out from the shadows stepped the dark silhouette of a man. He'd been standing there the whole time, hidden behind a glass box ad for *Cars 3*. The back of his heels teetered on the curb, and his head was slumped forward, staring down at the wet pavement like he was standing on the edge of a cliff, considering the jump.

"Getting on?" said the driver. She was built like a bouncer, hair tied back in a short ponytail, broad forearms covered in tattoos.

The man on the curb slowly looked up. He murmured something indecipherable. An apology? Whatever he'd said, his voice was thin, like his vocal cords might snap—rusty guitar strings wound up too tight.

He stepped off the curb and pulled himself up onto the bus, bringing with him a manic anxiety that buzzed around like a swarm of unseen flies. Even from my spot near the back, I could see how gaunt he was, skeletal almost. Dark shadows settled in the pockets of his face, and his patchy beard did nothing to hide hollow cheeks; he looked twenty and seventy years old at the same time. He steadied himself on a yellow handrail. He cleared his throat, buttoned up a dirty jacket, and fixed his tousled hair. A failed attempt to look presentable.

Normally, I would've drowned out whatever was about to follow with music, but a few weeks back I'd loaned my headphones to my sister, Jemma. She had predictably lost them. She promised to get me new ones "soon," but Jemma was even more penniless than me, so for now I was stuck listening to reality.

The driver leaned slightly away from the man, as if his chaotic energy might be contagious. She pointed at the ticket scanner and said something about fare. The man nodded like an overeager bobblehead. He started patting his pockets, making a show of searching for a ticket we all knew he didn't have. Been there, done that.

"I must've," said the man. "Oh shoot." He looked at the floor, like the ticket might be down there somewhere. He looked up, motioned at a nearby seat. "You mind if I just? I—I can spot you next time, I—"

The driver interrupted him, grumbled something that sounded like "you said that last time."

"P-please," the man stammered, "I got, I have, I need—just . . . please?" He shuffled past without waiting for an answer. The driver caught him by the elbow, pulled him back with ease, and shoved him toward the door. He caught his balance on a yellow handrail. "I can't. I have to—"

The driver jutted her pointer finger toward the exit.

The man peered over his shoulder, down at the crooked bus stop. The surrounding woods stood unmoving. Blackberry underbrush tangled up between the trees like barbed wire. In the streetlamp's orange glow, the forest felt like some monstrous nightmare waiting to pounce on unsuspecting prey. Spiderlike.

"Miss?"

I looked back to the front of the bus—the man was staring directly at me now. Why do they always lock onto me? I diverted my gaze, his tired face still stamped into my retinas—bright green eyes, strangely well-kept teeth. He probably had braces as a kid. At some point, somebody cared enough about this guy to pay for orthodontics. What went wrong—

"H-hey miss?" His thin voice butted into my thoughts. "Miss?"

I kept my eyes glued to the seat in front of me. Reading a line of Sharpied graffiti again and again:

LIVE, LAUGH, MURDER

He kept trying, looking right past the other passenger and locking onto me: "Could you spot me a couple bucks?"

I couldn't spot him a dime. Hell, I could barely afford my own transit pass.

The driver finally intervened. "Off. Now." She rose to standing, nearly a head taller than the man.

He looked down at the floor again, then looked to me one last time, wounded puppy dog eyes. I could only offer a pitying blink. He turned to the other passenger, started to open his mouth, and—

"OFF," the driver repeated.

He slinked off the bus, and started walking up the road at an uneven gait.

The driver slumped back down, pulled the door lever shut. The bus hissed back to life. The driver signaled onto the unbusied road, giving the man a wide berth as we passed.

I turned and looked through the back window. The man shrank farther and farther into the distance until the bus rounded a sloping bend, and he disappeared behind a black wall of trees. My focus shifted to the window's reflection. I furrowed my brow.

The other passenger—the woman in the blue rain jacket—had twisted in her seat. Her eyes were blurry chunks of coal in the dark glass. Unblinking. *Was she staring at me?* I could almost feel those blurry eyeballs, boring down into the back of my skull like two hand-powered drills, grinding the bone into dust. I turned to meet her gaze, but she twisted away, once again looking straight ahead. Motionless.

Late night bus weirdos, I reasoned. Only a matter of time before I joined the club. Maybe I already had. I leaned back into my seat, crossed my arms, and shut my eyes. I listened to the drone of the engine, felt its low hum against my back. Somehow, I drifted into that purgatory between sleep and waking. Nonsense imagery rose and fell in the shifting dark—phantoms of dreams and nightmares:

Grass-stained bootprints. Rushing water. The scent of fresh coffee. Diesel. Darkness. Cold, buzzing light. Glossy black plastic. Scratchy fur. Green button eyes. Darkness. The stench of vodka. Chlorine. Bluish-green carpet. Numbered rooms. Darkness. Lawn mower. White truck. Darkness. Red light. Darkness. Blue light. Red light. Blue—

"Miss."

My vision stuttered open. The driver was a few rows up, collecting litter with a garbage claw. "Last stop," she said.

I looked out the window. A dim square of a parking lot hemmed in by white pines. A glowing sign read:

Windfall Transit Center

I gazed down the aisle—the woman in the blue rain jacket was gone. Good. I hoisted up a Pikachu backpack that hadn't been replaced since middle school. Its yellow skin had long faded down to piss white, and its lightning bolt tail had been torn off in a playground scuffle. I clambered up the aisle.

The driver stepped aside, letting me pass. "You shouldn't be traveling alone after dark," she said.

"Thanks," I replied without looking back.

As my sneakers met the cracked asphalt, I pulled out my phone and tapped into Google Maps. NO SERVICE. I poked my head back onto the bus. "Hey," I said. "Which way is Brooksview Heights?"

One short trek up a dark and narrow road later, I came upon the neighborhood's entrance. It was impossible to miss. A pearly white sign, flanked by gauche Greek pillars and lit by flower bed spotlights. Golden brass letters proudly declared:

BROOKSVIEW HEIGHTS

The surrounding woods, unruly and windswept, only made the sign stick out all the more. I could already envision the three-story mansions, the perfectly manicured lawns, the luxury cars sitting pretty in every single heated driveway. Barf.

I slipped out my phone again. Google Maps was back in service here. Of course it was. Brooksview probably had its own direct line to Silicon Valley. I pinched my fingers against the cold screen, zoomed out, and . . . fantastic. Grace Carnswel's property was tucked away at the highest, farthest corner.

2
QUAINT

As I wheezed my way up the steep and winding streets of Brooksview Heights, I couldn't help but appreciate how accurate my premonitions had been: manicured lawns, three-story mega-mansions, walls and gates to fend off the masses. A strange lack of luxury cars in the driveways, though. Or, for that matter, any cars at all . . .

In fact, many of the houses were dark and looked like they'd been sitting empty. Summer homes? I could barely afford rent on my dingy ground-level apartment, these people had backup mansions.

A rustling noise drew my attention to a cluster of petunias. The petunias sat in a rounded flower bed, dead center of a recently mowed lawn. The mower's dark green lines had followed the flowerbed's curvature, perfectly spaced concentric circles.

I hadn't done landscaping in years, but still, I often found myself judging the work of other landscapers. This was a solid 9 out of 10. One point docked for leaving grass clippings on the flower bed.

The petunias rustled again, and out hopped a chocolate-brown rabbit. It was nibbling away on a stolen petal. Fight the system, I guess.

The higher I went, the larger the properties became. Many of them looked to be full-on acreages now. Grand lodges surrounded by towering pines, with guest homes bigger than most actual homes. And the steep, winding road had leveled out, straightened.

The stretches of dark forest between each property grew longer. Streetlamps became less frequent, until they disappeared entirely. Now, every time I passed a house, the distant glow of the next one was the only thing guiding me farther. Soon the smooth pavement turned to rough asphalt, and there was only darkness ahead. I checked my phone. Grace's house was allegedly three hundred yards away. I looked up and narrowed my eyes into the pitch-black nothing.

The faintest flicker of orange was shimmering between the distant trees. I continued forward, heedful. It was so dark now, I had to use my phone light to avoid tripping over potholes.

Every little sound stood out here: trees creaking like old doors slowly swaying back and forth. Branches snapping like faraway gunshots. Then, the soft pitter-patter of raindrops began to stammer in stops and starts, like the sky was on the verge of bursting into tears. It started pouring. By the time I reached Grace's lonely driveway, I felt, and probably looked, like a grumpy swamp goblin.

I took in my surroundings. This dead-end turnaround, encircled by Douglas firs, was lit by a single, moth-infested streetlamp. Beneath its orange glow was a jagged boulder, crooked numbers affixed, "5637."

The only address here.

Its gravel driveway led up through the trees and veered off into the dark. Great, another hike.

As I rounded the driveway's bend, Grace's house crept into view, and . . . it wasn't what I'd expected. Nestled into a sloping rock face, the abode was a relatively modest two-story rancher. Rectangular, with large windows all around, and wood-slat walls painted olive green. The flickering glimmer of a fireplace cast long shadows out over the surrounding trees. The house looked warm, welcoming even. Sure, the land alone likely cost over three million bucks, but compared to the rest of Brooksview Heights, it was almost quaint.

Right then, the front door swung open and out slipped a shadowy figure. The shape paced forward, off the front stoop, down a flight of concrete steps, and onto the driveway. A motion light snapped on, revealing the figure to be a young woman, probably about my age. Her arms were tightly crossed. And the closer she got, the more obvious it became: she was annoyed, angry even.

As she passed me, she met my eyes and, with a flick-of-the-wrist salute, said, "Have fun."

Tough interview?

I peered over my shoulder, watching as she marched off, leather boots crunching against the gravel. She looked a little overdressed for a caretaking gig. It made me self-conscious. Is that what people up here expected the help to wear? Was I going to lose this job because my 90s parachute jacket looked like a Value Village reject?

She climbed into a glossy black Mini Cooper and drove off. Wouldn't that be nice.

Behind me, a voice called out, "Macy?"

I turned back. An older woman was standing in the doorway, shielding her eyes from the motion light's harsh glare. Her face was hidden by the shadow of her hand.

I cleared my throat. "Ms. Carnswel?"

3
TROUBLESOME PEOPLE

Grace Carnswel held open the door, smiling patiently down at me as I ascended the concrete stairs. Grace looked to be in her late sixties, early seventies. She wore gray jeans and a scratchy-looking sweater, yet managed to retain an air of poised elegance. I sized her up to be the kind of rich person who went shopping for her own groceries, and did her own gardening instead of hiring a landscaper. Probably had a Costco membership and bought her clothes at Ross. The kind of person folks in town would describe as: "Down to earth. Worth a fortune, but you'd never know it."

These types of rich people were always a wild card. Some ended up being relatively pleasant, while others tended to be even nastier than the Rolex, spray-tan, sports-car types. It's easy to fake humility when you don't have to worry about making rent.

I slowed on the stoop, wringing out my wet hair. "Sorry I'm late," I said, "Traffic was—"

"No need to apologize," said Grace. "I know we're out of the way."

"Niceness" made me uncomfortable, especially when it came from people I didn't know. Still, I recruited the muscles of my face to form what I hoped was a convincing smile.

Grace ushered me inside and pulled the door shut. "Feel free to hang your jacket." She gestured to an old Victorian coatrack. An olive-green rain poncho was hanging from one of its hooks.

The poncho was large, almost reaching the floor, and its shiny plastic surface was streaked and spattered with long-dried mud. I pulled off my parachute jacket and hung it up beside.

"Love the colors," said Grace.

"Hm?"

"The jacket."

"Oh, thanks," I said. "It was my dad's."

The jacket was a chaotic collage of pastel greens, blues, and purples—more than a few sizes too big on me, but comfortable. Nostalgic in a bittersweet kind of way.

"Good taste," Grace said, seemingly sincere.

As I started pulling off my wet shoes, Grace drifted deeper into the house. I rose to stand and was about to follow, but a framed panorama caught my eye. It showed an ocean inlet, stormy skies, rocky cliffs, and a white sun cresting over a distant horizon. Something about the gloomy scene drew me in. My blurry reflection was superimposed over the dark clouds. God, I looked exhausted. I opened my eyes a little wider, tried to appear more awake, more employable.

"The Windfall Inlet," said Grace. "My husband took that one . . ."

I turned to look at her. She was running her eyes over the image, a hint of irritation pulling at the corners of her mouth. "It's always the first thing visitors notice. Not exactly a welcoming impression, but that's David for you."

Grace tucked a silver strand of hair behind her ear. Her gaze dropped to a glossy white rotary phone on a side table. I hadn't seen a landline phone in a minute. Let alone a 1960s relic like this.

Grace turned away and strolled farther into the living room, or at least, that's what I assumed it was. Here, everything existed in the same, open-concept space: kitchen, dining room, living room. Considering the exterior, it all looked pretty on-brand. Well-maintained mid-century furniture—a tasteful palette of soft blues, light browns, and other earthy colors. Expansive windows gave way to a view of the surrounding forest.

I wandered forward.

Wood panel walls were covered with photos. A collage of memories—most filled with happy, smiling people. The fact big happy families actually existed always weirded me out. When I was a kid the whole concept of multiple cousins, aunts and uncles, family reunions, it all seemed like stuff made up by Hollywood. What little extended family I had lived all the way up in Canada, and the one aunt who'd lived close had passed away years ago. My dad's side of the family was sparse to the point of barely existing, and my mom's side, well she walked out when I was five, so—

Dishes clanged, interrupting my rumination. I turned to see Grace rifling through cupboards in the kitchen. "Can I get you anything?" she asked. "Tea? Coffee?"

"No thanks . . ."

She stopped rifling, gave me a scrutinizing look, and said: "Are you . . . okay?"

I hated that question. It always came when I least expected. Felt like a mirror suddenly being thrust into my face, exposing a zit I didn't even know was there.

"Sorry." Grace went back to rifling. "You look . . . a little under the weather is all."

Gee, thanks.

"I'm good," I said. "Just tired." The stock answer to unexpected queries about my state of mind.

Grace started filling a kettle at the tap.

I popped my neck and tried to appear less "under the weather." Smile, Macy, SMILE. You are happy. Happy, enthusiastic, and dependable. You are great at making eye contact, super-confident and very likable, you are the best candidate for this job!

With another fake little smile glued to my face, I continued to observe my surroundings. In the far corner sat a wood-burning stove, fire roaring. Even from across the room, I could feel its radiating warmth against my skin. The fireplace was cast-iron black, with a glass door and a crooked chimney pipe leading up to the ceiling. Despite matching the overall decor here, it felt oddly out of place—like it had been torn from some remote lodge and brought here against its will.

Behind me, Grace chimed in, "Nothing beats the warmth of an old-fashioned fire, wouldn't you agree?"

I looked back and gave a noncommittal tilt of the head.

Grace was hunched over a kitchen island, flipping through a tin of herbal teas. She mumbled to herself, then turned back to the cupboards, and kept rifling.

My eyes flitted downward. An old VHS tape lay on the island. Along its side was a white sticker, with neatly written words in black Sharpie:

Do not watch, unless permitted by Ward of the House

"Please," said Grace, "make yourself comfortable." She gestured toward a beige couch. I hesitated; it probably had a price tag over ten times my net worth.

"Uhh, my clothes are still a bit damp," I said.

Grace scoffed, waved a hand. "It's just a couch."

Wary, I perched myself on the edge.

Grace set the kettle atop the stove. She turned a dial, the hollow click, click, clicks of a gas burner failing to ignite. With a grumble, she reached above the fridge, her hand blindly searching through a wooden tray until it found a lime-green wand lighter. She used the lighter to start the burner, then set the lighter back into the tray.

She strode toward me, settled down into a brown leather armchair, and lifted a printed copy of my résumé from the coffee table.

"So . . ." She squinted at the résumé. "Macy, uh . . . Mew . . . luns?" She butchered the pronunciation in a way that was almost impressive. "That's . . ." She grimaced. "Certainly an interesting surname."

I fought back my deeply ingrained instinct to reply with sarcasm, to say something snarky and pointlessly combative. For the sake of employment, I kept my politeness filter on. "Yeah, I think it's Irish."

"How is it pronounced?"

"Mull-ins."

"Well, Macy *Mullins*. Why are you here?"

Because I'm broke and desperate.

"Because, I just, I like rewarding work, that helps people."

Grace, without skipping a beat, said, "You and me both." Then she went off on a tangent. "I used to volunteer at a homeless shelter downstate. My husband never understood why. He believes giving people 'handouts' only causes more trouble. But I always remind him what they say about troublesome people . . ." She trailed off, meeting my stare. I maintained eye contact. *How long is too long? Should I blink? Why isn't she saying anything? Is she seriously waiting for me to ask:*

"Oh." I cleared my throat. "What do they say?"

With a peppy smile, Grace answered, "Troublesome people are often people in trouble."

I nodded—it was actually a pretty good saying.

Grace, back on task, ran her eyes up and down my work history. "So you have a certificate in graphic design?"

"Mhm."

She frowned, flipped over the résumé, and flipped it again. "I don't see any design work on here," she mused aloud.

I couldn't tell if she was being rude on purpose or simply lacked self-awareness. Maybe somewhere in the middle.

"I uh . . . I ended up choosing a different path." That was another way of saying: Nobody wanted to pay me for my labor. That's not to say people didn't offer me "great opportunities." After I graduated there were plenty of requests to work for "experience" and/or "exposure." But, shock of shocks, landlords don't accept "experience" in lieu of rent.

Maybe you just suck at graphic design, Macy. Ever thought of that? My inner monologue always ensured that I stayed "humble." Humble and miserable.

Grace glanced down again. "And you were a caretaker for the last three years?" She looked up.

"Yeah, it was just part-time, freelance, mostly," I lied.

"Freelance." Grace clicked her tongue. "Are you registered?"

"No, not yet. Working toward it." Another lie. I wasn't working toward anything. Sure, I knew some of the basics, but in reality, I wasn't really a caretaker at all, at least not in the technical sense. Three years back, I'd become the legal guardian to my younger sister. Not that she needed, or wanted, much guarding. Never made a dollar doing it, yet sometimes, especially in those early days, it sure as hell felt like a job.

Grace shifted her weight, eyes back to the résumé. "And before that you were . . . mowing lawns?"

"Landscaping," I corrected. "Maintenance landscaping. I was the lead supervisor."

"So you supervised the lawn mowing?"

"Sure." I breathed out my nose, again unable to tell if she was being rude on purpose.

I had been second in command at Mullins Mowing. Dad's very own one-truck, two-employee business. Of course, both employees were his daughters, and of course, I left those particular details off my résumé. I also left off a three-month stint at Starbucks, and a string of other jobs that ended in catastrophe.

Grace, already out of questions, looked around, a forlorn expression creasing the lines of her face. "You're probably wondering where my husband is."

I hadn't been. Not until she brought it up. Considering it was a caretaking job, I'd just assumed he was bedridden somewhere.

"Well . . ." Grace turned back to me, weighing her next words carefully. "I should've been more up-front about this in the ad, but . . . three months ago my husband . . . he actually passed away."

I leaned back, felt my brow wrinkle with befuddlement. All I could get out was a confused: "Oh . . . ?"

"It's been tough," Grace smiled sadly, "but we were long prepared for it." She pressed a thumb into her palm, kneading small circles.

Clammy unease shuddered over me, like a bunch of tiny insects had emerged from the pores of my skin.

Grace studied me, picking up on my obvious discomfort. "I really hate to surprise you like this," she said, "but if you let me explain, you'll understand why I had to . . . bend the truth a little."

A little? My toes curled. If I hadn't been so desperate for money, I would've walked out right then and there.

Her cheeks flushed red. "Don't worry, I'm not asking you to take care of a ghost or anything like that . . ." Her knee bobbed up and down. "I just need someone to maintain a general upkeep of the house while I'm away this weekend. That's all."

"So . . . a house-sitter?"

She nodded, face turning redder. "Why didn't I just say that in the ad, right?"

"Right . . ."

"David, my husband," she continued, "he was a little eccentric, to put it mildly. He had very specific upkeep routines for our property, and on his deathbed, he made me promise to keep them going. I've been doing that, diligently, but it's getting tedious. I need a break, and I don't want to miss my granddaughter's birthday. She's all the way down in Florida, you see."

I crossed my arms and ground my teeth together. "I still don't understand. Why not just put out an ad for house-sitting?"

"Well," she gave a thoughtful pause, "as you can imagine, requests like that tend to attract . . . undesirable candidates. But, more importantly, though the upkeep routines themselves are rather innocuous, my husband's reasoning behind it all might disturb some. Right up until his passing, he truly believed his routines were preventing certain . . ." She searched for a word, and settled on: "consequences."

More than a few questions shuffled through me. Morbid curiosity prompted me to ask, "And those consequences are?"

She grimaced again. "Unfortunately, that's privileged information, only for those who accept the position. Same goes for the routines themselves."

And there's the rub. There's the reason Mini Cooper stormed out in a huff. No, who am I kidding, she probably stormed out the second she learned about the dead husband. If only I was financially stable enough to do the same.

Grace sighed, again reading my expression. "I know. I know. But David was very adamant: the fewer people who know about all this, the better." Another somber memory passed over her face. "Of course, none of his reasons have any real backing—simply the quirks of an unwell mind. Complete nonsense."

My politeness filter was slipping. "Then why bother?"

Her brow furrowed. "Pardon?"

"If it's all nonsense, and your husband is . . ." I stopped myself from saying *dead*. "Why keep following his routines at all?"

Grace leaned back, crossed her legs, and tapped a finger against the leather armrest. Her left eye twitched. "Because I made a promise to a dying man," she said, "and I'm a woman of my word."

That hung in the air for a good three seconds.

"Fair enough," I said. "Sorry, this job isn't for me." And with another fake smile, I pushed off the couch and marched away. Everything else aside, there was no way I'd agree to a job when I didn't even know what it was. For all I knew they'd be sacrificing me to the Devil.

Grace lingered in her chair, watching me go, looking like she wanted to say something else, but was unable to get it out. Her disappointment was almost audible, like a chorus of tiny violins had begun to play. I was probably just one more rejection in a long line of interviews. Not my problem.

I stepped around the corner and retreated into the foyer. As I pulled on my dad's old parachute jacket and started tying up my sneakers, Grace hovered into my periphery. Right on cue, she chimed in, "Oh, I forgot to mention."

I looked over my shoulder.

"I'm sorry to be so persistent," said Grace, "I really am. And I completely understand if the job isn't right for you. Believe me, I'm painfully aware of how strange this all sounds, I hate to be so vague. I just . . . I really have a good feeling about this interview."

A good feeling? About that dumpster fire?

And then, with a gentle smile and a pleasant voice, she went for my weak spot. "Would you at least be willing to hear what the pay is?"

4
DESPERATE TIMES

I sold out.

Grace offered me six thousand bucks. For *two* days' work. Half up front, the rest after the weekend. BUT WAIT, there's more: depending on how well I followed the routines, a three-thousand-dollar bonus on top. Nine grand total. With a deal like that, not selling out would've been selling out.

Grace had even paid to Uber me back home. "Oh my," she had said. "You took transit, all the way out here? Poor thing. I didn't even know the bus still ran this far . . ."

"Yeah, my car's in the shop." I lied again. Part of me was scared if she learned how broke I truly was, she'd call the cops on me or something. *Yes, Officer, you heard me correct: there's a filth-stained brokey in my home.*

Now I was staring out the Uber's window, watching the dark woods sweep by again, appreciating the heated leather seats and the lack of cold buzzing lights.

The car KER-THUMPED over a pothole, and my Pikachu backpack

jostled in the corner of my eye. A rectangular shape was pushing out from Pikachu's belly, like it was about to shit a brick. Right, the VHS tape. With the whole nine grand of it all, I'd almost forgotten about the job itself. The so-called "upkeep routines."

After I had agreed to the position, Grace handed the VHS to me and said, "This will detail everything you need to know." Apparently, she hadn't even seen it herself. "David already explained it all to me in person." She'd paused. "And, to be honest, I'm not sure if I'm ready to see him again quite yet, even if it is just a video . . ."

She had told me David would've insisted that I watch it alone, reminded me of his belief that "the fewer people who knew about the upkeep routines, the better." But she'd said all this with a tinge of patronization, constantly reiterating that it was all "superstitious nonsense." Still, I couldn't help but sense a nagging hint of doubt behind her words—like an atheist worrying that maybe, just maybe, hell was actually real. After all, she was taking it seriously enough to pay my sorry ass nine grand . . .

The upkeep routines couldn't be that bad. Right?

bzz. bzz. bzz.

My phone buzzed against the side of my leg. I slipped it out and tapped the screen. A notification from my bank, simply labeled: "IMPORTANT." My stomach dropped. Was my balance below ten dollars again? Did I get hit with another overdraft fee? The bank loved to charge me money when I didn't have any.

My finger hovered over the notification.

If I pressed it, my banking app would open—something I actively avoided at all costs. DON'T LOOK. Those two words just about summed up the entirety of my financial planning. I'd even memorized the precise location my checking balance would appear on-screen. That way I could cover it with my hand whenever I needed to open the app: if you can't see it, it can't hurt you. Little-kid logic. A-toddler-covering-their-face-to-hide-from-a-monster logic. But the monster always found a way to rear its ugly head.

Anytime I used my card for anything, my heart nearly exploded from panic. The seconds after tapping, BEEP . . .

"PROCESSING" . . .

and . . .

"APPROVED."

Hallelujah, praise the Devil.

Of course, these days "DECLINED" was becoming the default. And somehow, even that was its own little "blessing"—particularly cruel card machines loved to hit me with:

"DECLINED—INSUFF FUNDS"

Go ahead, say it louder for the people in the back. At least with "DECLINED" I could mumble out a "Huh, my card's a little wonky."

"Yeah," the clerk would say, "our machine does that all the time." Both of us knowing full well my current balance was less than a two-dollar bottle of Pepsi.

I tossed my financial baggage to the side, clenched my teeth, pressed the bank notification, and . . .

$3,000 wire transfer received from Carnswel54@aol.com
Note: payment 1 of 3 for housesitting & upkeep

Three thousand dollars.

It was the highest amount of money that had ever sat in my checking account at one time. And only the first of three payments at that.

I actually did a stupid little fist pump right there in the Uber. Felt like I'd just pulled off the heist of the century. I thought of all the things I could buy: new headphones, concert tickets, a backpack that wasn't falling apart—

Slow down there, Macy, don't get ahead of yourself.

As per usual, my good mood was cut off at the knees by that little voice in my head. A voice that I usually drowned out with music. An ever-present companion that always ensured I never felt too happy for too long: *Whoa there, Macy Mullins, careful now, you let that feeling get too big and it just might turn to joy. And we all know what joy turns to . . .*

Shit. Joy always turns to shit.

You have responsibilities, Macy, never forget that. You have bills to pay. You have a younger sister to provide for.

Grudgingly, I tapped back into my banking app. I paid off our energy bills, Venmoed our landlord (who'd done the courtesy of leaving an eviction warning on our door a few days ago), and made a grocery list. I tucked away my phone, and crossed my arms.

Maybe I could treat myself, just this once.

I pulled out my phone, added headphones to my list, and—

Don't forget Jemma's asthma inhaler. Grumbling, I deleted "headphones" and put down "inhaler." My sister's prescription had been sitting unpaid for at a Walgreens for six weeks now. Ninety-eight dollars.

My forehead started aching. I rubbed my temples, slow circles that did nothing to soothe the pain. The three grand had barely been sitting in my account for five minutes and it was already half gone.

My phone buzzed again. I tapped the screen.

JEMMA: Are u dead?
MACY: Not yet.
JEMMA: Shucks. ETA?
MACY: 45m
JEMMA: Cya soon, hate u lots!
MACY: Hate you too :')

5
BAD WEATHER

The few times I'd ventured out of state, nearly every conversation about my hometown went the same way:

"Where you from?" people would ask.

"Oregon," I'd say. "Salem, Oregon."

"Oh, the witch town."

"No. That's Salem, Massachusetts."

"Huh . . . didn't know there was two Salems."

And that's where most conversations about my hometown ended. Folks always seemed vaguely let down that I wasn't from the place "witches" were burned at the stake by crazed zealots. I suppose I was a little let down too. It's a good hook.

I used to be all defensive about my hometown—Salem proud—back when I was still a kid, and had the energy to care about such things. Salem was my favorite place in the entire world. But it seemed like most people outside Oregon didn't even know we existed. They all knew Portland, but Salem? How far is that from Portland?

"Salem is actually the capital city of Oregon," Childhood Macy would often declare unprompted. "We're right next to the Enchanted Forest Theme Park that was built almost entirely by one guy, and we have a bookstore with a cat." *All true, my sweet little Macy, but we are in the middle of watching a movie.*

My passion for Salem died alongside most of my other childhood passions: Duplo, Disney, and a stuffed rabbit named Doc. All relegated to the back corner of a dusty storage closet. Nowadays, the few times people asked me where I'm from, I'd just say "Oregon." If they prodded further, I'd reply with a flat: "Middle of Oregon." I no longer had the energy to educate strangers on the geographical history of witch burnings.

Maybe I'd turned into a cynical asshole, but when it comes to Salem, think of any highway town in America, and the image your mind conjures up will be close enough. Wheat fields, a Walmart, a downtown core with some old brick buildings, and a shopping mall with a Best Buy and a TJ Maxx. Throw in a few small businesses that boarded up their windows after Walmart moved in. Survival of the cheapest.

And the sky in Salem was gray for most days of the year. Sometimes the sky was gray for so long I forgot it was actually blue. But I never minded that part. I like "bad" weather. I like waking up to the sound of rain hitting the window. Makes me feel less guilty being a miserable wretch all the time. The sun is an overzealous extrovert, forever screaming things like: "Turn that FROWN upside DOWN." And "UP and at 'EM, camper. Let's JUMP out of bed and JUMP into a POSITIVE ATTITUDE."

Fuck the sun.

Give me rain, give me clouds, give me a dreary day inside with nothing to do but curl up on the couch, play video games, and rewatch *Over the Garden Wall*.

The click, click, click of the Uber's turn signal pulled me out of my brooding. My exit was up ahead. I looked out over the highway's shoulder, a flooded field stretching to a pitch-dark horizon. The outskirts of Salem.

An old hotel sat along the edge of that field. The Hawthorne Hotel. It had been boarded up last year because the field kept flooding. Its walls were covered in graffiti tags now, as if the building had walked into a tattoo parlor and asked for every piece in the book. Jemma called it the "Post Malone Inn," said a warlock had cursed the man to forever live as an abandoned hotel. My sister loved coming up with weird metaphors. Runs in the family, I guess.

A Denny's sat next to the Hawthorne. It had survived a few months longer than the hotel, but was boarded up all the same. Dad used to take us there for breakfast on special occasions. Miss that.

The Uber rounded onto the exit. The car rattled against the rougher asphalt as we passed a block of foreclosed homes. A giant billboard for yet another condo development loomed over the gloomy houses like an executioner. Gentrification creeping in from the north, a slow-moving alien invasion.

The billboards always looked more or less the same: AI-generated yuppie couples with bleached white teeth, dead-eyed golden retrievers, and happy children playing tennis. May as well add a pet unicorn, that would seem just as attainable. Come five years and this would all be Starbucks, Whole Foods, and corporate-owned rentals six times above whatever I could afford.

The Uber slowed to a stop in front of my place. "This it?" said the driver. He sounded skeptical. Most of the buildings in this corner of town looked straight-up abandoned, my apartment included: a one-story L-shaped building sitting squat and haggard before a gang of sorry-looking trees. It was a repurposed motel—the kind of motel you'd see in a 1980s slasher film. Brown water stains streaked down its white stucco face like cheap mascara on a rainy day.

"Miss?" the driver prodded.

"This is me," I said, gaze still fixed to the place I called home. I snatched up my backpack and stepped out. The Uber drove off before I could even reach the crooked sidewalk.

I strode past my apartment's outdoor "swimming pool"—it hadn't been functional in God knows how long. A flesh-pink tarp was draped over the deep end, like it was trying to cover a corpse at a crime scene. The tarp's far corner was peeled back, exposing an inky layer of sludge beneath—the kind of murk that made me think of Tarman from *Return of the Living Dead*.

My eyes flicked to a rusty sign posted above what was left of the diving board:

NO LIFEGUARD ON DUTY

I reached my stoop and dug out my keys. As I turned the lock, I couldn't help but notice the remnants of masking tape goop on the door's white finish. That's where our landlord had left the eviction warning. I had stashed it away before my sister could see. Still got flashbacks every time I came home, though.

It's a scary, violent feeling being threatened with eviction. And the letter's matter-of-fact legalese made it all the scarier. I was nothing more than a customer unable to pay their dues, and this was purely a business decision:

Ms. Mullins,
Unfortunately, we have not been able to resolve your overdue balance.
Failure to respond in a timely manner will result in the eviction of you and any other tenant(s). If we are forced to take legal action, further costs and fees may be added to your outstanding balance. This will have a detrimental impact on your credit record, which can make it challenging to attain rental housing in the future.
Please consult with a legal professional to understand your rights.
Thank you for your prompt attention on this matter.

Well, I'd paid it off for the time being—the Mullins sisters lived to fight another day. With my fingernail, I scraped off the last bit of masking tape goop and flicked it away into the shadows. I muttered to myself and shuffled inside.

Home sweet home.

6
ATTACK

Our studio apartment was barely bigger than a one-car garage. Two hundred and ninety square feet of brown shag carpet, puke-green walls, and a white stucco ceiling. It had a nook of a foyer, flanked by a storage closet, and a bathroom with a standing shower that never went above lukewarm.

I pulled the front door shut, and turned the lock. I hunched to one knee and started untying my sneakers. "Jemma?" I called out. No response. Only the muffled quarrels of our next-door neighbors.

Our TV was on, just out of view, muted. The only source of light. Its bluish glare threw watery shadows behind every pile of clutter. Clutter I'd nearly grown blind to, just like the faint smell of mold. "Jem?" I set my sneakers onto a shoe rack and pushed off my knee to stand. I hung up my backpack and drifted forward. Jemma's go-to spot, our pullout couch, was empty. We'd found the couch on the curb a week after we moved in—somebody had spray-painted "FREE" in red on the back side.

I looked to the TV, an old CRT set we'd also dragged off the curb.

Looney Tunes played on its shiny glass screen. Elmer Fudd peered down a black pit while Bugs Bunny snuck up from behind with exaggerated tiptoe movements, and an oversized mallet. Before Bugs could flatten Elmer, I reached for the remote, switched off the TV. Darkness.

I fumbled for the nearest light switch and CLICK . . . nothing. Right, faulty wiring. Our landlord always ignored repair requests. Of course he's on top of doling out eviction threats, but God forbid he ever has the time to actually fix anything. With no other light source in arm's length, I switched the TV back on, its watery glow once again filling the room.

I tossed the remote onto the couch and looked to our kitchen. No Jemma.

From the foyer, a quick and dull scrape rang out. Metal against metal. I turned back and leaned to get a better look. No Jemma in the foyer, but . . . the bathroom mirror caught my eye. The shower curtain was pulled shut, blue TV light shimmering on its polka-dot surface. There was something uniquely menacing about the sight. Like a malevolent presence was standing on the other side—that or an unbelievably irritating younger sister.

"Jemma?" I grit my teeth. When we were kids, Jemma used to hide on me, jump out and scream "Ack ATTACK" when I least expected it. But Jemma was seventeen now. Not a full-blown adult, sure, but old enough to not act like a toddler.

"Jem." I cleared my throat. "If you Ack Attack me, we're both gonna be in the news tomorrow."

More silence. Only the low hum-buzz of an overhead vent. Even the neighbors had stopped quarreling. I kept my gaze locked to that curtain, tension throbbing at the nape of my neck.

I felt stupid for getting so worked up over nothing, but . . . weird thoughts surface when I find myself in quiet and restless places. Notions from the deepest corners of my brain stir awake and crawl their way up into the living room, whispering stories of ghosts and monsters. Like right then I was thinking about the shower curtain's polka-dot pattern, red against gray. Clown skin, Jemma once called it. Made me imagine a former tenant had hunted down some carnival creature, hung up its hide here to dry. Maybe that creature would come back, skinless and shrieking, looking to reclaim its pelt. Weird, I know.

All that aside, when the shower wasn't in use, we always kept the curtain open. House rule. Ever since we were kids, we'd both had a creeping feeling that something terrible materialized behind the closed curtains of unused showers. We, or at the very least *I*, knew it was a bullshit superstition, but it was a superstition we never fully grew out of.

I narrowed my eyes against the polka-dot pattern, as if I could will myself to see through the plastic. Embarrassed, I finally shook off the paranoia, stomped over to the bathroom, flicked on the light, whipped open the curtain, and . . . empty.

I stepped back, groaning with annoyance. I turned to the only hiding spot left: the storage closet across the foyer. Sure enough the door was cracked, a thin slit of dark. I marched over, swung it open, and . . . no dumb sister here either.

I reached up and pulled on the light string. A single hanging bulb flickered to life, casting a cold fluorescent glow onto a precarious wall of cardboard boxes. Boxes filled with memories from our old house. Things we lugged around from place to place, things we didn't have the heart to pawn off. Not yet anyway—

"ACK"—the bathroom door swung open and Jemma leapt out from the corner behind—"ATTA—"

Before she could get out the second half of "attack," the door ricocheted off the shoe rack, whipped back, and bonked her on the nose.

Justice.

7
KLEPTO

Jemma slumped onto the couch, head tilted all the way back, plugging up a nosebleed with scratchy toilet paper.

"Seriously, Jem." I strode into the kitchen and pushed aside countertop clutter. "Are you three years old?" I hoisted my backpack onto the counter, unzipped it, started digging through.

Jemma, voice nasally through the tissue, said, "Would've got you if it wasn't for that meddling door."

"You're lucky *I* didn't break your nose first."

"It's not broken."

"Too bad."

Jemma shuffled farther back onto the couch, still looking up at the ceiling. She ran a hand through her hair, or rather, her lack of hair. She'd shaven it down to a buzz cut a week or so prior.

"Cheaper than Great Clips," she had said.

"I could've cut it, you know."

"Sure you could. Heck, last time you cut my ear too." She'd pointed at her ear, a pale nick of a scar.

I didn't argue. "Suits you, though," I had said. "Tired of taming the curls?" Jemma had dark brown curly locks, just like mine, just like Dad's.

"Nah." She'd shaken her head. "Miss Bamford said I'd look prettier with it longer, said people wouldn't think I was a boy all the time. So I buzzed it off just to see the stupid face on her face." She had cracked her mischievous little smirk.

Back in the present, I dug into the deepest corners of my pack, and fished out the VHS tape Grace had given me. It was cold to the touch, the outside chill lingering on its black and grainy surface. I set it down on the countertop, once again dreading whatever it might contain.

I considered bringing it all up to Jemma, but I hated being told I was wrong, even when I knew I was. *Especially* when I knew I was. My sister was the type of person who had no qualms calling me an idiot. No qualms immediately telling me if a new partner was a piece of shit, whether I was ready to hear it or not. She'd said of my first boyfriend: "That guy is not a human being, Macy, he's a bunch of little red flags stacked up in a trench coat." She usually ended up being right, but . . .

I turned back. Jemma's head was still craned, eyes on the ceiling as she waited for the bleeding to stop. I breathed out my nose. Part of me almost laughed. It would've been a humorless, agitated sound, but a laugh nonetheless. Hadn't seen her stupid goofball side come out in a long while. Sometimes forgot she even had it.

Jemma removed the tissue from her nose and leveled her head. She gave a thumbs-up: nosebleed cured. She met my gaze, clocked my annoyance, then quickly diverted, like a dog in trouble. "I got you a present." She motioned at our coffee table. There sat a brand-new, still-in-the-box pair of wireless headphones.

"I know I lost your old ones," Jemma said, "so I got these today, after school."

"Is that so . . ." I lifted the box, and turned it over like a private eye studying an unexpected piece of evidence. The cardboard, shiny and plastic-wrapped, was *almost* in mint condition. There was a thumb-sized hole near the barcode. Precisely in the place they would put those little security tags. "How much it set you back?" I asked.

"Hmm?"

"What'd it cost."

"Oh?" She tugged on her earlobe. "It was on sale."

"How. Much."

She picked at a loose thread on the couch armrest. "After the, after the sale . . . only like twenty bucks, yeah around twenty bucks give or take."

I checked the brand: Sylvo Sound. Fancy stuff, sixteen-hour battery life, high-res audio, real metallic finish. I'd never seen a pair for less than two hundred flat.

My sister broke the silence with a terribly inaccurate impression of me: "Wow, Jem," she said, "thanks for the gift, you're the best sister ever and—"

"Jemma." I held up the box, then set it down. "Thought we were done with all the klepto shit."

"Okay, first off, klepto is an offensive term." She blinked at me through her big round glasses, her cheeks turning a guilty shade of red. "And it wasn't stealing." She rolled off the couch, slinked into the kitchen, and started rifling through the sparse cupboards.

Jemma had a thing with shoplifting. Sometimes she stole necessities, but most times she stole for the sake of stealing.

"Jem," I said. "Taking something without paying for it is the definition of stealing."

"It's Walmart." She stretched an arm into a high cupboard and stood on her tiptoes. "They steal wages through profit and stuff. So . . . I'm just balancing the scales." She jimmied out a nearly empty box of Lucky Charms.

"Okay, Robin Hood." I crossed my arms. "And what happens when you get caught?"

"God, Macy." Cereal box in hand, she dropped back to her heels. "You're such a friggin' *square* now."

"Jem, I can't have you ending up in juvie or God knows where else. Prison? I mean, you're almost eighteen." I rubbed my temples. "How much have you stolen this week alone?"

"Only like . . ." Jemma slouched back toward the sofa. "Three things . . . ten or twelve things." She collapsed down in her usual spot, and started digging through the long-expired cereal, picking out marshmallows like she was panning for gold. She glanced in my direction again, met my death stare, and looked away. "All right, fine." She made her eyes go wide with annoyance. "No more stealing." She relented.

"Good . . ."

Jemma tilted her chin at the headphones. "So I'll take those back then?" The slightest hint of a smirk played at the corner of her mouth. She already knew my answer:

"Nah." I shook my head. "You owed me, anyway."

I held up the headphones again, ran my fingers over the fancy white box. Even I had to admit, they were pretty dang nice, but: "This is the absolute *last* thing you steal, all right? I can't afford to bail you out of jail."

"I'm done, retired, swear to God." Jemma raised a pinkie finger, then leaned back and cracked a smile. "I knew you'd like them, though." She scooped up the remote and switched the TV on, back to watching *Looney Tunes*. "Oh right," she said, munching away on a scant handful of dry marshmallows. "How'd your Brooksview thing go?"

My eyes swept to our kitchen counter, the VHS tape. A festering obligation I'd been pretending wasn't there. "It was . . ." I didn't really know what it was. I mean, I was already three grand richer than I'd been that morning. Well, one grand richer after I paid off the bills and everything, but still.

"It was . . ."—I landed on the word—"decent."

Jemma dug into the cereal box one last time, came up with a handful of stale bits and dust. She shook them back in and set the box aside. "So you got the gig?"

"Yeah . . ."

"Nice!"

Jemma slid a bag of blue licorice from her pocket, and started chewing away on a strand. She had always been a chewer: gum, hoodie-strings, fingernails. Didn't matter where she was, or what was happening, she always found something to nibble on. Lately, it was the licorice, perpetually staining her lips and teeth with blue. "How's the pay?" she asked.

"Decent," I understated.

"Cool." She finished a strand of licorice, pulled out a new one. "I started working on my résumé again by the way."

"Yeah?"

Jemma was even more of a job interview train wreck than I was. Not to mention she had zero references after she got fired from TJ Maxx for shoplifting. And even if she landed another job, she could only work evenings and weekends thanks to school. But she was trying at least. I appreciated that much.

My sister was still glued to the TV, chewing away as the blue light reflected off her round glasses, concealing her hazel eyes from view. Elmer Fudd, double-barreled shotgun in hand, was sneaking up on Bugs Bunny now. "So . . ." Jemma took another bite of licorice. "When do you start?"

"This weekend." I wandered over to the kitchen counter.

"Right," said Jemma, "and it's like a caretaking thing?"

I lifted the VHS, turned it over in my hand. "House-sitting . . ." I ran a finger over the Sharpied sticker:

Do not watch unless permitted by Ward of the House

Jemma looked over, forehead wrinkled. "I could've sworn you said it was careta—" Mid-word, her eyes dropped to the VHS. "What's that?"

8
STUFF

We actually owned a VCR. Used to be our dad's pride and joy, along with his collection of nearly two hundred films. Now all of it was gathering dust in our storage closet. Just more things we didn't have the heart to pawn off. I yanked on the light string. The bulb flickered to life once more, buzzing angrily.

Jemma hovered behind me, both of us craning our necks up at the precarious wall of cardboard boxes. None were labeled. After the bank foreclosed on Dad's house, we threw everything we had into whatever boxes we could find, lugging it all off like fugitives on the run.

I set a wobbly footstool on the vinyl floor.

"So . . ." Jemma nibbled away on another piece of licorice. "This woman just straight-up lied to you about her husband being alive?"

"Yeah, but . . ." I set one foot onto the stool, and pressed my weight down, testing its strength. "She didn't want weirdos showing up to throw parties at her place—"

"Didn't want weirdos? Yet she posted on Craigslist?"

"Look." Deciding the stool was strong enough to hold my weight, I stepped up, and reached to the top of the stack. "I'm not going to argue, it was weird, she was weird, but old rich people are weird, and . . ."

"And what . . . ?"

I slid out a filing box with something hefty inside. My shoulders tensed as I hoisted it down. "She didn't seem one hundred percent there . . . you know?"

"No, I don't know."

"I mean her husband only died a few months back. I think she's still . . . processing things." I handed the box to Jemma and said: "Careful, it's heavy."

Jemma grunted as she took the box from me. "Bro," she said, "you are going for the gold in mental gymnastics." She knelt down, popped open the box, and tilted her head. A shabby old stuffed rabbit sat atop a bunch of Youth League soccer trophies. Jemma held up the rabbit, turned it over. It was Doc, my prized childhood stuffie. He was missing an ear, and he'd been gutted of his cotton innards after a dog had snagged him from me on a kindergarten field trip. His torso looked like a torn and dirty rag, but his head was still perfectly round with big green buttons for eyes. I used to fall asleep holding him close every single night.

I held out an open palm.

Jemma handed Doc over, and started sifting through the soccer trophies.

Doc felt so much smaller than I remembered. His fur was scratchy to the touch; it had melted when my childhood self had thrown him in the dryer on a rainy day. I ran a finger over the cold plastic edge of a green button eye. Foggy memories began to surface—*bluish-green carpet, numbered rooms—*

I set Doc aside.

Jemma was still rifling through the trophies: "Mullins Mowing Soccer Tykes." Dad had sponsored our team back when his business was doing well. Back when he was still . . . Maybe digging through all these relics from better days wasn't in Jemma's best interest. Let alone mine, but, "Hey," I said, "I can do this on my own if . . ."

Jemma frowned up at me. "If what?"

"If it's, you know, memories."

"Memories?" Her frown turned into a devilish smirk. "God, you're such a crybaby."

I smirked too. Gallows humor, for better or worse, got us through a lot. "Whatever," I said. "Just don't come whining to me when you can't sleep tonight."

Jemma shrugged. "It's . . . just a bunch of stuff." She lifted up a trophy, read the plaque, and cringed. "Why do we even have these still? We were such little losers." She held it up for me to see. It was a "Recognition Award" (a.k.a. participation trophy), complete with a photo of our smiling team—a photo that Dad himself had taken with a disposable camera. I could almost taste the sliced oranges from that day, smell the fresh cut grass, feel my kneecaps stinging from a clumsy dive, and—

Without ceremony Jemma tossed the trophy back in the box and popped the lid on. She smacked her hands together in a dry CLAP, and looked up at me. "Okey dokey, NEXT."

We dug through box after box, memory after memory, until finally my hand, reaching, stretching into a shadowy nook, grasped the prize. Bulky, metallic, rectangular—bingo. I pulled and yanked, but the VCR was caught on something. Unable to see shit, I tried to maneuver it around, twist, pull—nope. Twist, pull—nope. My cheeks flushed hot. "Come on, motherfucking-stupid-fucking-fuck." I continued fumbling blindly, balancing on the stool, almost there, just about got it, twist, pull, it caught once more, but this time I powered through, wrenching back with all my strength—

The VCR broke free, whipped back, and flew from my grip.

Everything turned slow motion, the hefty player sailing straight toward Jemma's dumbstruck face, eight pounds of metallic bulk about to break her nose for real when—I caught it at the last second, nearly toppling from the stool in the process. A breathless, frozen moment, both of us staring blankly at each other until I broke the quiet: "Saved your life, dude."

"Nah, doesn't count." Jemma adjusted her glasses. "You're the one who dropped it, so it just cancels out." She spun on her heel and strode off toward the couch.

Ungrateful brat.

◆

Turned out we needed RCA cables too. So after another fifteen minutes of digging through bittersweet memories, we were all set. I went to pop in the tape, but stopped short. "Oh right . . . technically I'm supposed to watch this alone."

Jemma scoffed, incredulous. "No way, not after all that."

I looked back. She was sprawled across the couch, staring at me through those big round glasses, munching away on another strand of blue licorice. I knew she was gonna watch the tape no matter what I said. And part of me was relieved. I really didn't want to watch this thing on my own, but, I had to at least give her the courtesy of a warning. After all, Jemma was a little more . . . susceptible to believing far-fetched things. Let's just put it that way. I gave her one last chance: "They warned me, the more people who know about this stuff, the worse things will be. Apparently."

"I'm shakin' in my boots."

"Your funeral."

I popped in the tape, went to press PLAY, and—my sister had to get one last stupid joke in: "It's gonna be a Rickroll."

With a tired sigh, I pressed PLAY. As the tape whirred to life, I joined Jemma on the couch, pushing her legs aside to make room. We stared at the dark and silent TV, wondering if we'd put the cables in right when—

The screen turned solid *blue*.

9
VHS

The tape begins with a BLUE screen. A single tone plays, harsh and dissonant—rising higher and higher, building without resolve. Finally, after about seven uncomfortable seconds, it goes quiet. The screen turns black. The black gives way to reveal—

A blurry shot of Grace Carnswel's living room. Harsh sunlight pours in through large windows, overwhelming the image with blinding white. A man steps into frame, only the lower half of his face visible, a strong jaw with silver stubble. The image jostles—the focus adjusts.

The man steps back from the camera and plops down on a beige couch. He looks to be around seventy years old. Despite his age, he's athletically built, and there's a youthful spark in his dark brown eyes. "My name is David Carnswel." He speaks with a clear and direct timbre. "In this video, I will detail the necessary precautions in regards to suppressing the entity at 5637 Brooksview Heights." He chuckles bitterly, seemingly aware of how absurd that sounded. "I know what you're thinking." He sighs, presenting his wrists like the viewer should slap handcuffs on him.

"Lock him up: straitjacket, padded room." He lowers his arms, and the sun glints off a glossy white FitLyfe bracelet on his left wrist. "I get it. Believe me." He rubs his neck, kneading small circles. "But for the sake of everyone, let's move past that. Just . . . humor me, at least until the end of the video—"

Here, the tape glitches out, cutting to a stationary shot of an empty room—no visible windows or doors. Concrete floor, concrete walls, exposed ceiling with pinkish-white insulation. This image, likely a remnant of something taped over, holds for about three seconds, and then, like nothing even happened, the footage cuts back to David, still sitting on the living room couch.

He leans forward, looking directly into the lens. "It's crucial you pay close attention to every word I say—watch this video multiple times if need be." Despite his relatively calm demeanor, his eyes are filled with grave severity. The look of a man trying to appear sane as he attempts to convince you of something completely insane. He leans back. "On top of regular house upkeep, I've come upon several things that need to be prioritized. They're simple at face value, but it's crucial you don't mess them up."

His left eye twitches.

"First of all, this should go without saying, but it's important that you keep the house generally tidy. My mother always said a messy home is the Devil's playground, and turns out she was closer to the truth than she ever could have imagined. The messier the house, the more likely you run into trouble." He shifts his weight.

"Now," he continues, "on to specifics. Make sure you keep all the main- and second-floor lights off between three and four a.m. That's it. That's all. Don't worry about the basement lights. And if you have to use the facilities and can't see in the dark, feel free to switch on a light or two, that's fine, just don't let any of them stay on for more than three minutes at a time. Not *one* second over three minutes. Be vigilant. The

THE CARETAKER

lights have a nasty habit of turning on by themselves—I used to think it was faulty wiring, but . . . Anyways, always patrol the home during the so-called witching hour to ensure compliance. Got it? Great."

He leans forward, reaches out of frame, and brings up a white envelope. Written on its surface in black Sharpie:

IN CASE OF LIGHTS

"In the event you're dumb enough to fail this one, open the envelope. It will provide further instructions." He sets the letter aside. "And be sure to follow these protocols as they're presented; don't try to get smart with this thing, don't go looking for loopholes. Trust me, I tried taking all the bulbs out once, didn't end well." He rubs his jaw, a flash of dark memories clouding his eyes.

"Anyway." He slaps his knees, puts a smile on. "So long as you keep the lights under control, you shouldn't have to worry about anything else. It seems that the failure of one Rite often triggers the next. Of course there's always outlier events, so stay alert."

David shifts his weight again. "Okay, next thing. As you may have noticed, there's a lot of stray rabbits out here. Even with all our doors shut, the big-eared rats keep finding their way inside. If you see one within a fifty-foot or so radius of the house—you must lock all doors that lead to the outside. For some reason, don't ask me why, that seems to help keep them at bay. If, God forbid, you see one *inside* the house, especially a white rabbit, catch it, toss it back out. That's it. But catch it within ten minutes of sighting—if you don't, they'll start scratching at the hardwood. I've actually timed it out. At the ten-minute mark, they flat drop whatever they're doing and just start scratching at the floor, frantic. At that point, just leave them be, and open this." He reaches off camera, lifting another envelope into frame:

IN CASE OF RABBITS

He sets the letter aside. "Do not, DO NOT let the rabbit out after ten minutes have passed. Read the letter first—"

Again, the screen glitches, giving way to the same concrete room as before. But now, in the room's dead center, stands an unplugged tube TV. It's sitting atop a metallic pushcart, the kind of setup one might see being wheeled around a community college or a public library. There's a blocky VCR on the middle shelf. The image holds for about four seconds, then cuts back to—

The living room. It's night out, pale moonlight spilling through the windows. David still sits on the same couch, but he looks exhausted now, like a paranoid shut-in. Ghostly pale, with dark circles under his eyes.

"Okay . . . here's the last, and most important, one." He falls quiet, eyes snapping upward, peering somewhere off camera, deeper into the house. Silence. Only the tick, tick, tick of a nearby clock. He looks back at the lens. "The *Visitors*. They can take many forms, but they always have cold blue eyes. If anybody with cold blue eyes shows up at the front door, and I mean *anyone*, a grandmother looking for her lost dog, a cop with a warrant, if *anyone* shows up between six p.m. and six a.m., do not talk to him, or her, it—do not let them see you, and, most importantly, do NOT let them inside. Hide. Hide and pray you didn't forget to lock any of the doors."

David pauses, tilts an ear. More silence. Only that ticking clock. His shoulders tense, his neck strains and spasms. He turns back to the camera. "Don't worry about locking the windows. The Visitors won't even climb through an open window, they only use doors. And they won't force their way inside, not usually. They might ask to borrow the phone, say they need water, whatever. Believe me, I've heard it all." He clears his throat. "Most of them, if they haven't seen or heard you, will leave after thirty minutes or so, in which case the phone will usually ring and somebody will tell you what to do next."

David pauses again. He absent-mindedly clenches his left fist until the knuckles turn white. "On top of that," he says, "always do exactly what the person on the phone tells you to do. I can't overstate how important that is. They might call in the middle of the day, they might call at three in the morning, but they will only call when you're within earshot of the phone. And it's profoundly important that you follow their instructions to the tee—even if said instructions contradict anything else I've told you. And be sure to write down what they say; they rarely repeat themselves. Don't worry, they won't ask you to do anything . . . unbecoming, but their demands can certainly be . . . strange." He relaxes his fist, blood returning to his knuckles.

David holds up a third envelope, this one labeled:

IN CASE OF EMERGENCY

"Only open this when you feel like there's no other choice. Listen to your gut. If the time comes, you will know." With a deep inhale, he sets the envelope aside. "As I said before, I know you probably think I'm crazy, or this is some kind of sick joke, or something worse than a joke. I don't blame you. If it makes you feel better, don't even think about the weird stuff I've said, just tell yourself it's all basic upkeep. Routine maintenance. In fact, I don't even want you to believe me—so long as you follow the Rites, I don't care what you think."

He stares directly into the camera again. "But trust me. You don't want to become a believer the hard way." He pauses, letting another heavy silence fill the air. "Each time you mess up one of these Rites, things will get significantly harder. The presence, specter, entity—whatever name you prefer—this thing is vicious. Relentless."

He pops his neck. "The more Rites you fail, the more the entity will torment you, try to drive you into unimaginable misery. It will use your own memories against you, hurt you. It will weaken your grasp on reality, your perception of time. Do not underestimate it. And know this: as soon as you set foot on this property with intention to be its caretaker, you can't just quit. You must stick with it until somebody else willingly takes up the baton, so to speak."

He looks over his shoulder and peers out the window, toward the surrounding trees. He turns back. "I've set up a rope denoting the property's boundary. You can still leave during the day, but no longer than eight hours at a time, and ensure you always get home before the sun sets." He goes quiet, tilting his head as if he's heard something. He continues: "Right now, the entity's power is confined to this property, but if you fail to maintain the Rites with a reasonable level of consistency—a blood-red sun will rise, and the entity's influence will spread far and wide. Then, we all become believers the hard way."

Somewhere behind the camera, three hollow knocks echo—a fist thumping against glass. David turns rigid, waiting, as if he hopes the sound was only imagined.

Three more knocks, louder, more insistent.

He shoots up from the couch and hurries off-screen. His footsteps recede toward the foyer and then—

He rushes back into the living room, the camera wobbling with every step until he hoists it up. He hurries deeper into the house, the image blurring back and forth, back and forth—

The screen turns solid *blue*.

10
DESPERATE MEASURES

Jemma and I sat in silence, staring at the blue screen, dumbfounded by what we'd just watched. After about five stunned seconds, my sister turned to me and said, "This is a joke, right?"

I forced a shrug, slid off the couch, and crawled over to the TV.

"Bro," she said, "you're not actually taking this job . . . are you?"

I popped the VHS out of the player, switched off the TV, and looked back at her. "Grace already paid me the first chunk."

Jemma blinked at me rapid-fire, like I'd just said the stupidest thing she'd ever heard. "Oh *NO.*" She broke into another god-awful impression: "My name is Macy *Mullins*, somebody sent me money, whatever will I do?" She snapped out of the impression and stared me down: "You send the money back, Macy, send it back right this second. And NEVER talk to these people again."

I chewed on my lip, turned away, and met my dark reflection in the gray TV screen. I knew she was right, but: "I already spent—"

"And aren't they like multi-millionaires?" Jemma spoke over me. "Shouldn't they have a groundskeeper or, like, a butler for this? Don't you think it's a little weird they're hiring, no offense, complete randos off Craigslist? Like seriously, if it's so important, hire a professional house sitter or—"

"Jemma," I cut her off, "I . . . *We* need the money."

"No amount of money is—"

"She's paying me nine grand for the weekend."

"Okay, but . . ." Jemma paused, the number sinking in. "Nine grand?"

"Yes, and she already sent me the first third."

"Three grand?" Jemma narrowed her eyes, the gears of her brain churning back into motion. "Did you even sign a contract?"

My silence betrayed the answer.

"No contract? Oh my freaking GOD, am I losing my mind right now? Why would they pay NINE GRAND for ONE WEEKEND with ZERO paper trail?! This is the SKETCHIEST thing I've ever seen. Send the money BACK—"

"I already spent most of it on rent and . . . I still need to get your inhaler. I know you don't have a hundred bucks sitting around."

Jemma, losing a bit of steam, changed tactics: "Just don't show. Take the three grand and run. Does she know where you live?"

"Jemma . . ." I trailed off. It felt wrong debating when I didn't really believe in my side of the argument, but logic hardly mattered, that nine grand was . . . well it was *nine fucking grand*.

Jemma went on. "Nine thousand bucks is way too much for house-sitting, Macy. That's almost weirder than everything else combined—"

"She's rich," I said, "that much money is probably like a parking ticket to her, and—"

"With all due respect, why would she hire you? I mean, again no offense, but—"

"I got it, Jem. Thanks."

"Sorry. Just . . . The Mullins are not exactly house-sitting material." She gestured around our disaster of a studio.

I shrugged. "She seemed desperate. I think all the other prospects got spooked by the whole . . . rites of it all."

"Yeah, no shit." Jemma blinked at me again, unbelieving. "Did we watch the same video? Are you not the slightest bit freaked out?"

A twisting knot of anxiety was swelling in my gut. I pretended it wasn't there. "Sure," I said, "but if it's a prank, I take my 3K and run. And if it's just a delusional old guy, then I'm getting paid bank to do nothing for the weekend. Win-win."

"And what if it's neither of those things?"

This time, I blinked at her. "So . . . what if David is actually right?"

Jemma flushed red. "No, I don't mean *that*, but . . ." She fell silent.

"But what?"

She started chomping away on her licorice again.

"Jemma." I sighed. "I love you, but I'm sorry." I set a hand on the VHS. "Why in the fuck would a supposedly all-powerful demon be held back by dumbass routines?"

With an exasperated huff she said, "I don't know. Maybe it's a metaphor?"

"A metaphor . . ."

"Didn't like the 'all-powerful' God in the Bible let his son die to save humanity? I dunno, supernatural beings work in mysterious ways . . ."

"Uh-huh . . . So you're religious now?"

"God no." Jemma frowned, then switched strategy once again. "As your sister and your closest advisor—"

"Closest advisor?"

"As your voice of reason, do NOT take this job. Seriously, this Grace woman is trying to pass off a curse on you or something. Go back to Starbucks. Shit, go back to mowing lawns, anything is better than"—she pointed at the TV—"whatever the hell we just watched."

Starbucks was off the table for too many reasons to count. And lawn mowing? I used to find it oddly calming, but these days . . .

"Look," I said, "I appreciate your sisterly worry, I really do, it's actually kind of touching. But do you know how broke I am right now? How broke *we* are? Minimum wage won't even put a scratch in it. I can barely afford groceries, let alone rent. We are perpetually one month away from ending up out there." I gestured at the back wall, out toward an abandoned tent city in the boggy field behind our apartment.

Jemma went quiet for a beat, then said, "When does it start?"

"Tomorrow. It's just for the weekend, then I'm back home Monday morning."

"You do know Dad's birthday is on Sunday, right? Are you sure it's a good idea for you to be alone?"

"Jem . . ." I swallowed a lump in my throat. "I'll be fine, it's just another day—"

"Just another day?"

I backtracked. "No. Of course it's . . . I just . . . We *need* this money."

Jemma tried one last time. "What about the insurance payout?" she said. "Greg promised it's just around the corner."

Greg was our dad's insurance broker. The kind of timid fellow people often described with the caveat: "He's a nice guy, but . . ." The whole process had been a comedy of errors. Though, in Greg's defense, none of it was his fault. The company that had insured Dad's life went bankrupt. The policy had been transferred over to another place with a massive backlog. Then, right before his claim was about to be processed, *that* company went bankrupt as well. So we got transferred over to yet another company with an even bigger backlog. Most insurance policies are settled in a few months, but ours . . .

"Greg's been saying that for the last two years, Jem. I wouldn't count on it."

My sister, finally accepting it was a losing fight, slumped back into the couch. She dug another licorice from her pocket and started chewing . . . angrily. "I wouldn't take a million bucks to step within a fifteen-mile radius of that house."

She pushed off the couch, and began to march away, only to realize she didn't really have anywhere to go in our undersized apartment. She huffed back to the couch, plopped down. "Macy, I'm going to put this as politely as I can: if you take this job, you're a stupid fucking idiot."

11
STUPID FUCKING IDIOT

I lay awake on a fold-out cot, watching a lonely spider spin her web between the blades of a broken ceiling fan. I'd named the spider Rosey. I couldn't sleep. A slow wash of headlights beamed through a window, lending Rosey a monstrous shadow that yawned across the stucco ceiling, then fell back into bluish dark. I turned onto my side. Jemma lay on the pull-out couch, mouth half-open, eyes fully shut.

My gaze shifted to the sliding glass door behind her. The door led to our "patio," a grimy lip of concrete, cramped against a chain-link fence. I sat up, and swung my legs off the cot. My eyes wandered to the stove clock: 2:57 a.m. Quietly as I could, I rose to my feet, and slid on a pair of counterfeit Crocs. Then I put on my parachute jacket, and stepped outside into the cold dark. As I pulled the patio door gently shut, I stole another glance at Jemma, still fast asleep.

I slumped down into a bright pink plastic lawn chair. The flimsy chair bowed slightly from my weight, the brittle plastic forever threatening to snap.

This was my quiet space. The place I went to get away from it all. The place I went to think, ruminate. I leaned over and tilted up a dried-out planter. Beneath it sat my secret stash. A half-empty pack of vanilla-flavored cigarettes and a purple Bic lighter. I'd whittled the habit down to one or two smokes a week, but still, Jemma gave me shit: "It's the same thing that killed Auntie Pat," she had said after catching me red-handed a few months back. "And if Auntie Pat hadn't died, we'd be living in a Portland bungalow right now."

"Fuck Portland."

"Rent-free, Macy."

"Auntie Pat didn't even like us."

"She liked me."

I'd given Jemma a single shoulder shrug and taken another long drag, when she'd snatched the smoke from my hand, hurled it to the ground, and stamped it out. I had sat there, fingers still pinched in front of my lips as I murdered my sister with a point-blank glare.

Jemma hadn't flinched. "If you'd seen the things I'd seen." She'd stomped back inside, wrenching the patio door shut in her wake. Jemma had been at Auntie Pat's bedside in the days before she went. Never told me what she saw, but it can't have been good because she never told me what she saw. Still, despite Jemma being a narc about it all, the next morning I promised her I'd quit. Scout's honor.

But that was months ago, and Jemma was fast asleep, and I was stressed to hell and back, so I lit up a smoke, sucked in that sweet, sweet nicotine. *Hold me close, warm my bones, tell me lies, tell me sweet little lies.*

Woodbury Golds: Vanilla Flavor.

The same brand Dad used to smoke. He tried his best to hide it from us, but we always knew when he was going out to catch a fix. He'd grab his parachute jacket from the garage and say something like: *Going for a walk, I'll be back in a bit.* It was the jacket that gave him away. Whenever he put it on, he'd always come back smelling like tobacco and vanilla.

I never judged him for it. Jemma and I were handful enough for two parents, let alone one. He just needed time to himself sometimes.

I could relate. I feel less alone when I'm by myself. Throw me into a crowded party, throw me into the arms of someone who tells me they love me, that's when the feeling that I'm worthless screams the loudest—shoves me back to this concrete patio where I drag on vanilla cigarettes, dart my eyes wild on the zigzags of a chain-link fence, drown in self-pity.

Smoking always put me in a brooding mood. An angsty, fledgling poet sort of mood. Sulking in the shadows, listening to the highway rumble never ceasing, my face lit only by the orange glow of a death stick.

I brought the cigarette to my mouth, inhaled again. More chemical warmth fell over me. Exhaling, I scanned the musty bog beyond the chain-link fence. "Waterfront property," the landlord had joked. It wasn't even a natural bog, the water had flooded in a few years back, set up shop, and refused to leave.

I took in the view. On the far shore, the tattered remnants of the tent city clung to the branches of felled trees and wispy shrubs. Blue tarps, overturned shopping carts. Farther beyond that, the pale glow of the Oregon State Penitentiary bled up into a pitch-black sky. Guard towers, high walls, barbed wire. Plumes of paper-white steam rose from heating stacks and drifted westward.

My eyes lowered to the murky water. It reflected the night sky above, the leafless trees, and the distant lights of the prison. I imagined standing on the opposite shore, looking back at my apartment, seeing my reflected self down in the water, slumped in a plastic lawn chair. I often wondered about that mirror version of Macy, wondered if she was doing any better than I was, or if she was just really cold and drenched. Weird thoughts.

Somewhere out of sight, a dog began barking, then fell quiet at the howl of a passing train. I took another drag and let it out, slumped further back into my chair. I rested my feet up on a cinder block. I used to wonder if the folks in that prison had it better than the folks in the tent city did. The inmates had heating, and three meals a day, so that was something, but—

My thoughts grabbed me by the ear and pulled me back to Brooksview Heights, told me how stupid I was for even considering the job. Told me Jemma was right to call me an idiot. Of course I knew my sister was right. Not about the supernatural stuff, but about everything reeking of trouble. Red flags on top of red flags on top of red flags.

I sat there for a good while. Puff after puff. Thought of Dad again. What ran through his mind when he went out for a nicotine fix? Probably money. The mortgage. Yet another client lost to Done Right Lawns LTD.

I rose to my feet and flicked a half-finished cigarette to the concrete. An orange fleck streaming thin ropes of gray. I pressed my heel to it and swiveled my ankle back and forth more times than I needed to. Then I returned the Bic and the smokes to their hiding spot beneath the dried-up planter.

I stood there a little while longer, one hand gripping the fence, cold metal digging into the crooks of my bare fingers. I ran my eyes over the tent city graveyard—neon-colored tarps catching glints of the moon. The distant plumes of steam from the prison now rose straight up, blotting out the stars above. My hand fell from the chain link and dangled at my side. I thought about rent and bills and debt and eviction.

I expelled another long sigh, the fog of my breath cutting into blurry shapes through the links of the fence. A siren wailed in the night, red and blue lights blinking in the distant dark. The sound rose high, then faded back into the freeway rumble that carried over the drowned fields. I made up my mind right then and there. Turning back, I pulled open the sliding door, stepped inside, and muttered to myself:

"Stupid fucking idiot."

PART II

GAINFUL EMPLOYMENT

CONTACT

I always had trouble making friends. When I was a kid, I really put in the effort too, climbed out of my so-called shell, but . . .

Sometimes it felt like the whole world was playing one big song, all in perfect pitch and cadence, only for Macy Mullins to stumble in, honking away on an out-of-key kazoo: "HEY GUYS, MY NAME'S MACY, CAN I JOIN?"

Social cues would fly over my head like hurled rocks. And sometimes, when I least expected it, one of those rocks would crack off the top of my skull and knock me flat to the ground—a confused and blubbering mess, flailing around in the dirt, wondering why nobody ever invited her to anything.

A teacher said I'd make more friends if I got better at making eye contact. "It's rude not to look at someone's eyes when speaking to them."

I tried that too.

But every time I locked eyes with someone, I started overthinking: How long is too long? Should I blink? Am I blinking too much? Why did they stop talking? Oh, they just asked me a question, and I wasn't even listening.

I pretty much gave up on the whole making friends thing in middle school. I had my sister, and I had my dad, and that was enough human connection for me . . .

1
NO RETURN

My second journey to Brooksview Heights was far less eventful than the first. Grace had paid for another Uber, which meant no weirdos staring at me on the bus, no drifters arguing with the driver about fare, no uphill hikes through pouring rain. Just me in the back seat of a Honda Civic, with my brand-new pair of Sylvo headphones. Tuning out the world never sounded better.

Despite more protests from Jemma, I was set on seeing this through, at least for one night. Still, I swore I'd jump ship at the first sign of danger, told her she could call me anytime to check in. But those "compromises" weren't even close to enough: "STUPID! STUPID! STUPID!" Jemma had yelled as I marched out the front door. Preaching to the choir.

The Uber slowed to a stop at the foot of Grace's driveway. "Here you go," said the twentysomething driver. He had a wispy goatee, wore a Tapout ball cap, and was listening to a podcast called *Mind-Set Grind-Set*. Not a parody. I'd lifted a headphone more than once to hate listen. The host non-ironically said things like: "How a man orders his steak is directly tied to his level of masculinity." And: "If you're not on the property ladder by your twenty-fifth birthday, what are you even doing?"

I climbed out, grabbed my Pikachu backpack, and shut the door. The driver left at a steady clip, turning up his podcast to full volume. The host's nauseating drone leaked from a cracked window. "Once you enroll in our twelve-week program, females will be THROWING themselves at you—"

I threw my headphones back on, turned up the music: churning guitars, guttural screams, blast-beat drums. Deathcore. A genre Miss Bamford used to give me grief for listening to. Back in high school, she'd caught me doing the old earbud-up-the-hoodie-sleeve trick. She'd confiscated my phone right in front of the whole class, and frowned when she saw the album cover on its screen. Blood-red letters, contorted and barely legible:

(Unrelenting Desecration)

She dared popping in an earbud. Her face pinched with disgust, like she'd tasted something sour. She wrenched the earbud free, and lectured me about the dangers of listening to such filth, how it would only turn a nice girl like me into something bitter and uncouth.

Well, I did turn out pretty bitter, so maybe she was right. But just imagine how bitter I'd be if I couldn't vent my fury listening to death-core.

I stretched out my arms and shook life back into sleepy legs. The surrounding woods appeared far less ominous in the daylight. Sunrays caught droplets on the branches. Spotted toadstools were scattered about the gentle slopes. A bushy-tailed squirrel scampered down a nearby tree trunk. Maybe things wouldn't be so bad after all.

I took a couple of steps forward, only to lurch to a halt right before my foot met the driveway. Why did I stop? Puzzled, I paused the music, lowered the headphones. My gaze ran to the left side of the gravel drive. A thin white rope was tied around a crooked stump. The rope led far off into the woods, looping around a tree every thirty feet or so. I looked to my right: another rope. This one was tied around a mailbox post. It led up a rocky slope until it slipped out of view.

The property line?

David's warning echoed in my head: "As soon as you set foot on this property with intention to be its caretaker, you can't just quit . . ." I looked over my shoulder—the Uber crawled around a distant bend. I turned back, my feet still rooted to the spot. Ahead of me, the driveway veered leftward, giving way to a bank of Douglas firs—silent spectators awaiting my next move. And even though Jemma wasn't there, I could almost hear her chiming in through a mouthful of popcorn: *They're trying to drag this out for tension, but we all know what she's gonna do.*

Back when we still did movie nights with Dad—Jemma, to my chagrin, always provided us with her own commentary track. Usually consisting of shoehorned clichés like:

"Erhm, it's right behind her, isn't it?"

"Uhh, guys, you're gonna wanna see this."

"Oof . . . That's gonna leave a mark."

She was especially vocal during horror flicks, blurting out eloquent critiques like: "Do NOT go down there you STUPID PIECE of SHIT." Or "Just leave the HOUSE you FUCKING MUPPET."

The dumber the characters, the louder Jemma got. Back then, it annoyed the hell out of me. These days, I almost missed it. Almost.

Either way, her prediction was correct. I cursed under my breath, slung my pack over a shoulder, and started up the drive. My sneakers crunched into the wet gravel with percussive thwacks. I rounded the bend, and once again, Grace Carnswel's house crept into view.

Just like the surrounding woods, the abode looked a little different in the daylight. Still the two-story rancher I remembered, just a little . . . rougher around the edges. Dead leaves were plastered to the roof, a wet skin that looked like it might slide off, a reptile molting. The olive-green paint was chipped and faded in parts, like healed scars. The lawn was shaggy, more than a few weeks overdue for a cut. Still a nice place, far nicer than anywhere I could ever dream of living. And in a weird sort of way, the flaws made it less intimidating. More relatable. We all look a little less sharp under the brightness of day.

I forged ahead. The garage door was partially open, revealing a beige Volkswagen hatchback sitting in the inky dark.

Behind me, the faint sound of footsteps squelching against mud. I turned. Grace was making her way down a sloped trail in the woods. She wore a green coat, blue jeans, and hiking boots. "Macy," she said, "Lovely to see y—"

Her foot caught on a gnarled root and she stumbled forward, nearly toppling onto the gravel before catching her balance. I hurried over to help, but she shooed me away and chuckled. "Clumsy old fool." She swiped a strand of silver hair from her forehead, tucked it behind an ear. "So lovely to see you." She raised her arms for what I assumed was a hug. I turned rigid.

Grace froze, arms dropping to her sides. "Oh, I'm sorry." Her face flushed with embarrassment. "Not a hugger?"

I barely touched people I'd known my entire life. "I'm just . . . I don't—"

"No need to apologize." She removed a leather glove and lifted her hand for a shake. We shook. Her grip was firm. Her hand was cold. She put her glove back on and started up toward the house. I waited behind, still questioning every choice I'd ever made up until this point. My gaze landed on a security camera above the garage. A black and glossy globe, like the eye of a giant spider had been lodged between the wooden slats—

"Come on now," said Grace. "I'll give you the tour."

2
FAULTY WIRING

Grace shuffled into the garage, bending low to avoid the partially closed door. She was surprisingly limber for someone her age. "One moment," she said.

I waited outside as she rose to stand, the top half of her body concealed behind the garage door. A switch CLICKED in the dark, and the door heaved slowly to life, groaning upward.

She raised her voice, competing with the churn of metal against metal: "I was a bit worried you might take the money and run." The door continued to ascend, revealing Grace as she held her thumb to a pale switch. "For three grand?" She whistled. "At your age, I would've turned heel and never looked back."

Shit. Maybe I should've.

The door rattled to a stop, a plume of gray dust wheezing out from above. Grace cracked a smile. "I'd send the cavalry after you, though." She strode off and shimmied sideways to fit between the Volkswagen and a hefty workbench. I followed suit.

"I really appreciate you doing this," Grace said. "You wouldn't believe how many interviews I went through. I think everyone else got scared off. The paranoia in your generation." She pushed a swing-arm lamp out of the way, then squeezed out near the car's hood. She grumbled something about her own parking job. Then she stamped her muddied heels on the concrete, and started toward a white door.

As I continued shuffling between the car and the workbench, I inhaled the familiar scent of diesel and grass clippings. A DeWalt mower lay belly-up on the bench, abandoned in the middle of a repair. With a quick glance, I diagnosed the cardinal symptoms: dull blades and a broken drive belt. Memories started to surface and—

I looked away. An assortment of tools hung on a white pegboard above. Good selection.

I stepped out near the car's hood and scraped off my shoes just like Grace had done. She pulled open the door and waved me inside. We broached into the narrow foyer, greeted by that ominous photo of the Windfall Inlet. My eyes drifted down to the rotary phone beneath—after watching David's video, it stood out even more: *Always do exactly what the person on the phone tells you to do, I can't overstate how important that is.*

Grace hung up her coat and held out a hand for mine. I gave her the same parachute jacket I'd worn to the interview. As she hung it up, her nose twitched—her eyes flashed with concern. She cut right to the chase: "You smoke."

I cleared my throat. "Not anymore."

I was a terrible liar, just like Jemma.

"It's fine if you do." Grace kicked off her boots and placed them on a shoe rack. "But keep it outside."

I replied with a sheepish nod and slipped off my sneakers.

Grace strode around me and glided into the living room. "You can help yourself to anything in the fridge," she said. "And I've left the number for a pizza place. No one else delivers this far out." She hefted a large suitcase onto the kitchen island, unzipped it, and started to dig through. She paused every so often, listing off travel essentials: "Phone charger, toothbrush, neck pillow . . ." She glanced up. "Invoice me anything you buy food-wise. Just keep it within reason, no more than, say, a hundred dollars daily."

"That should be enough . . ."

As Grace continued sifting through her bag, I wandered forward. My gaze fell to that beige couch. The one David had been sitting on in the video. I wondered, not for the first time, how Grace had managed to cope with his bizarre routines for three months straight, especially considering she didn't even believe in them—

"All right." Grace zipped up her suitcase and clapped her hands together. "Tour."

She insisted we start on the second floor and work our way down. She led me up a staircase flanked by wood-paneled walls—more photographs of varying shapes and size. Most were filled with smiling family members at weddings, reunions. A few were gloomy wilderness landscapes, much like the one in the foyer.

At the top of the staircase was a long, narrow hallway with a low ceiling and a skylight. It was dark up here. The skylight, coated with dead leaves, did little to illuminate the space. There were rooms on either side, four in total, and a closet with shuttered doors at the far end. Grace had continued forward when—

t-t-t-t-tick-bzzzzzzzzzzzzzz.

A light stammered on at the end of the hall—a wedge of yellow glow spilling out from an open door. Grace halted midstep, huffed, then continued forward. More irritated than concerned. I lingered behind, a trickling sense of unease creeping up my spine, raising the hairs on the nape of my neck. I'd assumed nobody else was here . . .

Grace looked back, noticing my hesitation. "The electrical wiring in this place," she explained. "The lights turn off and on by themselves all the time." She kept moving. "You'd swear it was haunted, but it's just my dolt of a husband, rest his soul. He refused to ever hire an electrician." She leaned into the room, her face slipping from view. "And he made such a mess of the wiring, even the professionals can't figure it out now." The CLICK of a light switch flicked, but the light stayed on. She groaned, kept trying, flicking the switch up, down, up, down, *UP, DOWN*. Finally, the light snapped off. She stepped back, shaking her head. "I'm sure he talked about the lights in the video?"

I gave a leery nod.

"Honestly," she started back toward me, "the lights are probably the only *rite*"—she threw up air quotes—"you'll have to worry about. I just set an alarm for 2:50 a.m. every day and wander the house until four. That's why I'm so peachy happy bright all the time." She forced an exaggerated smile. She opened the door to my left, the smile evaporating. "Bathroom here," she said. "Feel free to use any of them, but this one's closest to your room."

Gray light poured in from a small window above the tub. The shower curtain was pulled shut, covered in that old "farmhouse and ducks" pattern that grandparents can't seem to get enough of. I made a mental note to open it after Grace left. House rule.

She stepped across the narrow hall, and opened another door. It led to a guest room that was nearly as big as my entire studio apartment. Which, frankly, meant it was just about the size of a standard bedroom. A shuttered window cast blurry lines onto a queen-sized bed. Across the room was a closet with bifold doors, open just a crack. A thin line of pitch dark.

I always hated that, felt like somebody was on the other side watching, waiting.

"This is where you'll sleep," said Grace. "I've cleared out the closet, though it looks like you've packed pretty light . . ." Her eyes fell to my ratty Pikachu backpack, still slung around my shoulder.

"I . . . I just brought enough clothes for the weekend," I said.

"Nevertheless," said Grace. "Feel free to use the closet. Or the laundry downstairs." She started out of the room, but I held there, my eyes drawn to something on a blue nightstand: another glossy white rotary phone, just like the one in the foyer.

"Does anybody ever call you?" I asked.

Grace stopped in her tracks again and peered back at me, her brow furrowed. "I'm sorry?" She looked confused, hurt even.

I suddenly realized how offensive the question could sound to a lonely widow—*Hey, do your grandkids ever call or do you just sit around the house all day turning off lights?* My mind had blurted it out before thinking it through. Something I did a lot. But in my defense, the question had been festering for a while, waiting to launch to the surface like a balloon held underwater. "Your husband . . ." I explained. "In the video he said sometimes people call, tell you to do things."

"Oh, I see." Grace smiled grimly. Her eyes turned restless, unable to decide what to focus on, flitting to a photo nearby, then the hardwood below, then a scuff mark on a doorframe, then to me. "I've never received a call like that. And . . . I don't believe my husband did either. David was . . ." She fell silent again, considering her words. "I know he can seem convincing in his beliefs, but he was not all there, especially toward the end. On more than one occasion, we'd be eating dinner, or watching TV . . . and he would perk up as if the phone had rung . . . He'd tell me to stay put, tell me he would answer. Always urgent. Then he'd hurry off to the foyer and speak to someone on the other end in hushed tones. I . . ." She paused a moment, clearly not enjoying the topic. "I listened in once or twice, and there was never anyone on the other end, just David, talking, waiting, then responding to the silence. Auditory hallucinations, our doctor later confirmed. You understand?"

I replied with a solemn nod. As bizarre as it sounded, it was painfully familiar. My grandma had conjured elaborate delusions when her mind started to slip. Sometimes, she would seem completely there, sharp as ever, then the next moment, she'd be talking to shadows like they were old friends.

Grace straightened her posture and got back to business. She gestured down the hall. "Master bedroom on the left, no need to go in there unless to turn off a light. And another guest room on the right."

Grace guided me down to the main floor. A long hallway led from the kitchen, farther back into the sloping rock face. Doors on either side, the hall stretched surprisingly far, then hooked rightward. As I followed Grace, she motioned at each door. "That's the den . . . That's the home theater . . . That's a bathroom with a Jacuzzi . . . Feel free to use any of them."

I'd definitely be using that home theater.

She slowed, pulled a green door shut. "That's the study . . ." As the door closed, I caught a glimpse of book-filled shelves, and an old wooden desk. She carried herself forward, slowing to another stop just before the corner. Her eyes were locked on a plain white door.

Silence slipped by until I asked, "What's in there?"

She tilted her head as if trying to recall some long-forgotten thing. "That's a storage closet." With a shrug, she turned away. As we stepped around the last corner, Grace halted yet again. The final door, the one at the end of the hallway, was wide open. A shadowy rectangle framing a staircase receding into darkness.

In a huff, she stepped over and pulled it shut. "That's the basement." She turned around. "The door opens by itself sometimes. Broken latch. Another thing David refused to hire a professional to fix." She strode toward me. "Only go down there if you absolutely must. There's a bit of a mold problem."

She brushed past me, but I remained still. "Why would I need to go down there at all?"

Grace paused, weighing the question. "Good point," she said. "Probably better you don't."

Jemma's movie night commentary chimed in: *Basement's where they hide the bodies.*

Grace and I stepped back into the kitchen. "The envelopes," she said, "are on top of the fridge, in a wooden tray. Don't open them unless you have to, and trust me, you won't have to. I never did. Anything else comes up, you have my number, shoot me a text." She smiled at me, and I sort of smiled back.

"Oh," she said, "and I'll send you the log in for the Ring app as well." After the interview, she'd mentioned how they had cameras set up in the common areas. It felt more like a warning than anything else: *I'm watching. Don't steal anything, you filthy peasant.*

A blurry shape, dark and small, zipped through the living room and disappeared upstairs. I tilted my head.

"Last thing," said Grace. "That's my husband's cat, Brownie. She's a little prickly, but she might warm up if you ignore her. Litter is in the garage, and she has an auto feeder. I trust you can handle those?"

"Sure." Normally I would've bristled at the added responsibility, but it was a welcome surprise. I tended to prefer the company of animals to the company of humans.

"Brownie's allowed to roam outside," Grace added. "She's a little murder machine, though. Might bring you a dead bird or two or three." Grace shook her head, clearly not a cat person. She went on, "And feel free to roam the property yourself. There's a lovely viewpoint of the ocean out that way." She nodded toward a glass panel patio door. "I do the trek every day. Get my steps in." She adjusted a FitLyfe bracelet around her wrist. A fancy Fitbit clone I only recognized because Jemma had compulsively shoplifted one a few months back.

Grace walked to the kitchen island and hoisted her suitcase down; it swung to the floor with a muffled THUMP. The impact caused a hanging picture frame to fall to a green rug near my feet. The frame stood upright for a moment, then flopped face down. Jeepers, was she smuggling gold?

"Toys for the grandkids." Grace answered my unspoken thought. She crouched at the fallen picture and flipped it upward. Then she rose to stand, and carefully hung the picture back in its place among the rest. She studied the image, her face shifting into an expression I couldn't read. Sadness? Regret?

The photo showed what I assumed to be a younger David. He looked to be in his early thirties, handsome in a small town sort of way—sandy brown hair, dark brown eyes, clean-shaven face. Sitting atop his broad shoulders was a young boy that looked just like him. And nestled up to David's side was a woman in her late twenties, bright blue eyes, jet black hair. I glanced at Grace's eyes, light brown.

Grace stepped back, tilted her head, and clicked her tongue. The photo was angled slightly off. She leveled it out with a delicate touch. "David and Caleb . . ." she said, more to herself than to me. "All right." She clapped a hand against the kitchen island and checked the time. "Before I go, do you have any other questions?"

I had more than a few, but at this point I figured it was better to keep them to myself.

3
RED FLAGS

I stood at the living room window, watching Grace's Volkswagen crawl down the gravel drive. Sunlight caught the windshield and ricocheted off into the woods—bright flashes that ran across the trunks and whipped back toward the house, vanishing before they hit the unkempt lawn.

The hatchback picked up speed when it met the asphalt, then slammed on the brakes so hard I could hear the tires screech from all the way up here. Black clouds of rubber smoke carried forward. A brown dot hopped across the road.

I squinted. A rabbit? It moved unhurriedly, hop, hop, hop, until it slipped into the ditch.

Grace set back on the gas, slowly this time. The Volkswagen carried off at a cautious pace, rounded the bend, and disappeared behind the slope of a muddy bank.

My shoulders released a tension I didn't even realize they'd been holding. My neck settled, my breath deepened. The same feeling one gets when the "boss" leaves, I supposed.

I turned from the window, only for my eyes to land directly on a Ring camera. It sat high atop a china cabinet in the kitchen's far corner—a little white cube with a black circle lens and a blinking blue light.

Why have cameras inside? I wondered.

Jemma chimed: *To stream to the dark web as they hunt you for sport.*

Sure, maybe, or perhaps they just want to keep tabs on the cat. Tabs on would-be house sitters . . .

Whatever the reasons, I didn't love the idea of being surveilled. I did my best to put the cameras out of mind, and started over to the fridge. I popped it open. Empty, save for condiments and a glass Tupperware filled with baby carrots. *Help yourself to anything in the fridge.* I slammed it shut, marched over to the couch, and plopped down.

It was only half past five, and I didn't know what to do with myself. There was too much space here, too much quiet. Quiet paralyzed me. Dragged my thoughts into places that made me want to crawl into bed and count pockmarks on the ceiling, stay asleep for weeks. It was one of the many reasons I filled my ears with music, white noise, anything to keep my head from wandering off into rooms it couldn't escape. But Dad always encouraged me to sit in silence. Try to accept the discomfort of inactivity, live with your thoughts. Don't push them away, acknowledge them like a passing cloud in the sky. Pretend to be sitting on a park bench. Pretend your thoughts were leaves floating by in a gentle breeze: *Oh, there's the thought that always tells me I'm a worthless fuckup that deserves nothing but heartache and misery, and . . . there it goes. It'll be back, and that's okay, but it's gone for the moment at least.*

It was counterintuitive advice, but the times I really stuck with it, really sat down and just allowed my thoughts to exist, it helped. Usually. Thoughts are sound, Macy, background noise like rain against a window or an annoying song on the radio. These sounds will come and go whether we want them to or not. Accept them as they are, not as right, not as wrong, just another external stimulus. Thoughts are sound. Thoughts are sound. Thoughts are . . .

Every little noise in the house stood out now: the ticking of a clock, the creaks and groans of the walls, even the water in the pipes. A faucet drip, drip, dripped, each impact seeming to echo in the space. I lifted my feet up onto the couch, hugged my shins, pulled them close. I rested my chin between my knees. *Macy Eleanor Mullins, what have you gotten yourself into this time?*

I shut my eyes.

t-t-t-t-t-tick-bzzzzzzzzzzz.

I opened my eyes. A foyer light had turned on by itself, casting a yellow glare against the photo of the Windfall Inlet.

It's just faulty wiring, I reminded myself.

Still, my throat tightened, mouth went dry. Unease gnawed in my gut, nibbling away at the stomach lining.

Calm down. I took a deep breath, in through the nose, out through the mouth. I shut my eyes again, tried to ignore the buzzing light, but a nagging voice formed in the back of my head, like a wriggling grub squirming between the gray matter: *Turn off the light*, the voice whispered. *Turn off the light. Turn off the light.*

I tried to ignore this compulsive little itch. Tried to watch it float on by like a leaf in a breeze. After all, it wasn't even close to David's so-called "witching hour," but—

TURN OFF THE LIGHT. TURN OFF THE LIGHT. TURN OFF THE LIGHT.

I groaned, rose to my feet, and dragged myself across the living room. I slowed at the foyer's threshold. My eyes found the light switch—right beside the photo of the Windfall Inlet. I shuffled over and switched it OFF. The light went dark, that nagging voice went quiet, and the wriggling grub evaporated. I stepped back, and—

Somewhere upstairs two soft thumps echoed in quick succession:

du-dum. Followed by a low creak. Another wave of unease bloomed in my stomach. It could have been anything. The house settling, a pine cone thudding against the roof, the footsteps of an axe murderer . . .

OUT! OUT! GET THE FUCK OUT!

Jemma's commentary shrieked. I did my best to ignore it. *Thoughts are sound.* I was nowhere near my sister's level of paranoia, but somehow the sound felt intentional . . . like whatever had caused it *wanted* me to hear. This was more of an instinctual hunch than anything else. A warning bell from deep within my cortex.

More weird, runaway thoughts followed: What if this was a terrible trick? What if all of Brooksview Heights was in on it? What if they were going to cut out my tongue, harvest my organs?

I scoffed at the absurdity. It was the same kind of brain-dead nonsense Jemma would've conjured up after gulping down one too many edibles, but still . . .

That soft thump looped in my memory: du-dum, du-dum, du-dum. I crossed the foyer and slowed at the foot of the staircase. It was still dark up there, scant rays of golden sun leaking through the skylight. I cocked an ear and listened.

Nothing.

I almost wanted the sound to repeat itself. Then I could chalk it up to the house settling—a pattern. I looked over my shoulder, back to the front door. The door's floor-to-ceiling glass panel framed the woods outside. Tree trunk shadows stretched long in the golden sunlight, a welcoming sight compared to the dark and narrow staircase before me. I looked to the coatrack, my dad's parachute jacket, then to my sneakers on the shoe rack.

Was I really considering walking away from six thousand bucks because of two little thumps and a faulty circuit? God, I was so pathetic.

Irked that Jemma's paranoia had rubbed off on me, I turned back to the stairs, gritted my teeth, and stomped upward, adding weight to every step. I could almost feel my younger sister hurling popcorn at me, little kernels pelting off my back, pop, pop, pop. *YOU'RE WALKING THE WRONG WAY!*

Honestly, Jemma, I thought, *this is reality, not a horror movie. In reality, most people, even relatively paranoid people, don't go running at the sound of a little bump, don't go calling the cops because a light bulb glitched out. Most people investigate, come up with a reasonable explanation, shrug it off, and move on. Now throw nine thousand bucks on the table, and you know what, I'm done justifying myself to you. You wouldn't go up the stairs, Jemma? You would run away tail between your legs, leave the house empty and go crawling back to your shitty little flat to get evicted and thrown on the streets? Fine. Congrats. You're smarter and cooler and wiser than your dumbass older sister. Happy?*

I paused at the top of the stairs, mentally drained by the imaginary debate. The hallway stretched out before me—all the doors were closed, save for the main bedroom at the far end. From within, another low creak rang out. A floorboard? Then a quick scraping sound, like a ragged inhale, or a calloused hand running over drywall: *schrrrrrp.*

My left eye twitched. *Just weird house sounds*, I told myself. *Old houses make weird sounds.*

I balled my fists into hardened clubs, carried myself forward with a resolute stride, slowed in the main bedroom's doorway and stood there.

This room, much like the rest, was rather unremarkable. Floral patterned wallpaper, a king-sized bed with a plaid duvet, a walk-in closet, and an en suite bathroom, but . . . something was off.

With my hands pressed to either side of the door frame, I leaned forward. This room felt a little colder than the rest. Drafty, even though the windows were shut. Outside, a soft breeze jostled the spindly branches of an oak tree, wooden fingers scraping against the glass: *schrrrrp, schrrrrp, schrrrrrp.* Well, that explained one sound, but . . . something else was wrong. Something I couldn't place. As I scanned the room, it felt like I was looking at a *Where's Waldo?* picture. Knowing full well that damned fool in a striped shirt was hiding in my line of sight, but not for the life of me being able to scope him out—

There it was. Atop a dresser in a dim corner: Brownie the cat. She was curled up on a crumpled sweater that probably smelled like Grace. Poor thing.

Her eyes cracked open, bulging wide at the sight of me. She shot to her feet. Her tail puffed up, her back arched. She stared me down. Macy Mullins, the big hairless ape that had intruded on her territory and ousted her human.

Even from here I could tell the cat was a beauty. A Siamese, tortoiseshell mix, black fur spackled with a chaotic mosaic of orangey browns and jagged whites. She had a golden line on the bridge of her nose, and each of her eyes was a different color. The left an icy blue, the right a dark brown.

I made a tsk-tsk-tsk clicking sound with my tongue, but she remained frozen. I hunkered down to a crouch, trying to make myself appear less intimidating, rubbing my fingers together like I had a treat. Tsk-tsk-tsk. She blinked at me once, twice, then relaxed. She slinked off the dresser like a spill of liquid. Her front paws hit the hardwood first, followed by her hind legs, two quick thumps in succession: du-dum.

Noisy little cat.

She trotted toward me, raising my hopes, only to bank hard right and disappear beneath the bed. *Ain't that just the way.* Grumbling, I pushed back to standing. Better to give her space, pretend I don't care. That's how you get a cat to like you. I left the door ajar, happy to blame all the creepy little sounds on Brownie. I marched down the hall, but only made it one step onto the staircase when—

t-t-t-t-tick-bzzzzzzzzzzzzz.

I peered back. The main bedroom light had stammered to life. A rectangle of yellow glow spilling out over the hardwood floor. My left eye twitched again. Another wriggling grub formed in my thoughts: *Turn off the light, Macy—if you don't, something bad will happen, something vile and contaminated. Turn off the light. Turn off the light. Turn off the light.*

I took a breath, and exhaled. I marched back down the hall, reached into the room, and flicked the light switch down. But the light remained defiantly on.

It was an incandescent bulb, unceremoniously screwed into a ceiling socket. There was no covering of any kind, and I could hear its electric current from across the room—hell I could almost feel it, buzzing around my ears like a crazed hornet. I flicked the switch up. No dice. Down. Nothing. Up. Down. Up. Down. UP. DOWN. UP. DOWN. The room went dark.

THANK YOU.

A peculiar sense of relief washed over me. A flash of damn near euphoria. Dopamine bliss. Everything had been made right in the world, all because little old me turned off a stupid light.

But the feeling faded quick, faster than it had come. So fast I barely remembered what it felt like at all. So fast I questioned if I had even felt anything to begin with. *My God, Macy, you are losing it.*

Halfway down the hall, I froze again. I turned, peering into the bathroom. That "farmhouse and ducks" shower curtain was still pulled firmly shut. I got that needling sense of something standing on the other side, and a whiff of sour rot. I huffed over and swung the curtain open. Empty. I sniffed the air. The smell was gone. Probably just a leaky pipe. Stop letting Jemma get to you.

I returned to my spot on the main floor couch, hugged my legs again, and stared out the window. Golden sunlight. Swaying trees. I tried my best to sit with the silence. Tried my best to view thoughts as sound, background noise. Tried to watch the parade of red flags and mental gloom float on by like clouds in the sky, leaves on a stream.

Thoughts are sound.

But my head was in a particularly cruel mood today. *Hey everybody,* one passing thought stopped to gawk and point. *Look, look*, it said in a nasally tone. *Macy Mullins is here.* Other thoughts slowed to join in: *Oh my. What an ugly, worthless excuse for a human being. She can't even provide for herself—*

Thoughts are sound—

—let alone provide for her sister—

Thoughts are sound. They are neither true nor false, they are simply—

—it's no wonder every relationship she ever had turned to shit in weeks—

Christ, they would not shut the FUCK up today.

Accept the thoughts, Macy. Thoughts are background noise, don't try to push them away, recognize them, let them be and—

—no wonder nobody wants to be around her, hell, she doesn't even wanna be around herself.

And look at her crooked little snaggletooth, can't even afford braces.

She has to take on the sketchiest house-sitting job in the world just to survi—

I stomped off toward the foyer, threw on my sneakers and jacket, and trekked outside. I pulled on my headphones and blasted Unrelenting Desecration at full volume. I wasn't angry, I just needed some air.

And my snaggletooth is actually kind of cute, thank you very much.

4
FEED

> 've set up a rope denoting the property's boundary. You can still leave during the day, but no longer than eight hours at a time, and ensure you always get home before the sun sets.

◆

With the soundtrack of explosive guitar riffs and guttural screams scoring my every step, I trudged across the overgrown lawn. My sneakers twist-squelched against post-rain muck, and the shaggy grass reached up past my ankles. The maintenance landscaper in me cried out: *MAINTAIN THE LAND.* If mowing lawns didn't remind me so much of Dad, I might've dragged that DeWalt out of the garage, replaced the drive belt, sharpened the blades, and cut this yard myself.

The trail began in the yard's far corner, next to an aluminum shed. Tree trunk shadows stretched ever longer, and the golden light grew dimmer. I checked the time, half past six. Still had a solid hour of light left. I would go see the lookout, clear my head before the real work began. Walk off the gloom.

It was something I often did when my inner monologue got too loud: change physical location. As if bad thoughts were tied to a certain time and place, as if they couldn't just up and follow me wherever I went. Sometimes I'd walk so far, I'd forget why I'd even started walking in the first place.

I pushed forward. The path guided me between lichen-spattered trunks, and up a gentle slope. The air was crisp, that bittersweet scent of fallen trees and the Pacific Ocean. I felt calmer out here, more at home in myself. I lowered my headphones—

Worthless fuckup, my inner monologue immediately started up again. *This stupid idiot is trying to tune us out—*

I threw my headphones back on and the thoughts were, mostly, drowned out. A wood pallet bridge led me over a small creek. I hoofed up another slope, followed the path around a mossy boulder, and—

Before I knew what was happening, I was falling in slow motion, the wet path below rushing up to meet me, a dull ache catching my left shin. My arms shot out in front, and my palms slammed into the dirt with a wet SMACK, saving me from a total face-plant. I held there in a pseudo push-up for a good few seconds, looking down at my sorry reflection in the chaos of a brown puddle. I looked back—my shin had caught that thin line of white rope stretched tight across the path like a trip wire.

I grabbed a crook on the mossy boulder, and pulled myself back to standing. I wiped the muck from my knees, and ran my eyes hatefully along the rope that had tried to kill me. The rope stretched far off in either direction, looping around the occasional trunk. This property was big. I'd been walking for about ten minutes, so at least several acres in this direction alone. Primo real estate on the Oregon Coast. Jeepers. How rich were David and Grace anyway?

I was about to carry on down the path, but something on the boulder's face grabbed my attention. Between the patches of dark green moss, a strange symbol was etched, no bigger than a drink coaster:

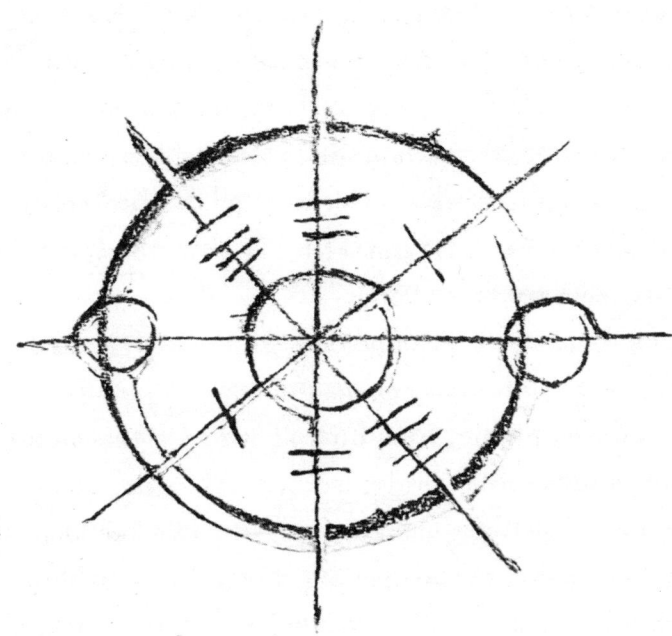

It looked oddly familiar. Maybe it was from some TV show, and kids had carved it here, but . . . I pressed my palm against it, felt the indents stamp into my skin. Somehow it felt ancient. Older than the rock itself, which made no sense at all, yet . . .

I shook off the feeling and turned away, but only made it ten steps before a horrid smell seeped into my nostrils—like rotten milk and open sewage. In the middle of the path, about twenty feet outside the property line, lay a dead rabbit.

I paused the music, and lowered my headphones. The rabbit's fur was a bright shock of snow white against the muddy path. There was no blood, no sign of injury.

Morbidly curious, I pinched my nose, stepped closer, and crouched down. It was definitely dead—its eyes permanently open, the irises a dull and milky gray.

I recalled a fun little YouTube factoid: the leading cause of death for the vast majority of vertebrates is "predation." A euphemism for getting eaten alive, torn limb from limb, fully conscious and shrieking as you watch the rest of your family flee in terror and realize you were never anything more than flesh and bone and marrow barely held together by tendons and veins. That's what a truly natural demise looks like.

But this rabbit looked like it had just flat dropped dead here. Struck down by some divine hand of nature. Disease was the most likely culprit.

I was finally ready to move on, when something began to pulse beneath the rabbit's rib cage. A rhythmic swell, accompanied by a wet and barely audible squishing sound: *ku-schlump, ku-schlump, ku-schlump.*

Was it breathing?

I found myself leaning closer, horribly, *stupidly,* transfixed.

The rabbit's belly was bloated, the pale skin partially transparent through thinning hair—*ku-schlump, ku-schlump, ku-schlump*—it wasn't breathing. Beneath its dead skin, a writhing mass of tightly packed maggots squirmed with embryotic unison. There were hundreds, maybe thousands—grayish-white incubating larvae. The skin was pulled so tight it made the maggots look like the wrinkles of a palpitating brain—*ku-schlump, ku-schlump, ku-schlump.* And I could almost feel them, as if they were teeming beneath my own skin, devouring me from the inside out—

Food for worms.

The intrusive little phrase jabbed into my thoughts like a dirty needle through my ear. A nightmare limerick:

Food for worms, food for worms, all you are is food for—

My lunch just about gurgled up my throat, but I forced it down, shot to my feet, and kept moving. As the trail bowed left and right, the rabbit's foul stench mercifully receded. *Food for worms . . .* I focused on my surroundings, and tried to think of other things. *It's just a dead rabbit, Macy. Breathe: In through the nose, out through the mouth. Walk: Left foot forward. Right foot forward.* A thick fog crept in from all sides, and the ocean's unending roar smothered the quiet. The trees ahead gave way to a gray sky.

The lookout?

The path spewed me out onto jagged rock. A semicircular clearing where nothing but lichen and moss could grow. The clearing went for about the length of a school bus, then cut sharply off. A cliff. I ventured my way to its edge, careful to keep my steps on the grippy patches of lichen.

One step from the edge, I peered over. Heights never bothered me; I'm not brave or anything, probably just apathetic. The rock stretched downward like dried candle wax, a picture-perfect ocean bluff. Winding roots ran between cracks in the surface. And there were gaps in the fog, brief windows to the crashing water far below. It was a long drop, two hundred feet at least, but even from up here the ocean's roar was near deafening—I could feel it, rumbling in my bones.

I sat down a few feet back from the edge, and rested my elbows on my knees. Took it all in. Not much of a view thanks to the fog, just a shifting smear of gray—as if I was sitting in the front row at a movie theater, looking at the sky from too close up. But the salty breeze was nice, and the roar of the ocean was loud enough to drown out the bad thoughts.

The Pacific Ocean.

Jemma, when she was really young, used to call it the "Specific Ocean." Dad and I never corrected her, until it was far too late and her classmates had poked fun at her for it.

I shut my eyes, took in another deep breath, let it out, opened my eyes, and—in the corner of my vision a dark shape shifted. My head turned, but nothing was there, only swaying trees—pillars in the fog.

Maybe I'd seen a branch or a shrub, shifting in the wind. Maybe I'd seen nothing at all.

I turned back, started patting my pockets, searching for smokes. This was an extra stressful week. I deserved a reward for seeing this job through. I'm not addicted, I just like the way it tastes. I kept patting my pockets, coming up short—did I leave them in my bag? Or did I—

CRACK.

I perked up like a startled rabbit, whirled my head to look over my shoulder. I scanned the woods. Another crack—snapping branches. A figure was traipsing through the underbrush. They wore a neon-blue rain jacket with the hood pulled up. One of David's so-called Visitors? No, it couldn't be, I was outside the property line, and—*it was all delusional bullshit anyway*. Still, I climbed quick to my feet and stood as tall as I could.

The stranger paused where the woods gave way to jagged stone. She had pale skin, red hair. The other passenger from the bus? I'd never seen her face aside from the blurry reflection.

She gave a friendly wave, and called something out. "Quite—huh?"

The ocean's roar drowned out most of what she said. I pointed to my ear and shouted, "CAN'T HEAR YOU."

The stranger smiled, cupped her hands around her mouth, and shouted something back, still indecipherable. I shrugged. She started toward me. She seemed harmless in the light of day. Sheepish almost. And even across the clearing I could tell she had kind eyes. I suppose I felt it more than I saw it.

Regardless, I took an instinctual step or two away from the cliff. Can't be too trusting.

5
LOOKOUT

The stranger continued making her way toward me, careful not to slip on the rock, stepping on the same islands of lichen that I had. She slowed to a stop beside me, both of us facing the gray void. I gave her a sidelong glance. Her red hair fell down in wet strings, sticking to freckled cheeks. "Quite the view, huh?" she said, gesturing out toward the foggy nothing. "Well," she added, "on a clear day, at least."

She looked to be in her late twenties. Her big eyes weren't a cold blue, they were dark green and, like I'd sensed before, kind. But up close I detected a shade of melancholy behind them, an undertone of sadness that looked to have settled in years ago. Maybe I was projecting.

She pointed to the right. "Without the fog here, you can see a wedge of open ocean that way." She pointed forward. "And the other side of the inlet over there. More cliffs. Lip of sand down at the bottom in low tide, but no way to reach it." She looked leftward. "On a really clear day you can see all the way to the flats. Out toward Eugene."

"Huh . . ." I said, my thoughts halfway between here and the house, thinking about that cryptic symbol on the boulder, the dead rabbit, and—

The stranger broke into my pondering. "Are . . . you doing okay?"

I gave her another sidelong glance. "What?"

"Everything okay?" Her voice was filled with concern.

"Yeah." I nodded. "I'm good . . . just tired."

"Sorry to pester you but . . . you never know out here . . ."

"Out here?"

She motioned at the gray nothingness. "The Windfall Bluff . . ."

I shook my head, still not following.

"There's . . ." She hesitated, untangling a knot in her red hair. "Some folks come out here when they don't see any other options."

"Ah, gotcha." I turned back to face the gray void. "Jumpers." A little blunt on my part, more speaking before thinking.

She went on, seemingly unbothered by my turn of phrase. "Yeah, there were at least three last year alone. That we know of."

I had no clue how to respond to that. "Wow," I said. "That's . . . rough."

She kept going, offering up more details I didn't ask for: "Most of the bodies are never found," she said. "With all the rocks and the waves down there, it's just far too dangerous to run retrieval operations."

Again, I didn't know what to say.

"Sorry." She shook her head. "Sorry, that's morbid, that's, I'm sorry." She shot out a hand. "I'm Lucy."

I looked down at her outstretched hand for a solid beat, then reached and shook. "Macy . . ."

"Macy and Lucy," she chortled. "Our names almost rhyme."

I offered a polite laugh. "Sure."

Lucy chortled again, oddly amused.

A stretch of uncomfortable silence followed. A gap in the fog passed by, the other side of the inlet faintly visible. Ragged hemlocks clung to rolling slopes, trees forever bent by the punishing ocean winds. The wall of grayish white returned.

I felt the need to say something, make small talk, if only to break the awkward silence. But when I started to open my mouth, Lucy beat me to it: "Not everybody calls it the Windfall Bluff," she said.

"No?"

"Yeah, some people call it the Weeping Hag's Cliff. But I don't like that name. It just, it doesn't have a good ring to it and . . . I think it's mean-spirited, calling an old woman a hag. I mean, we're all gonna be old one day. Hopefully." Lucy looked at me, like she expected a question. I pressed my lips into a straight line and nodded.

She looked away and continued talking. "Explorers," she said, "from like the 1700s, claimed they would see an old woman standing up here on moonlit nights. They said she always wore a tattered green dress, and that her 'wailing cries of sadness could be heard even over the ocean's roar.' They said seeing her meant a storm was coming. Said it was her tears that caused it." Lucy trailed into quiet.

Again, I opened my mouth to respond, and again, Lucy beat me to it, switching topics so fast it nearly gave me whiplash:

"I hike out here a few times a week," she said. "Just to make sure nobody is . . . you know . . ." Gulls cried in the distance, likely poaching eggs from sandpipers on a beach somewhere. Lucy went on, "I like to think me being out here saved at least a few lives. I've talked to a lot of folks who sounded . . . uh . . . pretty depressed." She paused. "Not that you look depressed or anything, I just mean a lot of people out here do."

Seemed like Lucy also didn't think much before speaking. I almost found it endearing in a sad, relatable sort of way.

After another short silence she asked, "You live around here?"

I shook my head. "Nope."

"I figured. You . . . you don't seem like the type."

I didn't know how to take that, compliment or insult? Maybe a bit of both.

Lucy added: "What I mean is, you seem too . . ." She fell quiet, searching for a word, looking around as if it might be out there in the fog. "You seem too grounded to live in Brooksview . . ."

"Thanks . . ."

"The people who live around here are, they're . . . they're uh . . ." Again she looked around for a word, this time finding it in the moss at her feet: "self-important."

"That's a funny way to say rich assholes."

Lucy snickered at this, snorted a bit, then apologized for snorting. I supposed she wasn't so bad. "So, Lucy," I said. "Where you from?"

"Portland, well Oswego, but that's technically Portland, right?" She looked at me, as if waiting for my approval.

"Sure," I said. "Oswego's Portland."

"That's what I always say, it's just easier to call it Portland." Lucy looked over her shoulder, back at the trail from where I'd come. She tensed her jaw. "You didn't use that path, did you?"

"Why?"

"It connects to private property, the owners are a little . . . prickly. Not a fan of visitors. Nice enough couple, but . . . prickly."

"Oh? I'm house-sitting for them."

She gave a perplexed blink. "For the Carnswels?"

"Yeah."

"Are you a relative?"

"No . . ."

She studied me, skeptical. "I'm shocked Mr. Carnswel even let you set foot on the property . . . You should be honored."

I considered telling her that David was dead, three months now, but I didn't have the energy. I gave a *beats me* shrug instead.

She asked, "Did they say where they were going?"

"Just . . . vacation, family stuff. You know them?"

"Uh-huh . . . I was their house cleaner a few years back, did some house-sitting for them too but, Mr. Carnswel . . . I'm sure you know, but he started losing it. I'm surprised he's not in a home by now." She looked at me. "Has he got you turning off lights at three in the morning?"

I gave a hesitant nod.

"Well . . ." She peered over her shoulder, almost like somebody might be listening in. "I should've quit way before I got fired, but the pay was so good. I'd do cartwheels and dress up like a clown for that kind of money . . ." She paused, and clicked her tongue. "There I go, again, taking over the conversation. My mom says I always make conversations about me. I don't think that's true, but my mom is right about a lot of things. One time she—" Lucy paused again, stopped herself.

"Why'd you get fired?" I asked.

Lucy shrugged, unperturbed by the question's bluntness. "The Carnswels were out of town," she said. "I slept through the 'witching hour,' and failed to keep the lights off. I woke up to an email from David saying that 'upon their return, my services would no longer be needed.'" She rocked on her heels, swinging her arms awkwardly back and forth.

A gust of wind volleyed up the cliff, cold spray spitting onto my chin. "Did . . . did you ever see anything?"

She stopped rocking. "Like rabbits?" She shook her head and crossed her arms. "No. Not in the house, but . . . we probably shouldn't talk about it anymore . . ."

"Why not?"

Lucy shrugged again. "I don't know, he just . . . Mr. Carnswel really seems to believe it, and . . . I don't think any of it's real, but . . . maybe we shouldn't talk about it, just in case." She laughed, a nervous, brittle-sounding chuckle. Then she shifted topic yet again. "I still come out here to do cleaning service," she said, "not for the Carnswels anymore, obviously. Just weekly tidy-ups for some of the other houses. It's decent pay, but the tips are garbage if you can believe that."

"I can," I said. Then asked, "You hiring?"

"Not anymore. Corporate's actually downsizing. Pretty sure my neck will be on the chopping block next . . . Maybe you'll have to save me up here soon." She forced another laugh.

I breathed out my nose. "I, uh . . . hope not."

More silence, but it didn't last long. Lucy continued oversharing: "My best friend and me, we grew up in Lincoln, came out here all the time in grade school . . . Zee. Her real name was Brienna, but we all called her Zee. She was a real troublemaker, I was a Goody Two-shoes, but we clicked like Legos. Lucy and Zee. People called us 'Lu-Zee.'" She chortled again. "We'd ring the doorbells on the mansions out here and hide in the bushes and watch the rich folk get all flustered but . . . people started putting up cameras, buying guns, so we stopped . . . Zee, though, she wasn't scared of *anything*. She would've kept going if I didn't rein her in . . . Zee didn't give a f-fuck . . ." Lucy pulled back a bit on the word "fuck," tripped over her syllables like she thought she might get in trouble for saying it.

She tapped her heel against the lichen-covered ground, three short taps. "Zee used to, she had this guitar and . . . she would play me songs sometimes, covers at first, but sometimes songs she wrote. I was the only person in the world who ever heard her singing voice and . . . Zee could sing. Like I mean *sing*. The kind of voice that made you close your eyes when you heard it, you know, gave you chills . . ." Lucy fell silent again, rubbed her nose with the side of her hand and sniffed, swallowed a lump in her throat. She swatted at the air, the same gesture one does when refusing a piece of cake. She looked like she was about to cry.

My toes curled, and a clammy discomfort ran up my neck. External displays of emotion mortified me. I was *horrible* at consoling people I'd known my whole life, let alone strangers I'd just met. Get me to comfort a sobbing human? Hell, I'd be more useful in an open heart surgery.

What was I supposed to do? Reach out and tap her on the shoulder, say, *There, there . . . chin up*?

"I'm sorry," Lucy blathered out, sniffed loudly, and collected herself. "You don't even know me. It's . . . Sorry. I'm trauma dumping, that's not fair . . ."

"Hey, it's all right . . ."

Lucy nodded, little bobblehead movements.

The fog was clearing now, but the sky was getting darker. On the sly, I pulled out my phone and checked the time. My sunfall mandate was approaching. And regardless, I didn't want to be traipsing through the woods in the pitch black.

Lucy scoped me looking at my phone. "You should probably get back home," she said. "It's gonna get dark soon."

"Yeah . . ." I glanced toward the cliff's edge, then back to Lucy's saddened face. "You uh . . ." My jaw tensed, relaxed. "You sure you're good?"

Lucy straightened up, sniffed. "Yeah, trust me, I won't . . ." She gestured weakly at the void, the rumble of waves crashing against the jagged rocks far below. "I'm . . . I'm not a fan of heights, and water. Trust me. I just need to be alone," she said—almost like I was the one that had intruded on *her* space. "I'm safe," she insisted. "Don't worry."

I saw truth in her eyes. I nodded. "Okay, good." I stood there a beat longer, giving her a chance to say something more.

"It was nice to meet you, Macy." She raised her hand for another shake. We shook.

"You too," I said. My hand slipped from hers, then I started back toward the trail. As I stepped into the woods, I looked over my shoulder. Lucy was sitting a good distance away from the cliff's edge, back turned to me. Her legs were crossed, shoulders hunched. She looked like a neon-blue tombstone against a darkening panorama. The last remnants of fog still lingered, cobweb strands across the sky. And a brilliant flash of purple pink seeped up into the gray, the westward sun setting over the Specific Ocean.

6
SHORTCUT

I walked back down the trail, bracing for the return of that dead rabbit's stench—but when I reached the property line, the rabbit was nowhere in sight. There was no sign of anything having dragged it off either. Jemma theories took the wheel: *It vanished into thin air—aliens abducted it.* My own voice of reason stepped up: A bird of prey must have swooped down and carried it off. A hawk or an eagle, maybe a spotted owl. Cold hard logic prevails again.

It was nearly dark out by the time I reached the house. The final rays of sunlight spilled up through the woods, caught the house's top corner, and painted over the olive green with light purple. A color that reminded me of a childhood neighbor—lovely Miss Wiersema. She only wore purple-pink, had four cats, and gave out big candy bars on Halloween.

I walked past the aluminum shed and stopped in the middle of the lawn. The house looked warm again in the evening light. Unassuming. But that only made me feel uneasy. Made my skin itchy. Sometimes I think I'm allergic to feeling safe.

It's when I feel safe that I start to feel scared. Like that feeling you get on a warm summer day when the lake water is just right, so you hold your breath and dive in and swim as far as you can before coming to surface, and when you take that first breath you feel like, for just a moment, everything is as it should be, like nothing in the world is wrong or ever could be wrong again, only for a disembodied voice to tap you on the shoulder and whisper sweetly into your water-plugged ear: *Not to worry, child, things will all turn terrible again soon enough, not to worry one bit*. I don't know, maybe that's just me.

I trudged up the sloping yard, climbed a flight of wooden steps, and pulled the keys out from my pocket. As I unlocked the patio door, my phone started buzzing. Video call from Jemma. I shuffled inside and pressed ACCEPT.

"BRO." Jemma was trekking down a dark suburban sidewalk; the phone was angled straight up at her chin, orange streetlights floating past above. "I tried calling you like three times, fuck hell." She'd started removing the "ing" from "fuck." No idea why. "Macy?"

"Yeah." I pulled the patio door shut behind me and locked it. "Service out here is shit."

"Oh my God-uh." I could hear the eye roll in her voice. "Of COURSE the service is shit. Is there a one-way bridge and a storm on the way too?"

"Funny."

Jemma chomped down on a strand of licorice, then held her phone up to show me where she was. Graywood Park. A few blocks from our place. A shortcut between two sports fields, cross a little bridge over a boggy river, then jump the fence of the boarded-up house, cut through the yard, and boom you've saved ten minutes. I knew the walk well, always took it when I couldn't afford the bus.

Jemma brought her phone back to its original POV, peering up at her chin. "Just had a job interview." She turned a corner and a whooshing sound started hitting the mic with every other step she took.

"Oh?" I drifted through the kitchen, and cracked open the fridge. I grabbed the Tupperware of baby carrots and shut the fridge. "How'd it go?" I asked.

"What?"

"How was the interview?"

"Not good. The manager only asked me like three questions and at the end he said: 'We'll keep in touch.'"

"Isn't that a good thing?"

Jemma grimaced. "That's exactly what I say to guys when I dump them: 'Hey ol' buddy ol' pal, let's keep in touch.' Fuck. Maybe they know I'm a klepto."

I tilted my head. "Isn't that an offensive term?"

"I'm allowed to say it. One sec." Jemma tucked the phone into her shirt pocket, the screen turning dark, the hazy glow of streetlamps through fabric. She grunted, the blurred light swishing upward until THUMP. Jemma slid the phone out. She'd just jumped the shortcut fence. She moved through an abandoned backyard, feet squishing against a long-neglected lawn. "Maybe I should start selling meth," she said.

"Maybe," I replied, only half-joking.

Jemma shrugged. "I got an interview at Target coming up soon, but . . . I'm not crossing my fingers." She let out a long sigh, clearly discouraged.

"Jem, it's okay . . . just, uh . . . just keep at it." There I go again, having no idea how to comfort even my own sister.

Jemma shimmied between a plastic garden shed and the boarded-up house, slipped out onto the driveway, and froze. "Ahhh shit."

"What?"

She strode forward and aimed the phone back at a billboard on the front lawn: "SOYA LIVING—NEW DEVELOPMENT COMING SOON." Below the caption was yet another AI-generated yuppie couple. Big fake smiles. They had a few too many teeth, and a dead-eyed golden labradoodle.

Jemma grumbled. "RIP Shortcut." She continued slogging down the street. "So how goes sitting the haunted house?"

I slumped into a leather armchair, and started snacking on the baby carrots. "I'm still alive," I said. "So that's something."

"Any rabbits yet?"

"Nope." *Not inside.*

"Creepy phone calls?"

"None."

"Visitors?"

"Zero."

"Just you wait." Jemma rounded another corner, her voice now competing with the rumble of traffic. "You're still leaving at the first sign of trouble, right?"

"Honestly, I don't think there's gonna be any." Didn't fully believe that one, but it was a nice lie to keep myself sane.

Jemma narrowed her eyes. "If you die there, it's your fault."

"Okay, victim blamer."

"Plus you're exploiting a lonely widow for her retirement funds."

"She's a multi-millionaire." I used Jemma's own logic against her. "I'm just balancing the scales."

"Whatever. Don't come crying to me when you're dead." She went quiet for a beat. "But if anything happens, get out of there, and call me."

"I will."

"Promise?"

I held up a pinkie finger. "Promise."

Jemma sighed, running a hand over her buzz cut. "If anything happens to you, I'm hooped, Macy. You know that right?"

"Hey, I've heard the foster care system is pretty solid these days."

"Ha."

"Maybe you'll get thrown in with a good family of God. Find the Lord."

"Kill me." Jemma stopped at an intersection, looked both ways, then darted across the street. A car blared on its horn, screeched to a halt. Jemma screamed: "Stupid FUCK!"

"Jesus, Jem, be careful."

She marched off down the sidewalk. "I had the right of way."

"Sure you did." I checked the time. "Look, I gotta try and get some sleep before the witching hour. I'm safe. There's no demons here, everything's good, and I hate you."

Jemma smiled. "Hate you too, sis."

My finger moved toward the END CALL button, but—

"WAIT!" Jemma cried out.

My hand jerked back. "What?!"

"Can I borrow twenty bucks?"

"Ugh." Borrow always meant "have."

"For bus fare."

"I'll send it, but I don't want to hear any more about me being stupid for paying our rent, all right? I already know I'm stupid."

Jemma held up a pinkie. "Promise."

7
GREMLINS

It was the comfiest bed I'd ever lain on, but I couldn't sleep. Normally, I might've popped a zopiclone or two, but I didn't want to risk dozing through my witching hour alarm. So I tried counting things. Counted the panels of the wood vinyl wall, counted the happy people in picture frames, counted the numbers on the rotary phone.

When I ran out of things to count in the room, I shut my eyes and started counting things from the past. All the times I'd been to Disneyland: 0. All the times I'd been to Enchanted Forest: 17. All the times I'd felt like a failure: I stopped counting.

I sat up. Moonlight poured in from the window behind me, forming a bluish puddle on the duvet. I turned to the closet. Its bifold doors were firmly shut. I'd made sure of that before bed—I'm not sleeping with a cracked closet, it's bad luck. I'd also opened every shower curtain in the house.

I looked to the hall. Brownie the cat was sitting in the open doorway, observing me with her mismatched eyes.

Hadn't I closed that door? I parsed back through a foggy haze of endless counting. Back to walking up the stairs, stepping into the guest room, and . . . I couldn't remember. Somehow, I managed to shrug it off. Maybe it was just easier to believe I'd left it open.

Brownie's tail started swishing, serpentine, moving with a mind of its own. "Hey, Browns . . ." I tried to sound aloof, pretend I didn't care. "Can't sleep either, huh?" I looked away from her, ran my eyes over a folded up quilt atop a chest at the foot of the bed. Red-and-white checkered pattern.

I looked at the time: 12:58 a.m.

The glossy white rotary phone pulled my gaze. That antique relic was another reason I couldn't sleep. It sat on the nightstand like a bomb that might go off at any second. Sure, Grace said the mysterious phone calls were just David's imagination, but . . .

I snatched up the checkered quilt from the foot of the bed, and tossed it over the phone. The quilt covered the circular nightstand, forming a little ghost child with checkerboard skin and a phone-shaped head.

A truly embarrassing level of relief fell over me. It was the exact same logic I used when hiding my account balance. What you can't see can't hurt you.

In the blurred edges of my vision, Brownie's head turned. I looked at her. She was peering off down the hall now, toward the staircase. I couldn't see the stairs from here, only a hazy cast of moonlight splashing up onto the wall.

Brownie's ears perked, and her head hunkered forward, like she was trying to get a better look at something she couldn't quite understand. Then, she slowly began to look up, one increment at a time . . . like she was watching someone ascend the stairs . . .

Blood rushed into my temples with an audible hum. The tendons in my neck pulled tight. I listened, absorbing the soundscape with hyperawareness, expecting to hear soft footsteps padding up the stairs, but only hearing pure silence.

My eyes homed in on the hazy moonlight against the wood panel wall—if someone was creeping up the staircase, I'd be able to see their shadow, but . . . there were only the framed photos of happy smiling people. Their smiles seemed to be mocking me now: *Why don't you take a little peek into the hallway, Macy Mullins? Take a gander at the staircase and see what Brownie sees.*

Brownie's head stopped moving, her neck craned sharply upward as if looking at someone impossibly tall. So tall their shoulders would've been hunched against the ceiling. Brownie blinked, mildly curious. Then she slinked forward, out of view.

My heart thumped a rising cadence. My feet swung off the bed, carried me over the cold hardwood. I lingered at the doorway, took a deep breath, and dared a peek into the hall. Brownie was descending the stairs, her swishing tail slipping from sight. No impossibly tall demons to be seen.

It's nothing. I leaned back into the room. *This is fine. Everything—*

—is FUCKED, Imaginary Jemma butted in. *Get out, get out, GET OUT! How many more red flags do you need!?*

It's just weird cat behavior, I countered. *Remember the stray Auntie Pat adopted? The crazy shit it used to do? Hissing at empty closets, bolting after invisible mice—*

YOU NEED TO LEAVE, NOW—

I tuned Jemma out. Slowed my breathing, and put on my blinders. It was only weird cat behavior. That's it. Nothing worth giving up nine grand for. I looked back to the bed, and checked the time again: 1:01 a.m. Only a couple hours until light patrol anyway, not worth trying to sleep at this point.

Pressing my hands to either side of the doorframe, I leaned out into the upstairs hall once more and glanced both ways. Still no demons in sight. Good. All the lights were still off. Even better.

Earlier that night I'd half-considered going to the fuse box and knocking out power for the whole place, but then I'd remembered David's warning not to get smart. *Don't go looking for loopholes, just follow the Rites as presented.* Besides, there was still a chance Grace would look at the cameras.

Couldn't afford to lose that bonus.

I trudged down the stairs. Moonlight cut across my shins, rising higher with every downward footfall. I slowed on the last step. What if it hadn't just been weird cat behavior? I leaned forward, turned my head toward the living room, the kitchen. It was quiet, dark. My eyes scouted for a ghostly outline, impossibly tall, looming in a darkened corner. There was nothing. I listened for footsteps—only hearing the hollow ticks of a nearby clock. I looked to the foyer, the front door. I marched over and checked the handle. Locked.

You're okay, Macy. Just two more days of this, and you're out.

I popped open the fridge, hunched forward, and squinted. My gaze swept over condiments: ketchup, mustard, relish, and why was I looking in the fridge? I pushed it shut, stood back up, and checked the time again: 1:04 a.m. Still two hours till the witching hour. How was I going to kill that much time?

◆

The home theater was even better than I'd imagined. Rocking a ninety-two-inch 8K OLED TV, 7.1 surround sound, heated leather recliners, and a fully stocked minibar. An obscene display of wealth I could get behind. Snatching up a universal remote, I plopped into a La-Z-Boy recliner, kicked up my feet, and . . .

I scanned the menus, searching for a streaming service, but there was only: color calibration, factory settings, and other stuff I didn't give two shits about. I entered a random channel number and—

Static. I changed channels. More static. I pressed the GUIDE button. Nothing. They didn't even have cable? Doesn't every person over sixty have cable? I threw up my hands, about to concede, when I turned to see: a floor-to-ceiling shelf filled with old VHS tapes. It sat in a dark corner behind the minibar. I must have been too distracted by the giant TV to notice it before.

I moseyed over.

It was an impressive selection. Everything from *Jaws* to *Contact* to *Lord of the Rings*. A lot of crossover with my dad's collection. After a bit of perusing, I settled on the first Gremlins. *A truly problematic classic*, as Jemma the cinephile would say. I popped the tape into a VHS/DVD hybrid player, pressed PLAY, and slumped back into my recliner. But before Stripe and the Mogwai had even tricked Billy into feeding them after midnight, I dozed off.

Darkness.

8
SLEEP WELL

Darkness.
    Cold buzzing light. Chlorine stench. Glossy black plastic.
    Darkness. Scratchy fur. Green button eyes.
Red Light.
Darkness
Blue light.
Darkness.
Red.
Darkness.
Blue.

I stand in a windowless room, rough concrete against my bare feet. In the shadows ahead: the faint outline of a bone-white door—blue TV light shimmers from beneath it.

Where am I?

I drift forward, first floating, then walking. My hand grips a cold brass knob, and my wrist turns. The door is locked. I can hear voices on the other side. Jemma's voice, and my own. I press an ear to the door, and hear Jemma ask: "Where are you going?"

I hear myself reply: "A friend's place."

"When are you back?"

". . . Tomorrow."

I can hear Macy's footsteps, padding across our apartment. I can hear her putting on Dad's parachute jacket, tying up her shoes, and rising to stand.

". . . Macy," says Jemma.

"Yeah?"

"This isn't a dream . . ."

"What?"

"It's a memory . . . this isn't a dream, it's a memory . . . this isn't a dream, it's a memory . . ."

The muffled sound of a door creaking open. Macy's footsteps leaving.

"This isn't a dream, it's a—"

Click. The sound of a door softly shutting.

Silence.

I take a small step back from the bone-white door and look around the concrete room. The ceiling feels closer now.

Where am I? How did I get here?

The sound of *Looney Tunes* begins to play on the other side of the white door. Cartoon explosions, orchestral music. I can hear Jemma laughing, but it sounds wrong, forced, "Ha. Ha. Ha. Ha."

I knock on the door, and call out my sister's name. The laughter only grows louder. "HA. HA. HA. HA." I try the knob again. Still locked. Then, in the darkness behind me, something moves: a low and guttural click, followed by a wet and fleshy SQUELCH against concrete. The sound evokes the image of a giant mouth, puking out a tumorous bloat. A mouth with cracking lips, bleeding gums, and a gray tongue.

I look over my shoulder. Only shadows, pitch-dark, stagnant, then—headlights snap to life, two eyes of brilliant bluish white in the distant dark. From behind the locked door, Jemma's forced laughter turns to weeping. Long and sorrowful moans of anguish. Icy coldness seeps around my sock-covered feet. I look down. From beneath the crack of the door bleeds a thin sheet of water. It spreads across the concrete, fans out into the shadows on all sides.

The headlights go dark, and Jemma's weeping turns to a single phrase, two words looping on repeat: "I know—I know—I know—I know—I know—"

The water begins to rise. Reaching my ankles. A terrible realization finally hits, sudden and violent: I'm going to die here. No, worse, I'm not going to die, I'm going to live. Forever. Eternally drowning in a concrete room.

The water reaches my shins.

I spin back to the door, start ramming my shoulder against the scarred wood.

The water reaches my waist.

My shoulder throbs with pain, each impact heavier than the last.

"Jemma," I shriek. "HELP ME!"

"I know—I know—I know—I know—"

The water reaches my neck.

"Jemma, PLEASE!"

"I know—I know—I know—"

The water reaches my eyes.

"I know—I know—"

The water reaches the ceiling.

"I know—"

9
PICKUP

Bzz. bzz. bzz.

When my eyes stammered open, blue light from the TV screen was flooding the room. My heart banged against my rib cage. Had I been having a nightmare?

I slowed my breathing—in through the nose, out through the mouth.

bzz. bzz. bzz.

My phone kept buzzing slow circles in the recliner's cup holder. I tapped the screen and brought it to my face. LED glow assaulted my corneas.

> REMINDER: 2:50 AM—ten minutes until LIGHT PATROL!

Right, the entire reason I was here. Slightly calmer, but still groggy, I stepped out of the room and dragged my feet down the hall. Fragments of the nightmare stuck to my brain, shrapnel without context: icy water, locked door, concrete—I know—I know—I know . . .

Using the job at hand to distract myself, I continued down the hall, checking each room, not bothering to open the doors. Even standing up, I could see well enough beneath the cracks—no light on in the study. No light on in the bathroom. Kitchen . . . nada. I made sure all the main- and second-floor lights were still off, double-checked the locks, and . . . a whispering thought tapped me on the shoulder, told me to cross the living room, take a look out the window. With my feet planted firmly in the kitchen, I peered over my shoulder. My left eye twitched.

Look out the window, the thought repeated.

I tried to ignore it, file it away under sleep deprivation, but next thing I knew I was crossing the living room. I stopped at the window. Through the trees, all the way down in the dimly lit turnaround, sat a white pickup truck. Motionless. Dark. I narrowed my eyes. Even from this distance, even through the trees, I could tell it was a Ford Ranger, early 2000s. The same make, model, and color as Dad's old truck . . .

. . . Was it?

Yet another stupid and childish thought. Of course it wasn't Dad's truck. That was impossible for two simple reasons:

Firstly, this truck didn't have a garish Mullins Mowing logo plastered to its side. A logo that Dad himself had let thirteen-year-old me design. It was a janky cartoon version of him, smiling through a thick beard and giving his signature thumbs-up. The proportions were off, the line work embarrassing, but Dad had said it was perfect.

The second, and more obvious, reason it wasn't Dad's truck was painfully straightforward: Dad's truck was over fifty miles upstate, rusting away at the bottom of the Willamette River. Ever since that night he slipped off a rain-slicked road, barreled through a guardrail, plunged into the water, and never came back up. The police couldn't even salvage the wreck—the water was too deep, the currents too strong. Dad, or whatever was left of him, was still down there too.

Three years ago, a few weeks after Dad's business fell apart, he went out for a drive. It was strange timing, because we were halfway through

Back to the Future, one of his all-time favorites. But less than ten minutes into the second act, Dad had pushed up from the couch, grabbed his keys, and told us he'd be "back in an hour, maybe two."

One hour went by. Two hours. Five. And then—

Three sharp knocks at our front door. Jemma and I looked at each other. Why would Dad knock? He had a key.

It wasn't until another round of door-knocking that I finally got up, trudged over, and answered. Of course, it wasn't Dad standing on our doorstep, it was a couple of cops. I don't remember what they said—I was too stunned to listen.

All I could do was stare past them, watching the lights of their cruiser flash red and blue. Red and blue. Red and blue. Lights that coated our front yard, painted the lawn that Dad himself had mowed the day before. His grass-stained bootprints still visible on the concrete walkway. Red . . . blue . . . red . . . blue . . . red . . .

Later, I learned a witness had captured everything on their dashcam—Dad's truck slipping off the road, barreling through a guardrail, and nose-diving into the Willamette River below.

As the cops spoke, their words sounding muffled and distant, the only thing I could feel was a growing tightness in my chest, right between my lungs. A terrible, twisting sensation that felt like at any moment, the entire world might shatter.

That feeling never really went away.

Ever since, I'd been teetering on the edge of a cliff—always on the verge of toppling. Sure, over the years, I'd gotten better at hiding it, better at coping. And there were moments, sometimes even hours or days, where it almost faded out, turned into white noise. Yet more often than not, whenever that tightness between my lungs loosened its grip and the teetering sensation receded, it was only masked by an even worse, festering emptiness. A miserable nothing that, once it felt comfortable enough, began to argue with terrifying persuasion:

The world might just be a better place with one less Macy Mullins in it. Maybe you should stop teetering altogether and let yourself plummet.

It goes without saying that I never did. Never could. I had to take care of Jemma. I had to be there for my little sister. That doesn't mean I never thought about it, though . . .

Soon enough this existential rumination turned to a bitter hostility at the world in general. It doesn't matter how deep your pain is, how much you wish you could've said one last thing to somebody before they disappeared forever . . . None of that matters. The world keeps on moving. The errands and the debt and the dishes, it all keeps on piling up.

Two days' bereavement.

That's what my employer allotted for grieving. Two business days to process forty-six years of a lifetime cut short. I still remember the day I got back to work, not even a week after Dad's funeral.

Fussy man in a fancy suit: "Excuse me, miss? Miss? I asked for cream in my coffee."

Red light . . . blue light . . .

"Yeah, it's over there, by the door."

"No. No. You don't understand. *You* told me you put cream in it. I walked all the way to my car before I took a sip and realized."

Red . . . blue . . . red . . . I stared blankly down at my reflection in the bar top, wondering how Macy in the mirror world was doing. Part of me hoped she was doing worse, part of me hoped she was doing better. Maybe her dad was still kicking. Then I got jealous. Fuck her. Red . . . blue . . . red . . . blue—

"Miss? Can you look at me when I'm talking to you?" The fussy man waved his hand mere inches in front of my face. I envisioned breaking his fingers, snapping them backward like folding chairs, crack, crack, crack. I looked up at him, slow.

He lowered his hand. "Are you deaf?" he asked.

I stared him dead in the eyes, looked right into his soul, and . . . faked an "employee of the month" smile. "I asked you if you wanted *room* for cream. So I left *room* for cream."

He paused, a hint of trepidation, like I was a snake that had just reared its head, and might strike at any given second. He puffed his chest and frowned. "I . . . I don't appreciate that tone, miss. Can I speak to . . . Do you have a higher-up I can—"

Red, blue, red, blue, red—

"Miss? Are you even listening to me?" He raised his hand next to my ear, pressed his thumb into a finger, and: SNAPPED. I didn't even flinch as the brittle sound shot into my ear canal, fracked down into my cortex, and disturbed the slumber of some deep and ancient wrath I'd never felt before. SNAP. "I'd like to talk with your supervisor," he said. "Miss?"

SNAP. Closer. SNAP. Louder. SNAP.

Every inch of my being wanted to jump the counter and kick his fucking teeth in. But in the name of compromise, I snatched an iced coffee from a passing tray, and whip-chucked it onto his fancy little suit.

Management, believe it or not, considered that "cause for dismissal."

I don't regret ruining that asshole's day. I'd do it all over again if I could. But . . . losing that job kicked off the long fall that led me here, turning off lights in a stranger's house at three in the morning. And in the months after Dad's funeral, I deeply, *profoundly* started to relate with the phrase: Misery loves company.

I'd find myself in a Walmart, scrounging the discounts to put any amount of food on the table. Barely able to put one foot in front of the other, only for Pharrell Williams to start chirping over the storewide speakers:

Because I'm happy
Clap along if you feel like happiness is the truth

On the days I could barely drag myself out of bed, that song made me want to stick a steak knife in my ears.

And I'm not proud of it, but there's a part of me—deep down, festering in a dark and squalid room—that wants everyone else to feel just as miserable as I do. At least it wouldn't be so goddamn lonely.

The pickup truck's headlights snapped on, interrupting my silent brooding, pulling me back into my body, into the present. The headlights, two eyes of brilliant bluish white, pitched a flat column of cold light across the turnaround, up the driveway, through the forest, and into the living room. For a strange, timeless moment, everything felt paralyzed, as if the entire world had frozen solid. Then, the truck lumbered to a start, pulled a U-turn, and unceremoniously drove off.

I stood there, watching the red taillights until they floated around a distant bend and disappeared into the night.

My phone pinged again:

3 AM, Witching Hour.

With a sigh, I turned from the window and got back to work.

It's just a truck, Macy. Just a truck . . .

10
OFF

Make sure you keep all the main- and second-floor lights off between three and four a.m. That's it. That's all. Don't worry about the basement lights. And if you have to use the facilities and can't see in the dark, feel free to switch on a light or two, that's fine, just don't let any of them stay on for more than three minutes at a time. Not one second over three minutes.

◆

"Light patrol" was simple enough. I walked the house in the same exact pattern again and again:

1. Start in the main floor hallway. Any lights on here? No? Good, move on.
2. Check the living room/kitchen/dining room. Any lights on here? Nope? Good. Move on.
3. Traipse upstairs, and repeat. Repeat. Ad nauseam. Then repeat again.

I was almost disappointed none of the lights were turning on by themselves. This was just . . . mind-numbing. I was a sleep-deprived zombie, shuffling back and forth, back and forth, doing little more than nothing. It felt like a dead shift at Starbucks, one of those painfully slow days that almost made me miss the customers.

But it was on patrol loop 26 or 27, when things got "interesting." I was fighting to stay awake, blasting music in my headphones, opening my eyes as wide as humanly possible. I just had to hold on for a few more minutes, then I could crawl into bed and fall asleep.

I slogged into the main-floor hallway, checked each room one by one—no light, no light, no light. I turned back, rounded into the kitchen, and halted. Somewhere in my brain, a warning sharply registered, like a pin pricking at the base of my neck, poke, poke, poke, a nagging sense that I had missed something. I lowered my headphones, took a few steps backward, and leaned into the hallway . . .

Sure enough, at the far end, a thin sheet of white glow was slipping out beneath the crack of the storage room door.

In a huff, I marched over and swung it open. Harsh brightness slammed into my retinas. I raised a shielding hand.

I glanced around. By all appearances, it was nothing more than a plain old storage closet. Stainless steel shelves filled with household supplies: paper towels, garbage bags, and . . . light bulbs—dozens upon dozens of spare light bulbs in little square boxes. Everything looked to be in its right place, save for a glossy black garbage bag, neatly folded on the ground at my feet. I bent over, picked it up, and—my gaze caught something sitting next to an old vacuum: a collapsable metal cage, shiny white with a few remnants of straw scattered inside. The kind of cage reserved for smaller pets, hamsters, guinea pigs . . . rabbits? I set the bag back on the shelf. A sleep-deprived question finally surfaced:

Why am I standing in a storage closet?

Jemma shrieked, hurled popcorn, *TURN OFF THE FUCKING LIGHT.*

Right. I twisted my head both ways, searching for a switch, but there was nothing. I back-stepped into the hallway and there it was, directly beside the doorframe. I clicked it off.

Darkness returned.

Relief, overwhelming and bizarre, fell over me. An echo of that feeling from before, but tenfold stronger. Like nothing I'd ever felt. Like a blissful jolt of pure, unfiltered dopamine, injected straight into my bloodstream. As if I'd just escaped a vicious bear attack in the nick of time, leapt onto a passing train right before the beast's claw snagged me by the ankle. Now I was standing on the caboose, riding off into the sunset as I watched the bear shrink, shrink into the distance. Smaller. Smaller. Gone.

I exhaled long, breathed in deep. All the tension in my body relaxed—more stress I didn't even know I'd been holding melted away like butter on toast, but . . .

What if the bear was doubling back around to the next station, what if I pulled in to find him waiting with a plaid bib and oversized cutlery, what if . . .

What if the light had been on for longer than three minutes?

I groaned. Maybe I should just go to bed, deal with it in the morning. I clearly wasn't in a productive state of mind, but . . .

Grace's voice echoed in my head, *Your bonus will depend on how well you follow the routines . . . routines . . . routines . . .*

Was this a test? Did Grace somehow turn the light on remotely? Was she watching me through the Ring cameras, gauging my compliance? She couldn't be that crazy, but . . . what time was it in Florida anyway? It was 4:01 a.m. here, so that meant—

I stopped myself, focused on the task at hand: How long had the light been on? I pulled up the Ring app on my phone, opened a list of cameras, and tapped: "Main Floor Hallway." The screen snapped to a night-vision, fish-eye view with surprisingly decent resolution. There I was, standing at the hallway's end in real time. My neck was craned at a sharp angle, the glow of my screen making me look like a frizzy-haired little gremlin hunched in the dark. I straightened my posture.

I looked up and around until I scoped out that blinking blue light. The camera, nestled up in the ceiling corner where the hallway began.

Using my thumb, I scrubbed the footage back to 3:55 a.m.

11
SEVEN SECONDS

I let the footage play on the Ring app. A good thirty seconds of empty hallway B-roll went by, until my past self wandered into frame and slouched her way down the hall, barely awake.

As she went, she checked each room one by one—looking down at the crack of every door. At the end of the hall, she gave a little thumbs-up that I only half remembered and started back toward the camera. She meandered out of frame, and then . . . at precisely 3:56:35 a.m., no more than one second after past Macy had exited the hallway, the storage room light snapped ON by itself. A thin line of stark white pixels beneath the door.

A sickly feeling shifted in my gut—like some parasite had stirred in its sleep, and bumped up against my spine. I looked to the actual storage closet right beside me. I made an instinctive retreat to the living room, eyes flicking back to my phone as I moved. *It's just another ill-timed electrical glitch*, I told myself. *Just weird timing.*

On the screen, the hallway continued to sit empty, the light beneath the storage room door still glowing bright. I scrubbed forward. Thirty seconds. One minute, and . . .

My past self snapped into center frame. I scrubbed back until the moment she entered: twenty-seven seconds after 3:57 a.m. One minute and fifty-eight seconds left until the three-minute mandate. She was moving stupidly, infuriatingly slow. God, I felt like Jemma, fighting back the urge to spew obscenities at the screen. Past Macy, completely oblivious to the now glaringly obvious storage room light, checked each room one at a time, then, stopping short of checking the only light that was on, the stupid moron idiot turned herself around, dragged herself back up the hallway, and once again disappeared from view. I held back a rage-filled scream.

Five seconds clicked by until Macy slowly leaned backward into frame and, FINALLY, saw the storage room light.

Thirty-seven seconds left . . .

Hurry, Macy. Hurry. She jolted out of her stupor, marched down the hall, swung open the door, and . . . stood there doing nothing.

Every single voice in my head shrieked at once: *TURN OFF THE FUCKING LIGHT.*

Fifteen seconds left.

Slowly, ever so slowly, Macy bent forward, and picked up the neatly folded garbage bag, then set it on the shelf.

Five seconds left.

She continued standing there, staring into blank space, until . . . she burst into action, fumbled around for the light switch, and . . . SNAP. The storage room went dark.

Seven seconds over the three-minute mandate.

12
UNDERPERFORMANCE

In the event you're dumb enough to fail this one, open the envelope. It will provide further instructions.

◆

Three minutes, seven seconds.

The light had been on for three minutes and seven seconds.

Seven seconds over the mandate.

Seven whole seconds.

Thoughts are sound, thoughts are background noise, thoughts are— three minutes and seven seconds.

You fucked it up, Macy. You fucked everything up like you always do.

Three.

Minutes.

Seven.

Seconds.

Once again, that bizarre dread twisted in my gut, even stronger than before. Like I'd done something morally abhorrent, something vile and contaminated, something against the very order of nature itself. Why did I feel so awful?

It was just a light.

Yes, my slipup put the bonus at risk, but as Grace had told me: *Plus a 3K bonus, depending on how well you follow the routines.*

That language left a lot of wiggle room. A little mess-up here or there didn't rule it out.

No, this was something deeper than money, this was a voice of prophetic doom, whispering to me that maybe, just maybe, David Carnswel was actually right. Perhaps something evil beyond reason truly dwelled on this property, maybe I was the only thing standing between it and the rest of humanity and—

I grit my teeth, pushed down the stupidity. Jemma had gotten to me yet again, that was all. There was no such thing as evil spirits, let alone spirits kept at bay by something as stupid as a light switch. I was just worried about the bonus, that's all this feeling was: the familiar threat of financial ruin. The specter of "DECLINED—INSUFF FUNDS."

If I wanted to keep my bonus, I needed to open that stupid letter and follow whatever stupid directions were inside. Wonderful.

Resigned to my fate, I went over to the fridge, stood up on my toes, and pulled down the wooden tray. I set it on the counter, flicked on a nearby light, and started sifting through. The tray was chock-full of random odds and ends: old receipts, a flashlight, the lime green wand lighter, a FitLyfe bracelet, and—tucked below a flyer for funeral homes—three envelopes held together with a red rubber band.

I lifted the envelopes, and hesitated—a chrome-plated switchblade was lying beneath them. My brow wrinkled. I reached and brought the switchblade into the light. Its handle was cold to the touch. The chrome reflected my face, warped and narrow like I was being squeezed through a straw. I slid my thumb over the smooth, metallic surface, scouting for the switch until CLICK—the blade popped out with a hefty and satisfying SNAP. Carved into its side were scratchy initials:

C.C.

Something Carnswel?

Knife in one hand, envelopes in the other, I walked over to the brown leather armchair, flopped down, and switched on a lamp. I set the letters on the coffee table, side by side.

IN CASE OF LIGHTS—IN CASE OF RABBITS—IN CASE OF EMERGENCY

I held up "IN CASE OF LIGHTS." Then, with a surgeon-steady slowness, I slid the blade into the envelope's fold, careful not to tear the paper. The letter felt oddly significant in my hands, sacred even.

I moved the blade slowly along with delicate care until the envelope flapped open. Inside was a piece of folded-up paper. I flattened it against the coffee table and . . . it was blank. I turned it over. Blank . . .

I held it closer to the light and saw, centered at the top of the page in tiny blue ink font:

FOYER

I flipped it again, double-checked the other side. Nothing. That's it? I twisted in my seat and looked back toward the "foyer." I set the paper and the switchblade onto the coffee table, rolled out of the chair, and padded over. At the threshold, I poked my head around the corner. The foyer was just as it had always been. A narrow nook with a shoe bench, a side table, and the old Victorian coatrack.

I strode forward and checked the front door—locked.

Good.

I peered through the door's glass panel, and surveyed the forest. It was oppressively dark. The only source of light, aside from the moon, was that streetlamp way down in the turnaround. The white truck was nowhere to be seen. I rubbed my neck, massaging a stubborn knot below my ear. I was about to turn away, when . . .

Outside, down at the base of the concrete steps, a motion light snapped on. Stark white, like a camera flash frozen in time. The sharp glare lent every little bump a pitch-black shadow: slight mounds in the gravel driveway casting pointed fingers toward the woods.

I lingered, my body motionless, my eyes frantic, searching for whatever had set off the light. There was nothing I could see.

I imagined a skinless carnival creature hiding around the corner, both hands raised to its mouth, nibbling away on overgrown fingernails, preparing to reclaim its pelt with giddishly evil anticipation, when . . . out hopped a rabbit.

Anticlimactic, sure, but with the context of everything—it put me even more on edge. This rabbit wasn't white, though; it was a patchy mix of brown and black. It hopped to the base of the steps and nestled down, a little ball of fur. Its ears suddenly shot straight up, and it lurched to its hind legs. It looked toward the forest.

I scanned the woods, trying to see what it was looking at, but there was nothing out there, nothing between the dark columns of the trees, nothing *I* could see at least.

The rabbit bolted, bounding down the driveway, kicking up gravel as it went. It zipped across the turnaround and out of view.

The motion light snapped off.

Darkness returned.

Once more, David's cryptic words played out in my head, *the failure of one Rite often triggers the next*. Was the storage room light to blame?

I berated myself for even having the thought. Sure, it was another case of peculiar timing, but there were a lot of rabbits out there. I shook my head and turned away. *Just go to sleep, Macy.*

Maybe I should double-check all the locks first, though. Just to be safe.

13
RELIEF

As you may have noticed, there's a lot of stray rabbits out here. Even with all our doors shut, the big-eared rats keep finding their way inside. If you see one within a fifty-foot or so radius of the house—you must lock all doors that lead to the outside. For some reason, don't ask me why, that seems to help keep them at bay.

◆

I checked the door that led to the garage first. Yes, still locked. Relief. I checked the patio door next. Yup, still locked. Relief. Wait, did I lock the front door? Yes, of course I did, literally thirty seconds ago. Or was that just how I remembered it? Maybe my memories were lying to me. Or maybe it *had* been locked, and my dumb ass *unlocked* it.

I stomped into the foyer, and poked my head around the corner. Okay, it's locked. Wait, does horizontal mean locked, or should it be vertical? I went over and tested the handle. Locked. Relief. Okay, all doors that led to the outside were locked. But what about the patio door?

MACY. YOU JUST FRIGGIN' LOCKED IT.

Yes, I know that, but . . . what if I didn't?

This was getting out of hand. It wasn't even paranoia anymore, or at least not a paranoia I'd ever experienced. I felt like an addict, chasing little bumps of dopamine every time I checked a lock. *Relief, relief, relief.*

On top of that, these intrusive, repetitive thoughts were starting to feel like fragile glass tendrils, sprouting inside of my brain, interconnected. If I were to ignore them, leave those locks unchecked, the tendrils would shatter, and countless splinters of glass would be permanently stuck inside of my head like dollar-store glitter. What in the fuck was wrong with me?

Sleep deprivation, I reminded myself. *It's just lack of sleep, Macy, get some shut-eye. You'll be back to normal in the morning.*

Still, maybe, just maybe, I didn't lock the patio door. I wheezed out an exasperated groan. My feet carried me back across the living room, through the kitchen, and up to the patio door. Locked. *Relief.*

All right. I was done. I would just check the garage, one last time, just to be sure, then I would go to bed.

As I moved back through the living room, something caught the corner of my eye. I halted dead in my tracks. The letter. It was still sitting right where I'd left it, beneath the lamp's glow on the coffee table. But now, the previously blank side was covered in words . . .

I felt the blood drain from my face. Felt my skin turn cold.

I trooped over, reached for the letter, and stopped short. How did the words get there? Delayed invisible ink? Something that only appears when exposed to the air? Was that even a thing?

Leery, I lifted the letter, turned it over, and began to read.

14
IN CASE OF LIGHTS

If you are reading this, it means you have failed the first Rite.

(If you are reading this without having failed, stop reading now. Place the letter back in the envelope and reseal it immediately.)

Because of your failure, you will face a moderate setback in your personal life at some point in the next twenty-four hours. I can't say what exactly, it's different for every person, but it certainly won't be pleasant. From here on out, be on guard as the rabbits are much more likely to appear.

(The phone is more likely to ring as well, so keep an ear out.)

Aside from the above, there will be no further instructions, unless given to you through a different letter, or a phone call.

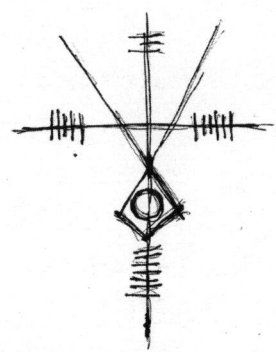

May the Last Enduring God
guide us gently back to sleep . . .

15
GET OUT

I lowered the letter, furrowed my brow. My sense of unease gave way to confusion, annoyance even. That's it . . . ? I'll face a "moderate setback" in my personal life? As Jemma would say: *I'm shaking in my boots.*

I folded up the letter, tucked it back into its envelope, and set it in the tray.

I stood there at the kitchen island, arms crossed. *May the Last Enduring God guide us gently back to sleep.* I pulled out my phone and googled the phrase. Nothing came up. I tried "Last Enduring God" on its own in quotes. Literally zero results.

Jeepers. David was even more off his rocker than I thought.

What about the magically appearing ink? Jemma butted in. *And what about the symbol—*

It's just a weird symbol, Jem. Doesn't prove anything.

Jemma went on: *The Devil himself could show up, and you'd gaslight yourself into thinking it was a trick of the light. Best case scenario, David was the leader of some crazy cult. Heck, he's probably still alive, living in the walls and—*

Seriously, Jem? This isn't—

GET OUT, NOW, YESTERDAY! she screamed over my train of thought, drowned out all other reasoning. Everything I'd been brushing off, big or small, came rushing up to the surface, like a mob of spiders scrambling out of a dark pit: the light turning on by itself at the exact moment I'd left the hallway, the compulsive urges to check locks, the "weird cat behavior." Everything.

I tapped into Uber.

> No rides available in your area at this time.

I checked the Coastal Connector bus schedule—next one wasn't for another five hours. I paced to the window, stared down the long winding driveway, and chewed on a fingernail. Maybe I could walk to the Transit Center, wait it out in the cold—

Macy, stop.

My own voice of "reason" butted in: *You are making oceans out of puddles. This, all of this, is nothing but the delusions of an old man. And if you leave now, you are leaving six thousand bucks—*

MACY, DON'T LISTEN TO HER. SHE'S AN IDIOT AND THIS HOUSE IS HAUNTED AND—

Both of you shut the fuck up.

I released a flustered groan—I NEEDED to sleep, figure this all out later. Hell, even if this house *was* undeniably cursed, the pay was probably worth the trouble. I checked the time—4:23 a.m.—I trudged over to the stairs, and stopped halfway up. I looked over my shoulder, down toward the foyer. Maybe I should check those locks, just one more time. Yeah, just one more check for safety.

Then I would go to sleep.

16
BAD THOUGHTS

After one last round of lock checking—*relief, relief, relief*—I crawled back into my offensively comfortable bed. I rolled onto my left side. The red-and-white quilt was still draped over the rotary phone—a little checkered ghost peering over the edge of the mattress. I rolled onto my right side, shut my eyes, and tried to fall asleep.

The sounds of the house conspired to keep me awake. An old pipe rattled somewhere in the ceiling. The spindly branch of an oak tree scraped against a window. And du-dum . . . even Brownie the cat. Though I would've struggled to sleep regardless of these sounds. Regardless of everything else going on.

Bad thoughts always come before sleep.

Thoughts that make me wish I couldn't think at all. Regrets and fears and what might have been. Most nights, the only way I can fall asleep is to convince myself that this version of me will blink out of existence, and the Macy of tomorrow will be forced to take over. A carbon copy Macy. Burdened with all my memories, all my failures, left to deal with the mess I'd left behind. Poor thing. But, just like me, she'd only have to cope for one day. Fall asleep, blink out in the night, leave her problems to the Macy of tomorrow, repeat, repeat, repeat.

Bad thoughts come before sleep. But the worst thoughts come in the morning.

In the morning there was always that moment, that blurred boundary between sleep and waking, where I smelled waffles and coffee, heard Dad singing old songs in the wrong key, Jemma laughing. Everything as it should be. I was back in my house, back in my home, and the last three years had only been a nightmare, oh thank God, thank God, thank God.

Some mornings I'd lie there, keeping my eyes closed for as long as I could, pretending it was all real. But sooner or later, I'd always come back to reality, find myself on a rickety cot, staring up at the blades of a broken ceiling fan, and Dad would die all over again.

Dad died three years ago, and he'd died eleven hundred and twenty seven times since.

Pull yourself out of bed, put on your work clothes, red, blue, brush your teeth, red, blue, get on the bus, red . . .

Then I'd spend the rest of the day waiting for the pattern to repeat itself. Dad would die again tomorrow. And the morning after that. And the one after that. But it wasn't my problem. Not anymore. It was the Macy of tomorrow's cross to bear . . .

And that promise, along with an unprescribed zopiclone or two, would lead me gently into sleep.

17
GOOD BUGS

Darkness. Red light. Blue light. Lawn mower. White truck. Darkness. Chlorine stench. Bluish-green carpet. Darkness—

Dad stirs awake, my tiny hand gripping his forearm. He rubs his eyes, glances at the time:

2:57 a.m.

He switches on his bedside lamp. His curly brown hair is messy, and he's wearing an old Fleetwood Mac T-shirt. Jemma stands behind me in the doorway, clutching a Super Mario blanket. I'm hugging a pillow. How old am I? The pillow turns into a stuffed rabbit, green button eyes, scratchy fur—Doc.

I tell Dad there's a spider in our room.

He pushes off the bed to stand, and rustles my hair. "Okay, kiddo," he sighs. "Lead the way."

The spider is constructing a web in the corner of our bedroom ceiling. Right above the top bunk headrest. Sharp and wiry legs, crawling between glow-in-the-dark planets and stars. It's just a house spider, but somehow it's bigger than a dinner plate.

"All right," says Dad, not a hint of fear in his voice. He trudges into the bathroom and comes back with an empty glass. He strides over to our little art desk and grabs a piece of lime green construction paper. The spider is small now. Dad barely has to stand on his toes to reach it. He carefully places the cup over the spider, then slides the paper underneath. He starts back across the room.

"Can I see?" Jemma asks.

Dad nods. He lowers to a knee. Jemma and I gather around. The spider scrambles madly against the cup, like it's trying to break through. I can hear its tiny feet ting-ting-tinging against the glass.

Dad says, "She's more scared of us than we are of her."

"She?" says Jemma.

Dad nods again, tells us the spider's name is Rosey.

He rises back to standing, and heads downstairs. We follow him through the living room, and out the front door, and onto the stoop. He slows on the walkway that cuts across the front lawn. A motion light snaps to life, spreading his shadow out over the yard, into the street. There's no traffic. Normally the road is busy, even at night. Dad crouches down. Sets the construction paper and cup onto the grass. He lifts the cup.

Rosey the spider doesn't move. So Dad gently jostles the paper until she scurries off. He stays crouched there, watching her go. Now he's wearing his parachute jacket, worn-out jeans, and grass-stained work boots.

Red and blue lights start flashing across the yard, but there are no police cars in sight. Jemma and Dad don't seem to notice.

"What if Rosey comes back inside?" Jemma asks.

Dad pushes off his knees to stand. "Then we'll let her out again."

I ask why he didn't just squash her.

Dad gives an amused smile. "Because spiders are the—"

For a split second, everything goes dark. When light returns, Jemma and Dad are gone. I'm left alone. Standing on the front stoop of my childhood home, clutching Doc tight as I shiver in the frigid night air.

Dad's voice calls out from the open door behind, "Macy, come on inside, you'll catch a cold."

I try to turn, but my legs won't budge. I can only move my eyes. I try to look behind me, try to see Dad one more time. My eyes strain to their farthest corners, aching, staring into blurry dark.

"Macy?" Dad repeats.

I try to speak, to call for help, but only a whimper escapes. The air grows colder, claws into my skin, burning.

Dad's heavy footsteps approach. My hopes rise. Maybe he'll carry me inside, maybe he'll save me. He slows to a stop right behind me, stands there for a moment, then releases a terrified gasp. "Oh God . . . No, no, no . . ." The fog of his breath plumes far above my head. I keep trying to turn my neck, to look back at him, to scream for help, but—

Dad slams the door shut—the lock turns, his muffled footfalls retreat deeper into the house. And just when I think it's the most terrible thing I've ever heard . . . another sound bleeds into my awareness—a strained and wheezing gasp. It's underscored by a guttural rattle, like an empty can of spray paint being shaken. My eyes dart forward. A looming figure stands in the center of our front yard—pale and thin—skeletal features horribly defined in the motion light's raw glare.

It's an old woman, no, not old, *ancient*. So gaunt her pale skin looks vacuum-sealed against her bones. She's standing with her back turned, arms dangling at her sides, completely naked, save for . . . wrapped around her head, a plastic bag, glossy and black—bright red electrical tape holding it in place around a withered neck. As she exhales, the bag slowly expands like an exposed lung . . .

She inhales, the bag collapses, wraps tightly around the shape of her skull. Another wheezing exhale, the bag expands . . . Inhale, the bag shrinks . . .

Terror, pure and cold, floods into my limbs like liquid metal—coats my tendons and bones, solidifies, and starts to constrict. Again, I try to turn back for the door, try to scream for Dad, but I can't open my mouth. Can't move. Can't even blink.

The old woman's wheezing grows faster, each rattling breath shorter than the last. And her arms begin to rise, inch by inch, until they are parallel with the ground. She stands there, arms outstretched like she's been tied to an invisible cross. With every quickening breath, her jutting rib cage swells against bloodless skin. Skin pulled so tight, it might just burst into shreds—like Saran Wrap stretched over ground beef—wrinkled tubes of grayish-white meat beneath. Wrinkled tubes that begin to pulse with embryotic unison: *ku-schlump, ku-schlump, ku-schlump*. Maggots. Thousands of them, squirming and writhing, devouring her from the inside out with eager abandon. Her breath keeps growing faster, faster, until she is hyperventilating and—silence.

She stops moving, mid-breath. A strange and monotone sound reverberates, the low buzz of humming through closed lips:

mmmmmmmmmmmmmm

The sound rises higher and higher without resolve. My terror rises in tandem. My psyche teeters, like I'm on the verge of toppling into a pit of rusty needles. And all the while, that horrible sound continues to rise, higher and higher—until it turns into a teakettle shriek, scraping my eardrums like jagged fingernails. The stench of vodka and chlorine fills the air, and then—

Silence returns.

The woman's arms fall back to her sides, limp. She stands there, shoulders slumped, then collapses like a tower of cards. Her skin is a bag of loose bones on the wet grass.

Another moment of silence.

A distant siren wails in the dark, then fades away.

The pile of loose skin starts to move, twitch and bubble, like water being brought to a boil. A shape begins to rise, the skin draping over it like a thin sheet—bones SNAP into place, new limbs forming altogether. Dozens of arms, dozens of joints. Screams and sobs of tortured pain score its every twisting movement, hundreds of different voices, and—

Don't look.

I force my eyelids shut. Darkness. I keep trying to move, clench my fingers, strain my toes, and—

Behind me, the sound of a lock turns, the door creaks open, and all at once my limbs jolt back to life—I spin on my heel, turning to flee inside, only to lurch to a stop.

The front door to my childhood home doesn't lead to a familiar foyer, it leads to a dark and narrow hall, numbered rooms on either side. An old hotel. *The Hawthorne Hotel.* Déjà vu hits me like a cold gust of wind—I've been here before. *When? Why?*

At the hallway's far end sits a white door—a thin line of red light bleeding out from beneath, exposing bluish-green carpeted flooring—patchy, and worn down to the boards, like elbow skin sandpapered to the bone.

Something behind me shifts, stuttering footfalls, dozens of them, thump, thump, thumping against grass.

I run, hurtle toward that white door, and grip the handle. Locked. Voices leak out from the other side, soft and gentle. Jemma's voice, my voice, a familiar conversation:

"Where are you going?" says Jemma.

"A friend's place," says Macy.

"When are you back?"

". . . Tomorrow—"

The voices go silent. I'm pounding on the door now, screaming, shrieking for help. But my screams are muffled, my lips are stuck together, the skin melting like candle wax.

Behind me, the cacophony of approaching footfalls slows to an ordinary cadence, two feet padding softly against carpet. The air grows even colder. I keep screaming, unable to make a sound. Keep banging on the door, unable to leave a dent, when—

The footfalls slow to a stop. The air shifts. The tendons in my neck spasm, my head starts to turn, but I force myself to look straight ahead, and stare at the white flecked paint of the locked door. *Don't look back. Never look back.*

An empty voice breathes into my ear, so close a frigid exhale brushes against my hair, so close I can smell the rot from within its bowels—like spoiled milk and open sewage. "Macy Mullins," the voice whispers. "I know you . . ."

18

A MODERATE SETBACK

I jolted awake in a cold sweat. The nightmare held vivid. I could still smell the rot, feel that icy breath, hear that terrible whisper: *I know you...*

I was used to having bad dreams, shit, I *only* had bad dreams, but never anything like that... it felt more real than my waking life...

bzz. bzz. bzz.

My phone vibrated against the top of a nearby dresser. I shook off the nightmare—*That's all it was, Macy, only another nightmare. Just a bad dream. Nothing more.*

I reached over and tilted the screen:

REMINDER—DAD'S B-DAY 2MORROW

Didn't I delete that notification last year?

Golden sunlight cut through the window blinds and sniped the corner of my eye. How long had I been asleep? I checked the time: 5:56 p.m. Jesus. Almost thirteen hours. That's what I got for taking a zopiclone on an empty stomach at five in the morning. Phone still in hand, I climbed out of bed and wandered into the hall, the horrible dream mercifully fading.

bzz. bzz. bzz.

What is it now?

UNKNOWN CALLER

Either a debt collector or a telemarketer. Feeling a little more wrathful than usual, I tapped ACCEPT and shouted "FUCK OFF."

Silence. And then, "Macy . . . ?"

It was a middle-aged man, a voice I recognized but couldn't quite place.

"Uh . . . this is Greg," he said, "your father's insurance broker."

"Oh . . . my bad . . . you, your caller ID said unknown so I . . ."

"No, it's okay, it's okay, I'm used to it." He gave a nervous laugh. "Anyways, is this a good time to talk?"

"Sure . . ."

Greg cleared his throat—something he always did before delivering bad news. "We've uh . . . We've had a bit of a moderate setback with your father's claim."

A moderate setback . . .

"It's still developing," Greg continued, "but last we heard the insurance company was, er, is . . . moving to deny you and your sister's payout."

That ever-present tightness between my lungs swelled, forcing my rib cage to expand. I took a breath. "Wasn't it supposed to be a done deal?"

"Well, it's uh . . ." He stopped himself, changed course. "There can be a lot of reasons for this sort of thing. We can send an appeal, but I have to be honest, Macy, it's uh . . . it's not looking good, and—"

"Greg. Why are they backing out?"

Silence.

"Greg?"

"They're saying new evidence has come to light that suggests your father's claim may be invalid . . . Anyway, as I said, it's uh, complicated stuff."

"Greg, just tell me."

"Well, uh . . ."

"Greg."

Again, he cleared his throat. "They're suggesting your father's passing may have been . . . self-inflicted. Or at the very least . . . his, uh, mental state is being called into question."

"Self-inflicted? Mental state? Greg, he didn't even leave a note, he—he drove into a fucking river. Self-inflicted!?" I spoke with fury, but it rang false. The possibility of Dad's death being . . . It always lurked in the back of my mind, but as with so many other things, I shoved it down and refused to acknowledge it. Dad never would have left us. Not by choice. Never. Even if he thought it would get us some big insurance payout. Dad wouldn't do that. Dad wouldn't do that. Dad wouldn't—

Before my thoughts could drag me into a spiral, I dissociated—hit the "emergency escape button." Ejected from my head like a pilot from a compromised fighter jet. Watched the tailspinning fireball from a floating distance. This wasn't happening to *me*, it was happening to a carbon copy Macy. Sucks for her, but it's not my problem. I was only a spectator, safely floating away.

"Macy," said Greg, "I uh . . . can understand your frustration, but with your father's company going under only weeks prior to the incident, his history of depression, and his previous attempt. It just—"

"Previous attempt?" I heard myself ask.

More silence.

"Oh . . . oh, I'm sorry, I thought you, oh shoot."

"Greg, what previous attempt?"

"I really shouldn't say any more."

"Greg."

"It uh . . ." Greg paused. "It was long before he had you."

A terrible silence.

". . . I'm really sorry, Macy." Greg finally spoke. "I thought you knew."

I didn't respond.

"Macy?" his voice crackled out from the speaker, but I was barely listening anymore. In fact, I'd lowered my phone about five seconds ago. Not because of anything Greg had told me. No, I stopped listening because down at the end of the hallway, curled up at the top of the staircase, was a brown rabbit.

19
HUNT

If you see a rabbit inside the house, especially a white rabbit, catch it within ten minutes of sighting, release it outside, and lock the doors. If you fail to do so, open the "IN CASE OF RABBITS" envelope for further instructions. Do NOT let the rabbit outside after ten minutes have passed. Read the letter first.

◆

The brown rabbit's eyes were a cold blue, so pale they were almost white.

As I stared it down, Greg kept talking on the other end. "Macy? Can you hear me? Hello?" I ended the call. Insurance headaches would have to wait for later. Right now, I had more important things to worry about. I tucked away my phone, started inching closer, and whispered a pitiful: "Hey there, little buddy." The rabbit tilted its head, doglike, sizing me up.

"We're okay," I said, trying and failing to sound harmless, "no one's gonna hurt you." The rabbit took a nervous shuffle-step backward, overgrown claws clicking against hardwood. It froze. I froze too.

Deathly quiet.

I slowly reached into my back pocket and pretended to pull something out. I hunched down, offered a clenched fistful of nothing, and made that tsk-tsk-tsk clicking sound with my tongue. "Here's a little snack." The rabbit's ears perked up, intrigued. Then, it took a cautious hop closer, sniffed the air, and glanced back toward the stairway. "C'mon, Doc," I coaxed. It struck me as a "Doc" kind of rabbit.

I clicked my tongue again, tsk-tsk-tsk.

Doc hopped closer, this time a little braver. My trap was working. After a few more sniffs, he hop-hop-hopped toward me. Almost there, come on, just a couple more hops and—

RIIIING.

The rotary phone went off like a gunshot. Doc, in a scrambling flurry, leapt down the stairs with two bounding hops, slammed to the foyer floor, and careened into the living room.

The phone kept ringing. So loud it hurt my ears.

Grace?

Scatterbrained, I hurtled into the bedroom, whipped the checkered quilt off the nightstand, and brought the phone to my ear. "Hello?"

Dead silence on the other end. I was about to hang up when—

"D-don't let it get away." The voice of a middle-aged woman. A voice I did not recognize. "Don't let it get away," she begged, as if her life literally depended on it. "P-please don't let it get, don't let it get away, don't let it—"

BEEP.

The call went silent, nothing but a low buzz on the other end. Profoundly disturbed, I set the phone back on the base and . . . *Catch the rabbit first, Macy, worry about whatever the fuck that was later.*

I shot out of the room, and barreled down the staircase. I pushed off the foyer wall, bounded into the living room. Head on a swivel, I looked to my right, my left. No rabbit in sight. Great. How much time did I have? I checked my phone: 6:11 p.m. Okay, probably until 6:20. Still moving, I set an alarm and tucked my phone away.

If I was a rabbit, where would I hide?

I dropped to my knees, placed my head flat against the floor, and started crawling, peering under couches, tables, any nook or cranny I could think of. Nothing. Nothing. Nothing.

A skittering scrape echoed from the back hallway.

I pushed to my feet, bolted across the kitchen, into the hall—past the den, past the home theater, the study, the Jacuzzi bathroom, the storage closet, the last corner, and—

The basement door was wide open, a gaping maw of inky shadow, and of course, there sat Doc—nestled in the doorframe's dead center. One false move, and this big-eared rat would plunge into the darkness below. I stood there, deadlocked, the seconds slipping away like sand.

I held out another clenched fist, and took a careful step forward, again making the tsk-tsk-tsk sound. But Doc wasn't falling for the same trick twice. He spun away and leapt into the darkness.

I hustled over and switched on the light—a warm incandescent glow flickered to life. I lingered. This basement, or at least the staircase leading down to it, looked nothing like the mold-infested cellar Grace had invoked. The steps were a spotless white vinyl, and the walls were a light hue of unblemished yellow. A chilly draft wafted up from below, forming goose bumps on my skin. I took one downward step and halted.

Jemma's popcorn commentary chimed: *Going into the basement alone? Classic fuckup.*

A fair point, but . . .

. . . don't let it get away, don't let it get away, don't let it—

I descended. At the base of the stairs, I grasped at the wall and flicked on another light to reveal a standard-looking basement. A garage-sized space with several rooms on either side. Glossy concrete flooring, stucco ceiling, yellow walls. No furniture, only a few empty shelves.

At the far end, receding into darkness, was another hallway, and: there sat Doc, waiting at the threshold, taunting me with a blank stare.

Before I even made it one step, he scampered off, overgrown claws click-clacking against the floor as he slipped into the uninviting shadows. Even though I couldn't see him, I could still hear his feet click-clack-clicking. He kept going, and going—*how long was this hallway?*—until silence returned.

My heart pounding, I strode over, checking the time as I went. Barely two minutes left. I stopped at the hallway's entrance, flicked the nearest light switch, and—

Nothing.

I tried again, up, down, up, down. Still nothing. I looked at the ceiling—no bulbs in the sockets . . . I leveled my chin, narrowed my eyes, and peered into the abyss. The hallway stretched about half the length of a city bus before plunging into darkness. Yellow walls. No doors . . .

The click-clack of Doc's paws returned, yet this time, he wasn't running away. His frantic skittering drew closer, closer. I hunched forward, cupping my hands near the floor like a goalie.

In a blur, Doc dashed out of the shadows, beelined right past me, zipped across the concrete, scrambled up the stairs, and disappeared from view. I gazed blankly at the staircase, about to bolt after him, when—

DING. DING. DING.

My phone timer went off. Ten minutes.

The familiar weight of failure draped over me like a drenched cloak, making my back ache. I marched forward, only for another nagging thought to whisper in my ear: *Take a peek over your shoulder, Macy Mullins.*

I slowed, almost involuntarily, and turned back to the darkened hall.

I squinted. My vision had adjusted, and . . . at the far end I could now see the faintest silhouette of an object. Despite the shadows and the distance, I knew exactly what it was: the TV set from David's video. Sitting atop a VCR pushcart in the hallway's dead center. It looked bizarrely sinister, looming in the dark. Yes, it was only an inanimate object, completely motionless, but somehow it felt alive. As if it might sprout eight segmented legs, sharp and wiry, then scuttle after me like a face hugger.

I turned on a dime, hoofed it back upstairs, broached onto the main floor, and slammed the door shut in my wake. No more basement. I trooped down the hall, rounded into the kitchen, and—

Nearly stepped on Doc.

He was just sitting there, right next to the island, not a care in the world. Not even scratching at the floor. Of course he stopped running *after* the time ran out.

I looked to the wooden tray resting atop the fridge. Fuck hell. I plopped the tray down on the countertop, pulled out the "IN CASE OF RABBITS" envelope, and tore it open. The letter was entirely blank, save one word:

FIREPLACE

The hairs on the back of my neck stood at attention. I looked across the room, toward the far corner. There sat the wood-burning stove, dunes of white ash piled against its glass door.

I held the letter up to the sunlight. The faint markings of other words were etched onto its surface. Another invisible ink trick. I waited, and soon enough, the entire message became clear.

20

IN CASE OF RABBITS

If you are reading this, it means you have failed to catch a rabbit within the ten-minute mandate. Hopefully, at this point, you have not let the rabbit outside. If you have, then go outside immediately, catch it, bring it back in, and continue reading.

In order to rectify your failure, a price must be paid.

You must burn the rabbit alive.

Horrific, I know, but this creature isn't real. It is a construct of the evil that dwells on this property. Even so, I implore you to leave the house while it burns. The screams of a dying rabbit, real or not, can be quite disturbing. Human-like.

(There is a wire cage in the storage closet, I recommend putting the rabbit inside it while building the fire.)

Unfortunately, the consequences of refusing to enact this Rite are three-fold:

1. You will suffer a devastating setback in your personal life.
2. The likelihood of a Visitor knocking at the door will increase by a factor

of ten (Remember: Visitors will always have cold blue eyes and introduce themselves with three knocks at the front door).

3. Going forward, you can no longer catch rabbits and let them outside, you must burn each and every one within five minutes of sighting.

For the sake of your own well-being, and humanity at large, burn this offering to avoid these consequences. It's a small price to pay.

You have until the clock strikes its next hour to decide.

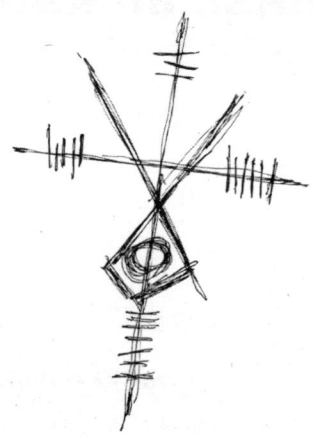

We defend even those who cast filth upon your name.

21
CLOCKING OUT

Nauseated, and a little confused, I lowered the letter. There was no way in hell I'd be burning a rabbit alive. This wasn't up for debate. It was a downright disgusting thing even to consider, but, again . . .

. . . what if this *was* real?

Not possible. It's only the ramblings of an unwell mind, and—

What about that moderate setback? Jemma reasoned. *What about the "don't let it get away" phone call? What about—*

SHUT UP. This isn't real. This isn't real. And even if it is, I am not burning a rabbit alive.

Okay, then how about that devastating setback? Jemma countered. *If losing Dad's insurance payout was "moderate," what in the fuck would "devastating" look like?*

The sun caught my eye, glinting off a nearby picture frame. Dusk was already creeping into the woods. Shadows pooling around the underbrush like a slow rising tide . . .

I checked the time: 6:56.

Four minutes to decide. Could I even make a fire that fast? I looked to the wood-burning stove—beside it sat a stack of old newspapers and a wicker basket filled with logs and kindling—

scritch-scratch-scritch-scratch-scritch-

The rabbit clawed at the patio door, desperately trying to get out.

"Doc?"

He spun at the sound of my voice. His ears were flat, his pale blue eyes filled with: *You're considering it, aren't you? You're actually considering burning me alive. You monster.*

I looked to the fireplace again, then back to the rabbit. I drifted over, one foot after the other. As I approached, Doc cowered against the door, petrified. After a few more steps, I slowed to a stop above him. I reached forward and unlocked the patio door. My hand lingered far too long before I pushed the door open and shooed Doc out.

He scrambled down the flight of wooden stairs, across the shaggy lawn and slipped into the darkening woods.

I stood there, watching him go, and breathed a long sigh of relief—I'd made the right choice. Now it was time to grab my things, and get out of—

Don't let it get away.

My left eye twitched, and my heart began to pulse—a terrible pounding like drums from the deepest level of hell. My insides began to itch, and a crushing weight pressed down on my shoulders, like I'd just made the biggest mistake of my entire life. As if this moment, right here, would haunt me until my final gasping breath. My nerves buzzed with dread, and—

Enough of this.

I was done. I locked the patio door, and rushed deeper into the house. *Grab your stuff, get out of here.*

It's a funny thing, caring about inanimate possessions during times of impending doom. There's a reason they drill it into you on airplanes: leave your baggage behind. A shocking number of people burn alive because their panicking brain told them they couldn't forget their carry-on. Well, I was the panicking idiot now, rushing upstairs to grab my ratty old Pikachu backpack, instead of just hauling ass outside like I should have. Though in my defense, I really needed a smoke.

I launched upstairs, three steps at a time. Burst into the guest room and—

Where was my bag? I'd left it right beside the nightstand. I know I'd left it there I . . . Fuck it. Time to go. I was back-stepping into the hallway, when, down the stairs, in the foyer below, three hollow knocks echoed at the front door.

22

VISITOR

If anybody with cold blue eyes shows up at the front door between 6 p.m. and 6 a.m., do not talk to them—do not let them see you, and, most importantly, do NOT let them inside. Hide. Hide and pray you didn't forget to lock any of the doors. Don't worry about locking the windows. The Visitors won't even climb through an open window; they only use doors. And they won't force their way inside, not usually.

◆

A cold knot welled in my throat, holding there like a chunk of ice that refused to melt. I looked down the stairs, into the foyer. I couldn't see the front door, but a hazy silhouette from outside spilled onto the hardwood and splashed up onto the wall. A vague shadow, unmoving.

KNOCK... KNOCK... KNOCK...

Don't let them see you. HIDE.

I slipped back into the guest room and, quietly as I could, pulled the door shut, then locked it. It was one of those flimsy "click the knob" locks, but I figured it was better than nothing. I pressed my back against the door, heart pounding. My options were . . . limited.

Option 1: Hide in the closet.

Option 2: Hide under the bed.

Option 3: Crawl out the window, drop two stories onto jagged, sloping rock.

Maybe I was overreacting. What if it was just a delivery guy wanting me to sign for something? I pulled out my phone, tapped into the Ring app, and searched for the front door camera, but . . . no connection. I pressed FOYER instead. The live feed took a few seconds to load:

A high-angle POV of the foyer interior. A figure in a yellow rain poncho and blue jeans stood on the front stoop outside. They peered through the glass, hands cupped against either side of a pixelated face, locks of red hair spilling out from their hood. Lucy . . . a wary sense of relief fell over me—yes, she was a bit of a character, but when I'd met her at the lookout, she didn't seem dangerous—

"Macy?" she called out, her voice tired and small. "Are you there?" She knocked again, this time with the palm of her hand.

THUMP . . . THUMP . . . THUMP . . .

The live feed was slightly delayed, so I heard the thumping downstairs a second or two before she knocked on the video.

My relief surrendered to doubt: What color were her eyes? I squinted at my phone, the image too pixelated to tell. I tried to think back to when I'd met her at the lookout, but my memories tripped over themselves like bumbling idiots: *Her eyes were green—nope, they were dark brown—actually, they were hazel, or maybe light brown?*

Lucy went on, "Macy, if you're there, I just . . . I'm . . . I'm sorry to bother you, but . . . I just . . . I need to talk to someone . . ." There was a deep sadness brewing in her small voice. A muffled sorrow, underscoring every syllable. She stepped back from the door and hugged herself tightly. She rubbed her arms, shivered.

Just stay hidden. Don't interact.

"Somebody . . . somebody was at the lookout last night and I couldn't . . . I couldn't save him. I tried, but . . ." She reached to knock again, then hesitated. She hugged herself for a second time, turned away, and plodded down the concrete steps. At the bottom, she looked over her shoulder, up toward the house. Even in the pixelated blur I could sense the burden of guilt in her posture. She trudged toward the garage, and slipped out of view.

I swiped my finger across the screen, going back to the list of cameras. I tapped on GARAGE — EXTERIOR. Another fish-eye POV popped up, this one a high-angle shot of the driveway, the darkening woods crowned the top of the frame. Lucy moved slowly along the bottom, still hugging herself. She walked in a straight line, but the fish-eye distortion made it look as though she walked along the curved edge of a miniature planet.

She stopped directly below the camera, leaned her back against the garage door, and slid downward, inch by inch, until she met the wet gravel. She sat there, arms wrapped around her shins, chin resting on her knees, staring out into the woods across the driveway.

I kept my neck craned to my phone, watching. Kept expecting Lucy to start crying, or maybe to get back up and knock on the door again, but she only sat there, staring into the forest. A pang of guilt rose in my chest, rose and fell, then rose again . . .

Don't talk to them. Don't let them see you.

Lucy sat there until the last rays of sunlight fled into the woods, and the sky turned dark. Then, with her back still pressed to the garage door, she slowly shimmied to her feet. She dusted off her blue jeans, and wandered across the driveway. The motion light snapped on, pitching her shadow toward the tree line, a distorted triangle.

The woods were cast in a grotesque light, clenched like the teeth of a rabid wolf, the gnarled stumps broken fangs. Lucy kept walking until she slipped through a gap between the trunks. The yellow of her poncho dissolved into the black, a shipwreck sinking into murky water . . .

I considered going after her, seeing if she was okay, but . . .

I closed the Ring app and tapped into Uber. I just needed to grab my stuff and get out of here. Now. Yesterday.

23
HEADLIGHTS

I never found my Pikachu backpack. Consider it an offering to the spirits of the house, along with my pair of Sylvo headphones and the last of my cigarettes. I tied up my sneakers in the foyer, quick, careless. The money was little more than an afterthought now. Jemma was right, at least partially: Something, *many* things, were seriously wrong with this place.

I pulled Dad's parachute jacket from the coatrack and raced to the front door. My ride was still twenty minutes out, but I refused to wait in the house. I shuffled onto the stoop, locked the door, tossed the key under the welcome mat, and started down the concrete steps. My left foot met the gravel and—

RIIIIIIIIIING . . .

I turned, peering up the stairs. The rotary phone continued to ring inside—muffled, insistent. I tried to keep moving, but my feet stayed rooted in place. Every bone in my body SCREAMED at me, BEGGED me to go back up the stairs, unlock the door, and answer the phone. *Just follow the Rites, Macy, everything will be okay if you just follow the—*

I set my jaw, spun on my heel, and stomped off down the driveway. The house seemed to pull at me from behind, like I was tied to it with an invisible tether. I severed the tie, picked up the pace.

As I crossed in front of the garage, the motion light snapped on. I glanced toward the spot where Lucy had been sitting. Her footprints were still clearly visible in the gravel, leading toward the pitch-dark woods. Yes, poor thing, but no way was I chasing her off into the night. I didn't even know if that *was* her . . .

Halfway down the drive, I could still hear the phone ringing. Faint, but ever insistent. Like an abandoned infant screaming for help: ANSWER ME. ANSWER ME. ANSWER ME. With every step farther the sound grew dimmer, fading into the night.

I stood beneath the lone streetlamp in the dead-end turnaround. My limbs quivered, and manic butterflies fluttered in my stomach. *You can't quit, Macy. You have responsibilities. You have a sister to provide for. And what if Grace comes after you for the three grand?*—

I pulled out my phone, and shakily dialed Grace's number. Three rings, then: "The person you are trying to reach is unavailable. Please leave a message after the tone."

BEEP.

"H-hey Mrs. Carnswel, I . . . uh . . ." I didn't know what to say— your husband's letter scared the shit out of me? Your home is cursed? "I uhh, I'm not gonna be able to keep watching the house, unfortunately. There's . . . there's been a, uh, family emergency. I . . . I locked the doors and left the key under the mat. I'm really sorry." *Please let me keep the three grand.* "Okay. Uh . . . hope you're good."

I ended the call.

I barely stood there ten seconds before continuing down the road— the Uber would have to pass me anyway. I didn't like being so close to the house; I could sense it through the trees behind, watching. I pictured the front door creaking open, never-ending arms writhing out like tapeworms, wending down the driveway to snag me by the ankle, drag me back through wet gravel, twisting and shrieking.

As I moved along the dark road, every noise from the flanking woods invoked a monstrous terror. A snapping twig conjured up the face of a grinning clown with blood-red lips, blunt teeth giving way to blackened roots. A rustling breeze: an arachnid abomination with pale blue eyes and human skin coated with thin, glassy hairs. I shook off the apparitions. Walked so fast I was practically jogging. Ahead, a low stretch of light swept up into the woods, settled onto the asphalt. Was it my ride? I checked the app, and . . . no service.

Headlights, two eyes of brilliant bluish white, floated around the distant bend, crawled toward me at an unhurried clip. The road became a spine, the trees on either side a towering rib cage, a mad sweep of probing light and skeletal shadow. The blinding headlights became the only things to exist in a black abyss. The vehicle moved with a menacing slowness, a great white shark through open water.

I looked back—the orange streetlamp was nothing more than a faint speck. I faced the headlights and lifted a hand to shield my eyes from the overpowering glare. As the car drew near, the buzz of an electric window rolled down. From the speakers within, a familiar podcast host imparted his wisdom: "No, no, that's the thing, man. Like you need to WANT to be high-value. The problem is you don't WANT it enough."

The first and only time hearing that voice would make me breathe a sigh of relief.

24
SICK LEAVE

I climbed into the Honda Civic's back seat, and yanked the door shut.

"Macy, right?" The driver adjusted his Tapout ball cap and looked at his phone. "Heading to Salem?"

"Yeah." I glanced at the surrounding woods.

The driver slipped out a pack of gum and started to unwrap a piece.

"Can we . . ." I shifted in my seat. "Can we get out of here?"

He popped the gum in his mouth and began chewing like a cow. He looked at me slow in the rearview, scratched his wispy goatee, and finally replied with: "Sure thing, boss." He set on the gas.

My hero.

We sped past the Brooksview mega mansions, the Windfall Transit Center, the solitary bus stop. With every mile farther from the house, more waves of relief fell over me, like a hot shower on a cold day. Purged my stress like a chorus of angels. Even the podcast, and the fact I was leaving six, *maybe nine*, thousand bucks behind wasn't enough to dampen my mood. We kept winding down the mountain roads, descending into the Willamette Valley, the orange glow of Salem blooming up into the distant night and—

Don't let it get away . . .

A dark thought flashed into my head. No . . . "thought" wasn't even close to the right word. It was more like a vision, so vivid I could nearly hear it, see it, like I'd been pulled out of this car and brought to another place entirely: rocky cliffs and windswept hemlocks, a pale blue sky, and . . . bleeding up from a distant horizon—a shock of blood-red light.

My heart pounded in my chest, each thump roaring: *DANGER. DANGER. DANGER.* My ears started ringing, a rising hum that grew higher and higher without resolve:

mmmmmmmmmmmmm

Another "vision" jolted through me: city streets running red with blood, countless screams of sorrow and misery. All of this happening because of me. Every soul on earth knowing it was my failure that caused their suffering.

The ringing in my ears only grew louder.

More imagery ran through me, carving into my brain like etchings into granite:

Rotting skin ripped from bone.

Hands with dirty, overgrown fingernails pressing into an exposed brain—*squelch, squelch, squelch*—the sound of laughter, turned to weeping, turned to desperate pleas for mercy.

A gaping chasm teeming with unclothed people—all of them screaming, *crawling* over one another like a writhing mass of larvae.

The visions of horror gave way to one last image. Something far worse than anything that had come before:

Jemma's lifeless body. She lay on concrete, facing the sky, rigid—stiller than a porcelain doll. Her round glasses reflected red light, concealing her hazel eyes from view. A thin line of crimson trailed from her ear, a pool of blood forming around the base of her skull, spreading out in all directions.

A devastating setback. A devastating setback. A devastating—

"YO. Are you good?" The driver's voice snapped me back into the Honda Civic. He was squinting at me in the rearview. And, judging by the frown on his face, he'd been trying to get my attention for a while now. He turned back to the road. "You better not upchuck in my car, man. Just had it cleaned."

I realized I was clutching at my stomach, shaking. "Just . . . just pull over . . ."

"Un-fucking-believable," he groaned. He signaled onto the shoulder, screeched to a halt, plumes of dust clouding into high beams. I fumbled for the handle, staggered out, and hurled my guts onto the side of the road. I could only take two or three breaths before hurling again. A disgusting puddle of stomach bile soaked into the hard-packed dirt at my feet.

The driver stepped out and looked at me, a hint of pity in his eyes now. "Just . . . get it out," he said, "no rush." He reached into the car and popped open the center console. He stepped back, holding a pack of smokes in one hand and a pack of wet wipes in the other. He handed me the wipes. "For when you're done."

I stuffed them into my jacket, gave a weak thumbs-up, and hurled again. More stomach bile. The driver turned his ball cap forward and leaned back against the car. He pulled out a Zippo, lit up a cigarette, took a long drag. I dry-heaved again and again, until finally, my stomach settled. I spat once, twice, stood up straight, and cleared my throat.

"Thanks," said the driver.

"What?"

He gestured his smoke at the bile. "For not doing that in my car."

"Sure." I cleaned the sides of my mouth with a wet wipe. My hands were trembling.

"You sure you okay?" he asked.

"Y-yeah." I shook out my hands and shoved them into my pockets, forced them to stop trembling.

The driver took one last drag, flicked the cigarette to the dirt and stamped it out. "Good to go?"

"Yeah."

We climbed back into the car. He turned his keys in the ignition, and steered onto the road. The tires hummed against the pavement, the dark woods blurred, the distant glow of Salem loomed ever closer, and . . .

"I need to go back," I said without thinking.

"What?" He blinked at me in the rearview.

"I'll pay you for the full trip, I just . . . I need to go back."

He studied me for a few seconds, then hit the turn signal. "You're the boss."

We drove in silence, once again passing the solitary bus stop, the Windfall Transit Center, the Brooksview mansions. The driver clearly sensed something was wrong, and decided not to put on the podcast. There was a human being in there somewhere.

With each mile closer to the house, that nauseating sense of doom diminished. The intrusive visions of death and terror had retreated into my subconscious, my memories. I still felt like shit, but it was a feeling I was well acquainted with. A feeling I could manage.

Of course, the last thing I wanted to do was go back to that house, but what I *wanted* held no weight. I *needed* to return to 5637 Brooksview Heights. Nothing less than the survival of humanity was at stake.

25
CHECK-IN

Maybe I'd lost my mind, but I now believed, with only the tiniest sliver of doubt, that David was right. My life, Jemma's life, every life on earth depended on those Rites. This belief, no matter how ridiculous, no matter how contrived, had dug its teeth into my psyche and refused to let go. Try as I might, I could not rationalize the unholy revelation away. I only prayed I hadn't fucked things up beyond repair.

The driver pulled to a stop beneath the lonely streetlamp's dim glow. "Gravol and electrolytes," he said. "And sleep. Lots of sleep."

"Thanks," I murmured, looking up the gravel drive. I gritted my teeth, swung the door open, and stepped out into the cold night. I turned back, started to swing the door shut, but stopped halfway. "Hey," I said.

The driver glanced at me, one eyebrow raised.

"Can I bum a smoke?"

He popped the center console, reached in, and tossed me a cigarette. He dug into a cup holder, produced a lighter, and tossed me that too. "You can keep it," he said.

It was a grimy little plastic lighter with the phrase "Live free or die trying" surrounded by angry-looking skulls. I replied with a flat "Thanks . . ."

When I swung the door shut, he wasted no time driving off: on to the next customer. The red taillights shrank into the night, leaving me on the dead-end road yet again. Turning back, I lit up the smoke, took a long drag, and walked up the drive.

The dark house crept into view. Now, its plainness only made it all the more unsettling, like a withered shrub in a line of perfectly manicured hedges. I took another long drag; chemical warmth filled my limbs, fading quick. *You're okay. Everything's okay.* I forced myself to continue: *You have to do this, Macy, you don't have a choice anymore. Right foot forward. Left foot forward. Right foot. Left.*

My phone buzzed—call from Jemma. I almost pressed decline, but she'd probably summon the National Guard if I didn't respond. I came to a standstill, took a deep breath, let it out, and pressed ACCEPT—

"BRO," she said. "Are my calls even getting through?"

"Sorry, sorry, just—shitty service again." I tried my best to sound calm. Didn't want to worry Jemma even more—she might come up here herself, get roped into this.

"Jesus, Macy." She groaned. "At least try sending me a text or something. I've been having a borderline panic attack for, like, two hours."

"Yeah, my bad . . . Everything's good here, nothing to report . . ."

"You promise you're okay?"

"Yeah, just . . . just t-tired." My voice shook a little, nerves getting the better of me. I took another drag. Exhaled.

"You uh . . ." Jemma cleared her throat. "You gonna be good tomorrow?"

"What?"

"You know . . . with it being Dad's . . ."

"Yeah, Jem, I'll be fine . . ."

"I . . . I can come up for the day if you want. I'm not spending the night there, but . . . if you want company during the day, I can come up."

I massaged a tight spot in my neck, the tendons spasmed and a dull ache radiated down into my shoulder. "I'll be good," I said. "Will you?"

"Yeah . . . just gonna play video games before my interview anyway, so . . . it's no big deal." Jemma paused. "You know I'm always here to listen though, right? Like whenever you need to vent or anything."

"Yeah of course, thanks, Jem . . . same here. I, uh, I gotta go, but we'll check in again tomorrow, all right?"

"Okay . . ."

I went to end the call, but—

"Macy?"

"Yeah?"

"Love you . . ."

"Love you too, sis . . ."

Before Jemma could question me further, I ended the call and continued up the drive. A familiar sound bled into the cold night—the rotary phone. Its muffled cries leaked from the house like a noxious gas. Had it been ringing all this time? The notion made my skin crawl. Made my skin shiver and twitch. Made me want to turn on my heel and bolt back down the driveway, but . . .

A devastating setback . . .

I needed to answer that phone. Every soul on earth was counting on me.

As I neared the garage, the motion light snapped on. I crossed over Lucy's trail of footprints and marched up the concrete stairs. I lingered on the stoop. My reflection gazed back at me in the front door's glass panel. The cigarette hung limp between my closed lips, an orange dot in a shadowy visage surrounded by a frizzy tangle of curly brown hair. I wasn't shaking anymore, my body too exhausted to appreciate how scared I was.

The foyer was dark, the phone still ringing from within. I spat out the cigarette and stomped it flat onto the concrete.

I flipped the welcome mat with my toe, scooped up the key, unlocked the door, grasped the handle, and pulled it open. I stood there, peering into the pitch black—the doorframe like the gaping mouth of a cavernous beast. Within its bowels, the phone cried out, each RIIIING almost making me wince. I could feel the sound in my bones, feel it buzzing against my skull. I took another deep breath, let it out. Then I stepped inside.

PART III
OCCUPATIONAL HAZARDS

WALK

I used to love mowing lawns.

Got to pop in my earbuds, listen to audiobooks and deathcore all day—tune out the world. I loved the sweet smell of freshly cut grass. Loved being outside. Loved the calming repetition, row after row. But now I can barely bring myself to look at a mower.

Not for lack of trying, though.

A little while after Dad died, I ran to the enemy: Done Right Lawns LTD. A big corporate franchise expanded down from Portland.

I quit in the first month.

Didn't give my notice, just stopped showing and blocked their number. Partly because I felt like a turncoat, but mainly because the second I touched a mower, yanked on that pull cord, felt the engine's hum against my palms—I'd find myself back in my early teens, mowing lawns on the weekend for Mullins Mowing. A few times I'd even see Dad again, in the corner of my eye, pruning a hedge or sipping coffee from a hefty thermos. Then I'd turn to see it wasn't Dad at all, it was just a stranger—half the time they barely even resembled him.

It made me think about this thing I learned on Discovery Channel: "phantom limb syndrome." It's where people who've lost a limb continue to feel its sensations—the bone, the skin, even the pain. But then they look down, only to be reminded there's nothing there, and the sensations vanish. I figure losing a person might be similar. The brain gets so used to someone being around, it tells you they're still here, even when they're gone and never coming back.

Phantom person syndrome.

Every time it happens to me, every time I think I've seen or heard Dad, only to turn and see a stranger—part of me wants to crumple to the ground, and burst into sobs . . . but I never can. I just stand there, numb. Red. Blue. Red. Blue. Nothing. Nothing. Nothing.

In the years since Dad went, I never cried, not once, not even at the funeral.

I'm no stoic, far from it. Cried a lot when I was younger, and never felt bad about it. Hell, I used to tear up watching sappy movies. Dad always told me it was okay to cry: "It's a good way to get the bad stuff out." But after he died, it was like that part of me just ceased to function. Went offline.

No matter how much I tried to get out the bad stuff, I couldn't cry out a single tear. I used to bring up old pictures on my phone, pictures of me, Dad, Jemma, all of us together. I'd scroll through, letting the memories hit me like a landslide. Telling myself it was okay to just fall apart, to drop to my knees and sob and gasp and weep like a star in the movies, but . . . I never could, I just felt . . . nothing.

Still, I'd keep trying, looking at photo after photo, memory after memory. Sometimes I'd even hear Dad's voice, steady and calming: *It's okay to cry, Macy, there's no shame in it. It's okay—*

Nothing. Nothing. Nothing. Only that ever-present tightness between my lungs. A corkscrew twist wrenching tighter, tighter, tighter, until it tore off my skin, ripped me out of the memory, and threw me into the driver's seat of a white pickup truck, falling in a weightless nosedive, dark water slamming into the windshield, shattering the glass.

Then I'd go back to feeling nothing.

Then I'd feel like a failure for feeling nothing.

Maybe I was grieving wrong. Grieving bad. Just another thing Macy couldn't do right.

I've long since moved those photos of Dad to a hidden folder. Haven't looked at them in well over a year. Don't have the heart to delete them, even though I want to.

If Dad was still around, he probably would've told me it was okay not to cry too. Told me it was okay to feel whatever I was feeling, even if that feeling was nothing at all. Told me it was okay to walk in the rain. That was another saying of his, "Walk in the rain." When it starts pouring out of nowhere, and you're gonna get soaked no matter what, don't scramble for cover. Just walk. Focus on what you can control. Accept the fact that you're gonna get drenched, feel whatever you're feeling. Focus on one breath at a time. In through the nose, out through the mouth.

Walk in the rain, Macy, just walk in the rain.

I guess it was good advice, but sometimes, when the rain falls so hard it threatens to rise past my neck, pull me into the depths and drown me, I have no choice but to run . . .

1
FURTHER INSTRUCTIONS

RIIIIING.

I stood in the foyer's entrance, my shadow stretching across the hardwood floor, leading my eyes to the glossy white phone, resting in its place beneath the photo of the Windfall Inlet. I pulled the door shut behind me with a soft click. I turned the lock.

RIIIIING.

I chewed on my lip and carried myself forward, wrapped my hand around the phone, held there for one, two, three seconds, then—

RIIII—

I brought it to my ear.

A wheeze of gasping air crackled out from the receiver, sharp and strained, like the first breath after decades of drowning. A bizarre image burst into my head: a windowless room, a red phone on a concrete floor. A figure sat hunched in the corner, spinal knobs jutting against the tight skin of an emaciated back. Skin so pallid, it was nearly translucent, skin that had never seen the sun.

Whoever this was, they had been suffocating for hours, decades, centuries, waiting for me—Macy Mullins—to answer that phone.

An impossible notion, with not a shred of evidence, but I knew it was just as real as those visions. I tried again, "Hello?"

More breathing, slower, deeper, and then: "M-Macy?" It was the voice of a young man, another voice I did not recognize. Strained and weak. Vocal cords that had not been used in a long, long time. Somehow he felt impossibly far from here, deep within the earth, or perhaps a different world entirely. Another incoherent thought, but—

"M-Macy Mullins?"

I opened my mouth, only for a thin cracking sound to escape. I swallowed. "S-speaking . . ."

"Oh thank God, thank God . . ." The relief in his voice was overwhelming, like he'd just avoided a fate far worse than death. "I—we thought you'd left . . ."

Questions raced through me, too many to count. "Who are you?" I asked.

"I-I'm not allowed to say—"

On his end, a high-pitched wail echoed in the distance, like a colossal merry-go-round turning in the wind. The stranger cleared his throat, on task: "Macy, you need to listen to me." He spoke with a measured but quick determination, every syllable imbued with grave importance: "You need to write down what I say. And you need to follow every word. Do you have a pen and paper?"

In the background, something began to tick, tick, tick. A clock?

"MACY," he snapped.

I flinched. "Y-yes?"

"Get a pen and paper. Now."

His conviction annihilated all my other questions. "One s-second." Frantic, I whipped open the side table drawer, and found a leather-bound notebook. I flipped it open, but all the pages were torn out. I set the phone face up, and hauled into the kitchen. I yanked down the wooden tray from atop the fridge, tossed it onto the island, started digging through. Coins, receipts, flashlight, FitLyfe bracelet, and . . . a ballpoint pen. I grabbed the pen, a crumpled receipt, and rushed back to the foyer. I crooked the phone between my collarbone and my ear, then flattened the receipt against the side table. I held the pen at the ready, hand shaking. "G-go ahead . . ."

"I need you to—"

That high-pitched wailing sound repeated, this time closer, louder. A teakettle shriek, like a chorus of humans, all screaming in unison. All screaming at the same pitch and cadence.

He waited for the horrific noise to fade, then continued in hushed tones: "I n-need you to listen to me very closely, okay?" His voice trembled with an ever-rising fear. A fear that seeped out of the phone and infected me.

"I'm listening." Even though I had no idea who this was, he spoke with such desperate urgency I couldn't help but hang on to every word.

He continued, "What color was the rabbit?"

"Brown."

He made a shuddering sound, a nervous exhale? Or a sigh of relief? "Is . . . is it still in the house?"

I hesitated.

"Macy."

"No . . ."

"How did it escape?"

"I uh, I let it out . . ."

"Okay, okay that's okay," he said in a jittery tone that clearly meant it wasn't. "Who knocked on the door?"

"A woman, uh, Lucy—"

"What did she say?"

"She wanted to talk, said s-somebody jumped at the lookout."

The stranger cursed under his breath.

On his end, another chorus of screams, even louder, closer.

He lowered his voice. "You have to follow her footprints."

"W-what?"

"When the clock strikes midnight, you have to follow those footprints into the woods."

The prospect of traipsing through the pitch-dark night, following footprints that belonged to God knows what, and led to God knows where—it was almost less appealing than burning a rabbit alive. "I'm not, there's no way I'm—"

"MACY." He seethed. "Did you, or did you not, agree to take over as Ward of this House?"

"W-what?"

"Just answer the question."

I thought back to the day before, the moment I crossed the property line, and stepped onto the driveway: *As soon as you set foot on this property with intention to be its caretaker, you can't just quit.*

I gave a tepid nod, then realized he couldn't see me. "I . . . I did."

"Good." He said this like he'd already known the answer. "Then do as I say. You are one thread away from unleashing something far worse than the most horrific imaginings of hell. Do you understand? At twelve a.m.—you follow those footprints into the woods."

I scribbled down:

at 12AM follo footprints

"Wherever they lead," the stranger went on, "someone will be waiting for you at the end. You have to calm them."

I wrote:

calm them

"Do NOT let them leave the property while in your presence—by any means necessary. And do NOT let them spiral. If they start weeping uncontrollably or, worse, rambling cryptic nonsense, you run. Run back to the house before they beat you there. Then lock the doors, and—"

"Can you slow down? I—"

"Even if they beat you to the house, do NOT leave, go back inside, lock the doors so more of them can't get in, wait for someone to call."

Barely able to process the insanity, I chicken-scratched:

they cant leav property—if they weep or spew cryptic BS run back 2 house b4 they do—lock doors—wait 4 call

"Macy, please," he said. "I live in a place where someone like you failed and . . . If the sun turns red, you—"

He fell quiet.

On his end, booming footsteps reverberated, muffled by a closed door, or maybe a thin wall. At first, I thought they belonged to something enormous, but I listened closer. They were the footfalls of many dozens, all walking in near perfect lockstep. Even when they staggered, the footsteps were synced, as if their nervous systems were strung together. A hive mind chorus. A nightmare drumbeat, getting closer, closer . . .

The man started whispering to himself, a strange and desperate prayer: "For w-we have seen your works and carved your vessels. For we defend even those who cast filth upon your name. For we—"

Many voices cried out at once, a grotesque and distorted shriek—
CLICK.

The call ended.

I stood there holding the phone, staring blankly at my bewildered reflection in the photo of the Windfall Inlet. My mind was about to start spinning, to try rationalizing whatever I'd just heard, but—

Follow the Rites.

I set the phone down, stepped across the foyer, and stopped at the door. I peered through its glass panel. Lucy's footprints led across the gravel driveway, into the darkened woods, disappearing between the columns of the trunks. I shut my eyes and rubbed my temples, slow circles that only provoked a worsening headache. I opened my eyes, once again staring at those footprints in the gravel. When the clock struck midnight, I would have no choice but to follow.

2
FOOTPRINTS

I paced the main floor back and forth, repeatedly checking the time:

11:58

The minutes had dragged by like hours. I'd scratched at my neck until red marks appeared. Chewed my nails down to the skin. I had to keep moving. Pace to the window, stare out into the woods, pace to the patio door, check the lock, pace through the kitchen, check the time, pace to the foyer, check the lock. Repeat the cycle. If I stood still for too long, my thoughts might catch up, swarm me like a legion of fire ants—devour whatever was left of my sanity. I had to keep moving.

11:59

There were brief moments where I could view the situation from a "rational" perspective, step back from it all. Scream at myself to leave the house. To call the authorities. To check myself into the nearest psych ward. To do anything other than what I was doing, but . . . none of that mattered. If I failed tonight, a red sun would rise in the morning and . . .

It was a fact more evident than existence itself. More inevitable than gravity. If I didn't continue David's Rites. If I didn't follow those footprints at midnight—Jemma, myself, every soul on planet Earth, would be doomed to unimaginable misery.

I pulled out the crumpled receipt, rereading it for the hundredth time:

at 12AM follo footprints—calm them—they cant leav property—if they weep or spew cryptic BS run back 2 house b4 they do—lock doors—wait 4 call

I tucked it away and—

12:00

I surged into the foyer, pulled on my coat, and tied up my shoes. I swung open the front door. It was raining, a spitting patter blotting the concrete steps into gunmetal gray. I snagged the olive-green rain poncho from the coatrack—a little big on my frame, more like a cloak than a poncho.

The forest looked even darker now, the shadows between the trunks an impenetrable haze. I rushed back inside, grabbed the flashlight from the wooden tray, then returned to the stoop. I switched on the flashlight—its beam cast over the driveway and hit the tree line, a circle of white glow exposing those terrible columns of wooden teeth.

Follow the Rites.

I pulled up my hood, stepped out onto the stoop, and shut the door. I started down the concrete steps. A storm was coming, I could smell it in the air, that alkaline bite you can almost taste. I rushed across the drive.

The rain tapped with hollow clicks against the poncho's hood. I paused at the edge of the woods—a muddled border of wet dirt, snaking roots, and stray gravel. The no-man's-land between civilization and the wild. I swept my light up into the wild. The forest rejected the intrusion, only allowing the beam about thirty feet before consuming it in shadows and branch. I aimed down at the dirt path. Lucy's footprints had turned to faint divots. The rain would wash it all away soon—

bzz . . . bzz . . . bzz . . .

I slipped out my phone:

REMINDER—DAD'S BIRTHDAY 2DAY

Memories of Dad shuddered through me, his smile, his laugh, and—
Follow the Rites.

I tucked away my phone, shoved down my feelings, and threw one more look back at the house—squares of light surrounded by shifting black. Brownie the cat sat perched in a living room window, a dark silhouette, ears pricked, tail swishing. Rain streaked the glass, and spattered shadows cast out over the muddied lawn below. I turned to the woods, and trudged up the trail.

Just follow the Rites, and everything will be okay.

Beneath the cover of the trees, the darkness was all-consuming, as if the world outside my flashlight's beam had ceased to exist. But the rain was softer, my footsteps turning from wet squelches to dry thumps then back again. On either side of the path, the trees seemed to be fighting for space, choking roots, stabbing branches—everything frozen in a desperate struggle for territory. Faces formed in the shadows, fleeting apparitions spawned by the flashlight's glare—eerie tricks of light that forced me to keep my eyes on the path.

Without warning, the rain stopped, replaced by a deafening silence. The smallest sounds magnified: snapping twigs, fallen pine cones. I kept my focus on the shoeprints, head down, hood up. In the absence of rain, the forest gradually came to life—chirping crickets, croaking frogs, even the occasional hoot of an owl.

The path took a sharp turn left, but the shoeprints continued straight off into the woods. I slowed, scanning the trees—white birches rising into the black like pillars holding up an unseen sky. The shoeprints led across a gray carpet of dead leaves. I continued forward, off the beaten path.

Lucy had traveled in a straight line, deviating only to avoid the occasional trunk or boulder. Soon, the birch trees gave way to gnarled oaks, twisted and leafless. The chirping crickets had suppressed all other noise, an unending drone that made it hard to think. *Keep moving, Macy. Keep moving.*

"I KNOW YOU," a voice rang out, the forest falling dead quiet in its wake. I whip-turned to face a crooked oak, a stone's toss away. The voice echoed faintly in the wet dark. It had sounded like a child—or maybe an adult who'd intentionally raised their voice to a falsetto shrill. I stood rigid, hot blood rushing into my temples. The voice had come from somewhere beyond that crooked oak. The trunk was covered in bulbous knots. Bulbous knots that looked like ruptured cysts, cracked and bloated, bleeding tears of long-dried sap. And . . . at the foot of the oak's trunk, lying atop a tangled mess of roots: My backpack. It sat there, like the lure of an anglerfish. Daring me to walk over. Daring me to crouch, pick it up, and lower my guard.

Keep moving. Follow the footprints.

I took a cautious step backward, when—

One of those bulbous knots slipped out of view.

The hot blood in my temples turned ice cold, the ground seemed to tilt. Something had been peeking out from behind that tree, watching.

Before I knew it, I'd spun around, and found myself sprinting in the opposite direction. My limbs had taken action without my brain's permission—but they weren't making me retreat from these loathsome

THE CARETAKER

woods—my legs were forcing me to go deeper. My flashlight's beam scoured the forest floor, picking up Lucy's trail once again. In any other circumstance, seeing what I just saw would have sent me screaming back to the house, but now, that compulsive need to fulfill the Rites, to seek relief, was just about overriding all my other instincts, survival included. This was less about saving humanity and more about scratching some insatiable itch. Still, I kept glancing back, kept bracing to see a pale figure with a bulbous head in close pursuit, but nothing was there . . .

Just follow the Rites, Macy. Follow the Rites and everything will be okay. Follow the Rites. The mantra repeated again and again, an all-consuming urge, like a rusty razor blade was lodged between my two front teeth. I had no choice but to try and flick it out with my tongue:

Follow the Rites, follow the Rites, follow the Rites . . .

3
WEEPER

The gnarled oaks broke rank to form a circular clearing. I froze, casting another skittish look over my shoulder—met only with the uninviting darkness and hollow silence. I turned back to the clearing. It was big enough to park a mansion, the dirt coated with more dead leaves and pine needles. There were small humps in the ground, dozens in total. Mounds of dirt evenly spaced apart. An image that made me think of unmarked graves, and buried bodies—

Focus, Macy. Follow the Rites.

I swept my light around, searching, but the trail of footprints had gone cold.

"Fuck."

I pushed forward, hunting for any sign of Lucy—a snapped twig, a shoeprint in the leaves, anything. A queasy sense of dread settled into my bones, yet again making me feel vile, contaminated, as if my shortcomings were against the very order of reality itself. An escalation of those feelings I'd had after failing to switch off the light in time, after refusing to burn the rabbit. The rain started up once more, beating a low pattern against the ground—

"ZEE?!"

My head shot up. The voice echoed around the clearing—a new but familiar voice.

"ZEE?!" it called out again. "WHERE ARE YOU?!"

My light swept over a fallen oak, and cut into a curtain of shadow. A muddied slope led up to an audience of white pines, standing at attention in the black. The trail of footprints snaked between their company. I looked over my shoulder again. My flashlight's beam snapped from trunk to trunk, no pursuer in sight. But a glowing speck hovered between the distant trees—the house?

"ZEE!"

I turned toward the voice. *Calm them.*

A gust of wind volleyed from the trees behind, prodding me forward. A flash of lightning exposed the canopy above. The rain thrashed against my face, and a distant rumble boomed. I clambered over the fallen oak. Blackberry thorns clawed at my poncho like they were trying to warn me about whatever lay ahead. I twisted free and continued up the muddy slope. As I crested the summit, my light scoped a figure standing about twenty feet away, clad in blue jeans and a yellow rain poncho. The figure spun toward me, raising a hand to shield their eyes from the flashlight's glare. "Zee? Is that you?" she asked.

I lowered the light—she lowered her hand. Red hair, freckled cheeks. It was Lucy, just as I expected, but . . . her eyes were a different color now. A pale blue, so cold they were almost white. I still couldn't remember what color her eyes had been when we met at the lookout, but they definitely hadn't been blue . . . or at least not a blue like this.

"I'm looking for my friend," she said. There was no recognition in her worried expression—to this "Lucy," I was an absolute stranger. "She's about m-my height," she went on, voice shaking. "Dark hair, blue jacket.

Her name is Brienna, but she goes by Zee, I was just . . . we were, I was j-just—" She broke into stutters, suddenly on the verge of tears.

Calm them.

"Hey, hey." I stepped closer. "I-I'm sure she's not far. Can I help you find her?"

Another flash of lightning cut into the dark. Lucy straightened up, sniffed loudly, and pulled herself together. Thunder boomed. She met my gaze, those blue, unnaturally cold eyes making my skin crawl. I stifled my unease: "I'm here to help, okay?"

"Okay . . ."

I opened my mouth, having no clue what to say next. It was beyond strange, trying to calm somebody else down, when *I* was the one on the verge of insanity. And I kept throwing glances over my shoulder, kept expecting to see a pale figure peeking out from behind a tree. Lucy hugged herself, apprehension growing beneath her icy blue eyes. Her anxiety only fueled my own. A vicious cycle.

"W-where did you last see your friend?" I finally said. "That's usually . . . that's a good place to start . . ."

Lucy motioned to the woods behind her. "Out that way, near the lookout." She slowly turned, and began to trudge off.

I remained still, surveying the darkness she was heading toward. The rain forged small rivers in the ground. Flat chunks of dead leaves shifting and cracking like peeled skin. The wind sent waves of murmuring protest through the trees, and—a flash of lightning revealed that pale, thin rope, no more than a hundred feet away, swaying in the wind with the cadence of a playground swing set. My heart jackhammered—

Follow the Rites: *Don't let them leave the property while in your presence, whatever means necessary.*

"Wait," I called out, sounding more urgent than intended.

Lucy looked back, she'd only made it about twenty steps, but that was a quarter of the way. She waited for me to say something. I stood there with my mouth agape, floundering, until: "Does your friend sing?" I had no idea where I was going with this.

"She does . . ."

"Yeah, I . . . earlier I heard somebody singing," I lied. "Back this way." I started off, and gestured for Lucy to follow, but she stayed locked in place. I slowed, turned, and raised an eyebrow, feigning innocent confusion. A howling gust of wind threw back Lucy's hood and fled through the trees behind, as if nature itself wanted her to leave the property. She pulled her hood back up and studied me, her cautious expression hardening to a stony glare. "Are you trying to trick me?"

"Trying to—" I blinked. "I'm trying to help—"

"Zee never sings outside."

"I know what I heard, I—"

"STOP," Lucy bellowed, her voice filled with a surprising resonance. "Just . . ." Her voice fell back to a feeble timbre, tired and defeated. "Please stop . . ." She rubbed her nose with the side of her hand and sniffed, swallowed a lump in her throat. "You . . . you're just like the last one . . . I— I just want to find my friend. It's my fault she—I just, I just need to tell her how much she, how much she—" Lucy drew in a slow, stuttering breath, the universal sound of *I'm about to start sobbing*, and—

"WAIT," I yelled again. She looked up at me, sniffling, still on the verge of tears.

"You're right," I admitted. "I *was* lying." That seemed to grab her attention. I went on, "but I was lying to . . . protect you, to protect both of us." She sniffed again, still skeptical, but willing to hear me out.

"Lucy," I took a careful step closer.

"How do you know my—"

"I'm just as scared and confused as you are, all right? But if we can't stay calm, then we'll never find your friend and—"

From somewhere in the darkness beyond that pale, thin rope, a voice began to sing. An unfamiliar song in a language I didn't recognize. It was a beautiful voice, slow and sorrowful, soft and lilting—the kind of voice that, in any other context, I might've shut my eyes and let wash over me, but here, now, it was like two pieces of rolled-up sandpaper twisting against my eardrums.

Lucy turned back. "Zee?!" She set off toward the property line and cupped her hands to her mouth. "ZEE!!"

Calm them.

"Lucy, no." I went after her, my pounding heart threatening to jump out of my throat. "STOP."

She kept moving, cried out again: "ZEE!!?" The singing continued unabated. Lucy picked up the pace. I surged forward and grabbed her by the elbow—she wrenched free, not even looking back.

"Lucy, it's not Zee." I kept following, just about ready to tackle her. "Zee doesn't sing outside, right? That's NOT her."

The property line was barely thirty feet away, Lucy half-running now, twenty steps, ten steps, five, and—

I pulled air from the deepest corners of my lungs, and boomed, "LUCY." She jerked to a halt, one step away from the property line. She spun back to face me. Even the singing stopped. I gritted my teeth, and lowered my voice to a deathly serious bite: "If you step over that rope, you will NEVER see her again. Do you understand? You will NEVER see Zee and it will be YOUR fault."

Lucy's pale face crumpled with befuddled shock, "I-I— What . . ." She was about to start crying again.

Shit. I'd gone too far. I backtracked: "But if you . . . if you come with me, we can save her, okay?"

"I don't, I don't, I—"

"Lucy!" a voice called out from the shadows beyond that pale, thin rope. "Where are you?!"

Lucy looked over her shoulder. "That's Zee . . ." But there was a hint of quivering doubt in her words now.

"It's not," I said. "It's not Zee, just . . . just come with me—"

"LUCY!" the voice cried out again. "HELP!!"

"It's NOT her—"

While the voice kept screaming for help, I kept saying whatever I could think of to coax Lucy away. She clenched her eyes shut, caught in a verbal tug-of-war. She balled her hands into fists, brought them up to either side of her head. She teetered—like a cut tree deciding where to topple. I fell silent. So did the voice. Lucy dropped straight down to her knees. "It's all my fault . . . It's all my . . ." She started hitting herself, smacking her temples with dull thwacks. The exact fucking opposite of calm.

I rushed closer, blathering, "No, no, Lucy, it's okay, it's not your—"

She pushed me away with a forceful shove. I staggered back, tripped on a rock, and fell flat on my tailbone—a shock of bright pain ran up my spine. The flashlight slipped from my hand, rolling to a stop in the muck. Its circle of white glow stretched across the forest floor, projecting Lucy's shadow onto a monstrous patchwork of poison ivy and blackberry brambles. She drew in another long, stuttering breath, and then . . . broke into wheezing sobs. Heaving and messy, sounding more animal than human. I sat there on my aching tailbone, dumbstruck—I'd never seen a sorrow like this before. With each gasping wail, Lucy's entire body shuddered, tears seeped from her eyes, streamed down freckled cheeks. The storm rose with her grief, the wind getting stronger, louder, and—

In an instant, as if an unseen and unheard director had just shouted *CUT*, the storm ceased, Lucy stopped weeping, and her face snapped to complete and total neutrality. She looked at me, pale blue eyes unblinking, empty. Then, with her voice barely above a whisper:

"Macy Mullins," she said, "I know you."

4
RUN

A slithering chill enveloped my brain, squeezed tight, and expunged a toxic cloud of putrid dread. Lucy shot to her feet, whipped past me, and vanished down the muddied slope. Next thing I knew I was hauling through the trees faster than I'd ever run in my entire life. In the smearing dark, the yellow glint of Lucy's poncho was my only guide. I'd left the flashlight behind, but that hardly mattered now. My pumping adrenaline, cold and electric, seemed to make the shadows brighter. And between the distant trees, that dim star blinked into view: 5637 Brooksview Heights.

Follow the Rites: Get back to the house before they do.

Get back to the house.

The phrase resounded with every pounding heartbeat, every thudding footfall: *Get BACK to the HOUSE. Get BACK to the HOUSE.*

Branches rustled at my flanks. Shapes emerged, yellow and blurred. More Visitors. Dozens upon dozens. All were clad in yellow rain ponchos. And all were running toward the house. I ignored the rising dread in my stomach, the throbbing ache in my tailbone, the burning pain in my lungs. I ran faster.

GET BACK TO THE HOUSE.

Branches thwacked against my skin, left behind stinging cuts. I ducked and weaved with an agility I hadn't employed since Youth League Soccer. I was focused. The most deeply motivated I'd ever been since . . . Youth League Soccer. *Eyes on the prize, Macy.*

My legs carried me over roots and rock. The trees were the opposing team, and I moved through them with ease. I'd left the other Visitors in the dust, but Lucy still had the lead. Not for long.

Thirty-foot gap. Twenty-foot. Ten.

Ahead of us, the house loomed ever closer, that dim star taking on tangible features: rectangular windows, the peaked roof, and . . . the door. The front door I'd been certain to shut was now wide open.

Lucy broke out of the woods, tripped on a gnarled root, and stumbled onto the gravel drive. She slip-scrambled to her feet. I was right on her tail now, mud kicking up from her heels, spitting onto my chin. *Get inside before she does. Lock the doors.* I recruited every tendon, every synapse, every muscle fiber, but my legs simply refused to move faster, and—

The motion light snapped on as we bombed up the driveway and beelined toward the front stoop. Our footsteps crunched against the gravel, thwack, thwack, thwack. I leapt forward, wrapped my arms around Lucy's waist, and tackled her. We sailed through the air, a strange and weightless moment that came to an end with a sickening CRACK. Lucy's face had met the sharp corner of a concrete step.

But she didn't so much as whimper. She only crawled, terribly silent, pulling herself upward one step at a time, dragging me along as I held on to her legs from behind, breathless and exhausted.

Still crawling, she looked back at me, her face awash in the motion light's unforgiving glare. Where her nose should have been was a caved-in gash, dark red, flecked with the stark white of broken bone and ruined cartilage. Blood seeped from the gash, streaming down her chin, her neck. And yet her cold blue eyes remained completely empty, apathetic.

She wrenched her leg free from my grip, raised it up, then promptly brought it back down. The muddy heel of her hiking boot met my eyes with a hollow THUNK. I didn't even feel the impact. My grip loosened, I tumbled backward, gravel crunched against my back. Then, the sound of footsteps. Footsteps sprinting up concrete stairs, into the house.

My vision tunneled, everything turned to crushing dark.

5
WARD

Existence was a hazy void. A blurred shuffle of incoherent stimuli. Darkness. Chlorine stench. Bluish-green carpet. Darkness. Glossy black plastic. Red light. Blue light. Red light. Blue light. Stuffed rabbit, scratchy fur. Red light. Blue light. Glossy black plastic. Red light. Blue light. Darkness.

Reality returned in five stages. The first was taste. The metallic bite of blood on my tongue, like a mouthful of dirty street pennies. The salty hint of mucus and long-dried saliva coating the back of my throat.

Touch came next. Thousands of little bumps molding against my back: gravel? Then a throbbing ache between my eyes, stinging cuts across my skin.

Sight came third. The hazy void reshaping itself into vaguely familiar surroundings. Concrete stairs. Olive-green slates. A dark sky dotted with stars like pinpricks in a black sheet.

Then came smell. Body odor and sweat. The earthy scent of concrete after rainfall. The bittersweet waft of rotting trees and the Pacific Ocean.

Right, I was on the coast.

Why?

I braced against the pain, turned onto my side. A motion light snapped on. A smeary mess of mud ran up the concrete stairs, footprints, handprints. All of it trailing toward a front stoop. I squinted. There were dots of blood too, spattered throughout the chaotic mud.

Last came sound. The electric buzz of the motion light, a slow breeze stirring through the surrounding woods.

I pushed myself up to sitting and took in a deep breath, exhaled. My lungs burned with a raspy sting. Had I been running? I shifted in the gravel, a low ache throbbing in my tailbone. Rolling onto my hands and knees, I pressed down against the first step and rose unsteadily to my feet.

I felt like a newborn calf learning how to walk. I nearly fell on the second step, but caught my balance on the wall. I started brushing dried mud off my pants. In my half-conscious daze, I thought I needed to look presentable—maybe I was about to have a job interview: *Get yourself together, Macy. Don't fuck this up. Don't fuck it all up like you always—*

Everything came rushing back at once. I was house-sitting for a dead man. No, not house-sitting—following Rites. Preventing a red sun from rising in the morning, protecting Jemma, protecting humanity, and—

My racing thoughts came to a violent halt, whiplashed by a horrid sight in the surrounding woods. My eyes widened. People . . . *Visitors*. Dozens upon dozens. Men, women, even children. All were clad in yellow rain ponchos, and all were standing perfectly still. Their faces empty and emotionless. They formed a loose perimeter that stretched across the gravel driveway and appeared to wrap around the entire house. The message, surreal and foreboding, was terribly clear:

You cannot leave.

6
INTRUDER

If they beat you to the house, do NOT leave, go back inside, lock the doors so more of them can't get in, wait for someone to call.

◆

I plodded up the stairs. Every step sent a ripple of jangling pain up my legs, into my spine. I slowed on the stoop. The front door was still wide open—the trail of muddy bootprints leading across the foyer, disappearing into the living room. A smear of red was streaked along the wood-paneled wall, a clumsy handprint. An image flashed through my head: Lucy's mutilated nose, blood pouring down her chin, her neck. Pale blue eyes unblinking in the motion light's glare. My shoulders tensed.

I took another deep, shaky breath. Exhaled. I stepped inside, pulled the door shut, and turned the lock. With my back to the wall, I inched forward, bracing for that yellow rain poncho to creep into view, those cold blue eyes, but . . . the bootprints led through the kitchen, and veered off into the back hall.

Lock the doors so more of them can't get in . . .

Keeping my eyes fixed to the darkened hallway, I arced across the living room. I checked the patio door. Locked.

I held there, eyes still homed in on the darkened hall and the muddy bootprints. What now? I fumbled through my pockets, searching for the crumpled receipt, but came up short. It must have slipped out during the foot race. I sifted back through a concussed haze of blurry memories:

Follow footprints at midnight.

Already did that.

Calm them?

Failed that one.

Beat them back to the house.

Failed that one too.

Lock doors.

Done.

Wait for call.

My eyes flicked to the foyer, the rotary phone. Maybe they already called? How long was I—

Click.

Somewhere in the shadows of the darkened hall, a door clicked softly shut. Silence. My gaze snapped to the wooden tray sitting atop the kitchen island. I grabbed the chrome-plated switchblade, pressed my thumb to the release—the blade popped out with its hefty and satisfying snap.

RIIIING . . .

I nearly jumped. I glanced to the foyer. Step by step, I backed toward the ringing phone, knife pointing at the darkened hall. I slowed to a stop, brought the receiver to my ear—

"Ms. Mullins."

I opened my mouth to respond, but—

"It's important you stay calm." It was the voice of a child, ten or twelve years old, speaking with the composed detachment of a debt collector. "Do not leave the house. Do not let your heart rate exceed one hundred and fifty beats per minute."

Just hearing that made my heart rate jump an octave. I slowed my breathing, put two fingers to my pulse, looked at a nearby clock and tried counting—

"Where is the Visitor?" said the child.

"S-somewhere . . . in the house?"

"Which room?"

"I, I don't—"

"Find out which room, come back and tell me."

I set the phone face up on the side table, stopped counting my pulse, focused on slowing my breath instead.

Knife raised, I padded alongside the trail of muddy footprints, through the living room, the kitchen, right up to the back hallway's entrance. I dared a peek around the corner. The hall looked like a deep space void, lit only by a thin sheet of warm light fanning out from beneath the crack of the study's closed door. The muddy prints led over white carpet, and slipped beneath that door. I hurried back to the phone. "She . . . she's in the study."

"So long as you follow the instructions I'm about to give," said the child, "the Visitor will not leave that room. Is that clear?"

"Yes."

"This should go without saying, but do not open the study door. And don't waste your time trying to barricade the door, if the Visitor wants out, it will find a way. If they start talking, do not respond. Do not wield any sort of weapon, it will only escalate things."

I dropped the switchblade.

The child continued speaking, calm and direct. "If you haven't already done so, lock all doors that lead outside. I'm going to assume you're writing this down. I will not be repeating myself."

I grabbed the ballpoint pen, started scribbling on my arm. Blue ink over blotchy bruises and red cuts:

dont leave house—keep bpm <150—dont open study door— if u follo Rites they stay in room—dont talk 2 intrudr— no weapon—lock doors

"When this call ends," the child went on, "you will have three minutes to turn on all the main- and second-floor lights. Ensure they remain on, even during the witching hour. If any picture frames fall, put them back up immediately, do not let a picture stay fallen for longer than one minute. Do not let a light stay *off* for longer than one minute—"

Barely able to keep up, I continued manically scribbling onto my arm:

lites ON, pics UP—1 min limit

"So long as you maintain these Rites until sunrise," said the child, "the Visitor will leave, a red sun will not rise, and you will be spared the devastating setback owed for refusing to burn the rabbit. But if you fail, things will get worse—expect another call."

CLICK.

7
BEATS PER MINUTE

I reread the barely legible scribbles on my arm:

*dont leave house—keep bpm <150—dont open study door—
if u follo Rites they stay in room—dont talk
2 intrudr—no weapon—lock doors—lites ON, pics UP—
1 min limit—follo these til sunrise*

My heart rate soared just trying to make sense of it all. *Focus, Macy. All you need to do is follow the Rites: keep the lights on and the pictures up. Follow the Rites.*

With two fingers on my pulse, I surged upstairs, hustled through each room and click, click, clicked on every single light switch. Even with all the chaos, each little click still hit me like a bump of pure dopamine: Click: relief. Click: relief. Click: relief.

I hurried downstairs, clicked on the foyer light.

Then the living room lights: click, click, click.

The kitchen: a click, and a BEEP for the stovetop light.

My pulse began to pound a mad rhythm against my fingertips. I came to a halt. *Breathe, Macy, in through the nose, out through the mouth.* I looked at the clock, tried counting again, when—

My eyes darted to the wooden tray on the kitchen island. I scoured through until I found the FitLyfe bracelet. I slapped it on my wrist, tightened the strap—a blue display came to life. Ten percent battery left. I fiddled with the buttons until:

122 BPM

Again, I slowed my breathing.

119 BPM

I crossed the kitchen, my gait a slow but steady tempo.

I froze at the hallway's entrance, and dared another peek around the corner. Every light was off, save for that thin sheet of warm glow fanning out from beneath the study's door, exposing those muddy shoeprints on the carpet. It was so quiet. I almost would've preferred the Visitor to be pacing around, rambling. The silence made me imagine her standing stock still, waiting for me to sneak past so she could burst out and grab me like a trapdoor spider.

My jaw clenched, relaxed, then clenched again—felt like I was revving up to plunge into ice-cold water. Fuck it. I surged forward. Skipping the study, I leaned into each room—click, click, click.

I'd started humming to myself, any song that came to mind: "Happy Birthday," the *Back to the Future* theme, "Happy" by Pharrell. God, I missed my headphones. At the hallway's end, I reached for the storage room light switch, and—

A low creak emanated behind me. I looked over my shoulder. At the base of the study door, that thin white line was now interrupted by two columns of black shadow. Utterly motionless. A rising swell caught in my throat—

Don't look.

I flicked on the storage room light and hightailed it out of there.

Just focus on your breathing. Follow the Rites.

I broached into the kitchen. Each and every light was still on, but . . . next to the fireplace, lying face down on a blue rug, was a fallen picture frame. I marched over, scooped it up, and hung it back on the wall. An old photo of David and Grace—

t-t-t-t-t-tink . . .

In the picture's reflection, the foyer light snapped OFF. I spun on my heel, rushed over, and flicked it back ON. The plastic switch was cold to the touch, like somebody had held an ice pack against it. In my periphery, a light on the second floor snapped OFF. I made my way up, two steps at a time. The bathroom light. I reached in, switched it ON, and—

THUNK.

Another picture had fallen, this one at the end of the hall, face up against the hardwood. *Breathe in. Breathe out. Stay calm.* I padded over, hung it back on the wall—

t-t-t-t-t-tink . . .

The guest room light stammered OFF. I stepped over, leaned in, snapped it back ON. It was cold too, just like the foyer switch. A shattering THUNK rang out from below—my heart bucked against my rib cage, tempo rising. I checked the bracelet:

132 BPM

Slow your breathing, in through the nose, out through the mouth.

I speedwalked down the stairs. A picture frame lay near the front door, surrounded by shimmers of broken glass. I kept moving, fast as I could without pushing my heart rate into hyperdrive. My sneakers crunched the splintered shards. I hunched down, hung the picture back up. A lamp in the living room snapped OFF.

Walk in the rain.

I *walked* briskly into the living room, switched the lamp back ON. Okay. I did an optical sweep for more fallen pictures, checked each and every light. All good. I moved into the back hallway and . . . at the far end, the storage room light was off.

My eyes flicked to the study, those two columns of black shadow still visible beneath the crack of its closed door. The Visitor hadn't moved a millimeter . . . I averted my gaze, and strode forward, one foot after the other. I switched the storage room light back ON, and had started down the hall, when—

A soft thump reverberated against the study door. I froze in my tracks and imagined "Lucy" standing on the other side, leaning with her forehead pressed against the door, arms dangling. Her nose a bloody gash, drip, drip, dripping.

A voice, small and quiet, leaked out—it spoke only one word: "I . . ."

I kept moving, not wanting to hear whatever else it had to say.

Walk in the rain.

I checked the kitchen, the living room, the foyer. All the lights were on, all the pictures up. I went to the second floor: all the lights were on, all the pictures up. I turned back, plodded down the stairs. The foyer was just as I'd left it—fragments of broken glass strewn across the floor, the switchblade on the side table.

I strode into the living room, the kitchen. All the lights were on, all the pictures up. I drifted forward and peeked into the hall. Every single light was on . . . save for one: the storage room at the very end. My focus snapped to the study's door. Those two columns of shadow. Fuck hell. I ground my teeth together, forced myself to carry on.

I covered my ears. *Walk in the rain, Macy, walk in the rain.* Shoulder

THE CARETAKER

against the wall, I *walked* forward, now giving the study as wide a berth as humanly possible. At the storage room, I lowered a hand, reached for the light switch, snapped it on, and—

"M-Macy?"

My hand froze in the middle of its journey back to my ear.

"Macy?" the Visitor repeated. It was Jemma's voice, an imitation so perfect, I almost questioned if it was actually her, but . . .

"Macy? W-where am I?" Jemma sounded scared, no, not Jemma, the *Visitor* sounded scared—a rising fear quivering beneath every syllable. "Macy, I don't, how did I, I don't know how I got here . . . I can't remember how . . . I . . ."

I snapped out of my daze, was about to cover my ears again, continue down the hall, when—the door handle started jostling. Before I knew it, I'd shot over and grabbed it with both hands. The jostling was weak, but I held tight, knuckles turning pale. "Macy, what the hell?" she said. "What are you doing?" The jostling grew stronger. I held tighter. Yes, the kid on the phone said the Visitor wouldn't leave the room, but . . .

As the Visitor kept trying to get out, I kept gripping the knob. "I'm scared," she said. "I don't . . . I can't remember how I got here—I think, I . . ." Her breath turned quick, shallow. The frantic sound of hands patting pockets, but the doorknob kept jostling. "I—I don't have my inhaler, Macy, I . . . I . . ." She drew in a gasping breath. "Macy, help, I—"

Her words trailed off, overtaken by panicked hyperventilating. But still the doorknob kept jostling. I shut my eyes, started humming—it did nothing to block out the horrifying sounds on the other side: the shortened breaths gave way to a long and guttural gasp like Velcro being torn apart. A heavy thump followed, glass breaking, feet kicking, high-pitched wheezing like the whines of a frightened dog.

141 BPM

It's not real, Macy. It's not real. It's not Jemma. Unable to think straight, I kept my hands clasped to the knob, waiting until the nightmare symphony finally trailed into . . .

Silence.

The doorknob stopped moving.

Dead quiet on the other side. As I stepped away and stumbled into the kitchen, my arms felt weaker, my body slower. And my thoughts took more effort, like molasses through a fine mesh strainer—

I imagined the Visitor's body lying face up on the study floor, a perfect copy of my sister, save for the eyes. I knew it didn't have hazel eyes like Jemma, like Dad. No, it had cold blue eyes, so pale they were almost white. Staring blankly up at the ceiling through big round glasses. Unblinking. Lifeless.

Then another image came to mind: a malformed caricature of Jemma, perched on top of the study desk, holding back a chorus of heinous laughter. Her head misshapen, her limbs too long, hands clasped over a grinning mouth filled with endless rows of Chiclet white teeth. Where her ears should have been were two dark holes, their insides encrusted with open sores.

I finally came to my senses and smothered the revolting image. *It's only trying to distract you, pull you away from the Rites.* I snapped back to the task at hand. *Follow the Rites. Lights on. Pictures up. Follow the Rites.*

8
HOLD ME CLOSE

Almost three hours had gone by without even a peep from the study. And I'd long stopped covering my ears altogether. After being forced to hear a highly detailed mimicry of my little sister dying from an asthma attack, I figured things couldn't really get much worse. My thoughts were numb, distant. *This isn't happening to you, Macy, it's just some poor carbon copy version of you. Walk in the rain.*

It was 4:15 a.m.—only two hours to go until sunrise. By now I'd gotten the whole "pictures up, lights on" thing down to a science. I knew the exact pacing I could keep without shooting my heart rate over 150. I'd even figured out a pattern: the fallen picture in the foyer was almost always followed by a light turning off in the kitchen, then the light in the storage room, then another fallen picture upstairs. Not once in the last three hours did it deviate from this pattern. It was like the Visitor had played its best "dead sister fake-out" card, and I hadn't fallen for it, so it gave up. A lack of effort I found admittedly relatable. Still, just to be sure, I'd texted Jemma to confirm she was safe, breathing, and not locked in the study.

MACY: Hey?
JEMMA: don't text me just one word it's terrifying
MACY: Sorry. Just saying hi!
JEMMA: K. ¯_(ツ)_/¯

My sister was alive and well.

I kept pacing the house, running on autopilot, getting more little bumps of dopamine relief each time I put a picture back up, each time I flicked a light on. And despite everything, part of me was almost finding a strange sense of purpose in it all. Yes, I was still miserable, but I was protecting the world from unspeakable suffering. I was protecting Jemma. Finally doing something worthwhile.

Around 4:37 a.m., a familiar sound leaked out from the study. I'd just turned on the storage room light, and was heading back down the hall when—

Once again, a thump hit the study door. But this time, the sound was so gentle, so quiet, I wondered if it had been imagined. I carried on, went back upstairs, and . . . no lights turned off. I did a double-check sweep: no lights turned off, no fallen pictures. A deviation in the pattern.

Thump . . .

Downstairs, that hollow sound repeated, louder. *It's fine, Macy, whatever this thing throws at you, it's fine, just ignore it.*

Fists clenched, I stomped down into the foyer. No fallen pictures. No lights turned off. Same with the living room. And the kitchen.

I looked to that hallway, one shade darker than it should be—now I could tell if the storage room light was off without even seeing it directly. I rounded into the hall. *Walk in the rain.* As I moved, I couldn't help but steal a glance at the base of the study's door. Only that thin line of white, no columns of shadow. I switched on the storage room light, and hurried back down the hall—

129 BPM

I quickly *walked* into the kitchen and—

Once again, Jemma's small voice leaked from the study, somehow crystal-clear, as if carrying through vents that did not exist. It said only two words: "I know..."

T-T-T-T-T-TINK...

I looked over my shoulder—the hallway was almost pitch dark... I stepped backward, and peered in. Every single light was off, save for that thin line beneath the study door. *Follow the Rites.* I shuffled forward, flicking the lights back on as I went. I finished at the storage room, rounded back into the kitchen: no fallen pictures, no lights turned off.

Living room: no fallen pictures, no lights turned off.

Foyer: clear.

Upstairs: clear.

I stepped back down onto the main floor and—

T-T-T-T-TINK...

Again, that back hallway turned one shade above pitch dark—nearly all of its lights snapping off in unison. The tightness between my lungs swelled. The Visitor wanted me in that hallway. I exhaled, and pressed forward. The study light was still on, that ever-present line of white, but once again, it was interrupted by two familiar columns of black shadow. I pushed onward—

Fake Jemma's voice leaked out, "I know you..."

Yeap, I get it, you know me, it's only like the fifth time I've heard it. I switched the lights back on, one at a time. I reached the storage room and—

"I know you tried—"

Don't respond. Thoughts are sound. I switched on the storage room light, carried myself back down the hall, and—

"I know you tried to leave . . ."

Sorry I wasn't dumb enough to fall for your fake asthma attack. I made it two steps into the kitchen and—

T-T-T-T-TINK . . .

Yet again, the hallway behind me went dark. I spun on my heel, started back.

"I know you tried to leave me," the Visitor continued in Jemma's voice. "Two years ago . . ."

I furrowed my brow, flicked on the first light. Two years ago? What was she talking about? I switched on the next light.

Jemma, the *Visitor*, wasn't finished: "I . . . I lied to myself about it for a long time." She, no not *she*, *it* paused. "But, deep down, I know you tried to leave me . . ."

I switched on the bathroom light.

Tried to leave you? Two years ago? In my sleep-deprived confusion, I just about said, *The fuck are you talking about?* But I stopped myself well before the words made it up my throat. Don't respond.

I switched on the next light.

It's just saying whatever it can to distract you. Don't respond. Never respond. It's only trying to get into your head. Trying to get your heart rate up. I checked the bracelet:

132 BPM

I switched on the storage room light, marched back down the hall, and stepped out into the kitchen—

"I know you tried to leave me." Jemma's voice resounded from above, again seeming to travel through vents that didn't exist. "I know you went to the Hawthorne Hotel . . ."

The Hawthorne Hotel.

A rotten chill ran through me. A shuddering wave of guilt starting at the base of my skull, radiating outward, like a rock hitting the surface of a frozen pond.

The Hawthorne Hotel . . .

Jemma didn't know about my stay at the Hawthorne Hotel. I'd never told a soul about it. I'd pushed it so far down in my psyche I forgot about it myself sometimes. There's no way Jemma could have known, and . . . *This isn't even Jemma, you idiot. It's messing with you, trying to hurt you, trying to pull you away from the Rites, and—*

I hurried to the foyer, covered my ears again, but that did nothing to block out the Visitor's voice. I could almost hear it in my thoughts now, feel it thrumming in my teeth:

"I know you tried to leave me." I was all the way in the foyer, but the voice was still crystal-clear. Speaking calm, soft. Yet there was the slightest hint of growing anger simmering beneath every syllable. "And that night, two years ago, when I asked where you were going and you just said 'a friend's place,' you looked . . . you sounded guilty. You always were a terrible liar—"

It's just bullshit, Macy, just ignore her, it's all FUCKING bullshit. I glanced around the foyer. No lights to turn on here. No pictures to hang—

I started upstairs, but I could not escape that voice. She wasn't even yelling; she still spoke soft and steady, yet no matter where I went, it always sounded like she was only one room away. Plug my ears, hum to myself, there was nothing I could do to drown it out. I had no choice but to listen:

"And when you told me you'd be back the next day, when you turned to walk out the door, it looked like . . . you looked like you were finally at peace, like that ever-present tightness between your lungs had finally gone away . . ." The Visitor fell quiet again. I searched for pictures to put up, lights to turn on, anything to distract myself, but there was nothing . . . I descended back to the main floor, each step filled with growing dread. I slowed in the living room and looked toward that hallway. It was dark again, all the lights switched off save for the study.

I floated forward, Jemma's voice seeping out from the inky black ahead: "I know you tried to leave me, Macy. I called you that night, do you even remember? Or were you too drunk?"

More old memories emerged, bobbing to the surface like dead fish. I pushed them down, only for them to come back twice as strong. It had been almost a year after Dad . . . Shortly after I'd been fired from yet another job. I'd been lying in bed for days, staring up at our broken ceiling fan, watching spiders spin their webs and suck the life from dying flies.

Red. Blue. Red. Blue.

That ever-present knot between my lungs had banked itself down to an old familiar nothing, that empty misery that told me the world just might be a better place with one less Macy Mullins in it. I was numb to that voice. Never listened to that voice. Never could. I had to take care of Jemma. I had to be there for my little sister, but . . .

There was a deeper level below all that emptiness, all that misery. An underground bedrock thousands of miles below the fear of catastrophe, below the cruel voices telling me to end things. A level that, two years ago, I plummeted into.

As I stared up at that broken ceiling fan, falling deeper and deeper into a pit I might never escape, this level caught me, cushioned my free fall like a soft blanket of peaceful acceptance. A chorus of warm voices seemed to ring out. Soothing. Gentle. Voices that spoke with the same reassuring tone as my father, steady and calming. Voices that wrapped their arms around me, held me close and whispered: *You know you don't have to keep fighting, Macy. You don't have to keep teetering. You can just let go. Let yourself plummet. That's okay too . . .*

"I called to ask if you were okay," Jemma, the *Visitor*, went on. "You said everything was good, said you were just tired, and . . . I was dumb enough to buy it."

143 BPM

I stumbled into the hallway. My breath coming in shallow sips. I fumbled for the first light switch, flicked it on, and started toward the next. The entire house seemed to sink into the earth as more terrible memories came rushing back, memories that always rested just below the surface of everything. Like reality itself was nothing but a thin blanket draped over a festering stab wound. Memories I pretended weren't real. Memories I pretended weren't mine. They were the memories of the Macy in reflections, the Macy forever drowning in puddles and bogs. The memories of a carbon copy Macy. I never would have left Jemma, I had to take care of my little sister, I had to be there for—

"I know you tried to leave me, Macy, just like Mom walked out, just like Dad drove into a fucking river." Jemma's tone, the *Visitor's* tone, began to shift, speaking through gritted teeth, speaking with a spiteful cruelty—a hateful and bitter fury, a hatred for Macy Mullins that almost matched my own. "I know you tried to leave me, but you couldn't even do that right. You thought a bottle of sleeping pills and a liter of vodka would be enough. You curled up with your childhood stuffed rabbit, tied a plastic bag over your head, and passed out on a king-sized bed at the Hawthorne Hotel, praying your air would run out in the middle of the night, praying you would blink out of existence, but you fucked it up, you FUCKED IT UP, just like you FUCK EVERYTHING UP—"

Ignore it, Macy, you're not the same person now. Just ignore it—

"You stirred awake, thrashing and whimpering, covered in bile and puke and drool—you hadn't taken enough pills and the bag ripped open in all your flailing. You FUCKED IT UP—"

I switched on the storage room light, and turned back down the hall. *Just focus, check the living room next, follow the Rites, follow the—*

"And you keep telling yourself the only reason you don't try it all over again is you need to take care of your little s-sister." The voice shifted slightly, warbled, like two voices had spoken at once. "But we both know the real reason . . ."

I rounded into the kitchen; all the lights were on, all the pictures up. Nothing to do but trace my path through the house and listen, listen and try not to scream back, ramble out a list of excuses, reasons for why I did what I did two years ago, despite knowing full well the effect it would have on Jemma, and—

"The real reason you don't try again is that you're just too fucking scared." The voice shifted once more. Now it was my own voice. Filled with a hatred for Macy Mullins that was unmatched by every soul on earth. Every soul except for mine. "You're too scared of failing," it continued. "Too scared of waking up half brain-dead in a hospital, cold buzzing light, chlorine stench, spoon-fed till you rot away in the dirt and realize that, just like Auntie Pat, just like Dad, all you ever were was food for worms, FOOD for WORMS, FOOD FOR WORMS—"

148 BPM

I needed to slow my heart. I slumped against the kitchen island, and slid down to the floor, hands against my ears, eyes clenched shut—

"You're an absolute WASTE of a human being, MACY MULLINS," my own voice screamed from the hallway. "You weren't meant to exist in this world. In ANY world. You'd be doing EVERYONE a favor if you just tried to LEAVE, just ONE MORE TIME, and—"

151 BPM

All at once: Every single picture frame fell to the floor with a mighty THWACK. Every single light bulb shattered into a hailstorm of glass.

Darkness.

And . . . finally, the Visitor's voice went silent.

I sat there in the dark, my back pressed against the kitchen island, surrounded by the broken glimmers of yet another failure. My fingers clawed into tangled hair, clawed so tight the roots ripped out with needling bites. And then, for the first time in nearly half a decade, I started to fight back tears. Red. Blue. I hit the side of my head with a closed fist. "Stupid fucking idiot." Red. Blue. *You have to turn the lights back on, replace the bulbs, put the pictures back up.* Red. Blue. *Get yourself together, Macy, you have responsibilities, you can't fall apart, you have to keep moving, you have to protect Jemma, follow the Rites—*

I tried to stand, but my limbs wouldn't move.

Red. Blue. Red. Blue. Red—

Tears welled from my eyes, trailed down my face, seeped into the cuts and stung—but these weren't tears of sadness, these weren't tears of grief—my teeth clenched down, bit into my lip until blood burst over my tongue—these were tears of rage. Hatred and bitter fury. Hatred for the house, the Visitors, the entire fucking world—but most of all . . . hatred for myself. Hatred for the fact that, only two years ago, I gave up. Hatred for the fact that I still thought about giving up every single day since. I couldn't even take care of myself, let alone Jemma, and—

I clenched a fist and hit the side of my head for a second time: "Stupid fucking idiot." The dull ache barely registered. I hit myself again, harder: "Stupid FUCKING idiot." Again: "STUPID FUCKING IDIOT." I kept hitting myself until my fist turned limp and the pain turned numb. I sat there, my dreary reflection gazing up at me in the scattered fragments of broken glass. I looked away. I took a breath. *In through the nose, out through the mouth. In through the nose, out through the mouth.*

And then . . . across the kitchen, around the corner, somewhere within the shadows of that darkened hall: a soft click, followed by the low creak of an opening door.

PART IV

DUTIES AND OBLIGATIONS

OBSCURE

I used to have a habit of breaking people's hearts before they could break mine. Defense mechanism. I knew it was wrong, but I still went ahead and did it. Can't even blame that one on grief 'cause I did it long before Dad ever kicked the bucket.

But, at the very least, I always waited until I saw the writing on the wall. People fell in love with me fast, then fell out of love even faster. The same pattern had happened so many times I'd lost count. Boo-hoo. Poor Macy.

Nowadays I have a habit of not dating anyone, that way nobody gets their heart broken. Win-win.

The last time somebody got the jump on me, broke my heart before I could break theirs, was in senior year. Avery Beckett. They were cool. They played drums and had a septum piercing and liked the same kind of movies I did. But less than four months into going steady they told me they "didn't not like me," they just "didn't see things ending well."

Fair enough.

After school that day, Jemma caught me sulking in the backyard. Sitting on our undersized swing set, staring at the fence. She asked me if I was okay.

Normally I would've just said I was tired, but "I got dumped."

Jemma was sifting through a handful of sunflower seeds, picking the ones without shells. "It's 'cause you're weird," she said.

I frowned.

Jemma went on, "You're like an obscure Midwest emo . . . jazz-fusion metalcore country band. Weird. You're not everybody's thing. Heck, you're not even most *people's* thing—"

"Jesus Jem, thanks—"

"But that's okay, you don't have to be. One day you're gonna find somebody and you'll be their *thing*. They're gonna be the biggest fan of Midwest emo jazz-fusion . . . metalcore country in the world. They'll know all your albums front to back, even the live stuff. They'll tell all their friends they loved you before you went mainstream."

I shook my head. It was a dumb analogy, but . . . it was the only post-breakup thing anybody had ever said that made me feel even one iota better. Sibling pep talks. Jemma was always better at those than I was.

1
SEE NO EVIL

So long as you maintain these Rites until sunrise, the Visitor will leave, a red sun will not rise, and you will be spared the devastating setback owed for refusing to burn the rabbit. But if you fail, things will get worse—expect another call.

◆

Across the kitchen, around the corner, somewhere within the shadows of the darkened hall: a soft click, followed by the low creak of an opening door.

The sound eviscerated my self-loathing, replaced it with a pure and dreadful focus—a pinpoint awareness that kept my eyes fastened to the hallway's entrance. I scoped for any sign of movement in the lifeless shadows. My ears strained, readying to hear the sound of footsteps plodding out from the study, but there was only silence.

Silence, and the tick, tick, tick of a nearby clock.

I imagined a crooked figure, tiptoeing down the hall with the exaggerated movements of a *Looney Tunes* nightmare. My survival instinct took over. I shot to my feet and started toward the foyer, sneakers crunching the remnants of shattered light bulbs and broken picture frames. I wasn't waiting for the Visitor to step around that corner. *Get out of here.* I swung open the front door, ready to make a run for it, but . . .

The other Visitors still stood guard in their loose perimeter. Vacant eyes. Empty faces. Maybe I could take my chances, bolt through a weak spot in their ranks, and—

Follow the Rites, Macy. Stay in the house, and follow the Rites.

Backing away, I pulled the door shut, turned on my heel, and climbed upstairs. The lights here were shattered too, a constellation of starry glints strewn across the hardwood—

RIIIIIING . . .

I surged into the guest room, brought the glossy white phone to my ear, and—

"Do not look at the Visitor." This voice belonged to an old man, monotone, completely void of any emotion, yet oddly familiar. "From now until sunrise, if you look directly at the Visitor for longer than three seconds, you will forget how to breathe." He paused. A muffled voice spoke in the background, baritone deep—warbling and indiscernible. When it stopped talking, the old man continued, seeming to relay whatever the muffled voice had said: "Do not let the Visitor get its hands on you. It moves slow, but you cannot leave the house. Your heart rate is no longer of consequence, and you can use anything at your disposal for self-defense." The old man fell silent again. The deep and warbling voice spoke for a second time. And once more, the old man waited for it to finish, then relayed its message: "The Visitor can hear your thoughts, so try to think of quiet things. Gentle memories."

For the last time, the warbling voice spoke in the background, then fell quiet.

"Avoid the Visitor until sunrise," said the old man, "or deal with it through force. If you survive, you will be spared the devastating setback and a red sun will not rise at dawn. Do not expect such leniency going forward."

CLICK.

The call ended.

I set the phone down. Hide or fight. Both options were far less than ideal. I backed into the hallway, peered down the stairs, and stood perfectly still. I tilted an ear, again straining to listen for any sign of life down there, when—

Slow footsteps reverberated—soft and plodding, thump . . . thump . . . thump . . . Each impact underlined by the clink of broken glass. The Visitor began to pace around the kitchen, or maybe the living room. I took a reflexive step backward, and the heel of my sneaker crunched a fallen picture frame. *Fuck.* I froze. The footsteps froze too . . . then started moving toward the stairs.

Thump . . . Thump . . . Thump . . .

My heart pounded, head swiveled. My eyes landed on the shower, reflected in the bathroom mirror. I took a long stride over broken glass, reached in, and turned on the water to full strength—praying the sound would drown out my footsteps. I darted back into the hallway and cracked open the main bedroom door as another distraction. I slipped into the closet at the end of the hall, pulled it shut, and peeked through the slats.

My view of the outside hallway was little more than a sliver: bare walls painted over by dim moonlight, shower steam pluming out from the bathroom. Those thudding footfalls ascended the stairs—slow but imminent. And just as the shadowy crown of a bulbous head crept into view—I shut my eyes and clasped a hand over my mouth.

Don't look.

The footsteps thump, thump, thumped steadily down the hall, crunching against broken glass. Heavy, dragging. I winced at the thought of bare feet pressing into shattered glass, jagged splinters sticking out from pale soles, trailing blood.

The Visitor paused.

A rusty squeak rang out, and the shower went silent. My eyes twitched open—in the bathroom mirror stood a dark and crooked shape, so tall its neck was craned to avoid bumping the ceiling. It started to turn, bending to fit through the doorframe—my eyes snapped shut again.

The Visitor's footsteps plodded out of the bathroom and continued down the hall, getting closer, closer. The floor shook with every approaching impact. The moonlight against my eyelids shifted to a darker shade. Then, everything turned still, like time itself had stopped.

I held my breath.

The floor creaked, and a silent exhale seeped in through the slats, brushed cold across my face. *It can hear your thoughts.* I tried to think of quiet things, gentle memories, but I could hardly think at all. I kept my eyes shut, breath held . . .

Another frigid exhale seeped through the slats and grazed my skin, this time carrying the metallic scent of blood—blood and chlorine. A stench so strong, I could taste it, coating my tongue like dust. I kept trying to think of gentle things, happy memories, and . . . my mind became a desolate wasteland, a flatlined heartbeat. Seconds unfolded like minutes. The floor creaked again, and the shadows against my eyelids shifted once more.

Silence.

The Visitor trudged off.

Thump . . . thump . . . thump . . .

I cracked one eye, just in time to glimpse the shadowy figure slip into the main bedroom. The image—briefer than a millisecond and obscured by darkness—burrowed into my thoughts like a bloated tick. The Visitor's limbs had been impossibly long, its skin wet in the pallid moonlight: a glistening sheen, like the underside of a freshly peeled scab.

From within the main bedroom, the sound of a door creaked open.

Scraping noises: hangers sliding over metal racks. My eyes flicked forward. The staircase at the end of the hall dared me to retreat into the foyer, grab that switchblade, and find a better hiding spot. Another door clicked open. The en suite bathroom? The Visitor was checking each door one by one—this closet would be next. A sweaty chill climbed up my legs, my torso, my face, like mercury filling a thermometer and spilling out at the top. My lungs caved in on themselves. I caught my breath. *Focus, Macy, Focus.*

I cracked the closet door and crept out. I moved forward with my back to the wall, doing my best to avoid stepping on broken glass. I picked up speed, stalked down the stairs, and eased into the foyer. My hand grasped the switchblade from the side table. Its chrome-plated handle was oddly reassuring, smooth and cold against my palm.

From above, the footsteps thumped. Another door creaked open. I navigated through the living room, step by step, stretching my legs to tiptoe onto islands clear of shattered glass. Where to hide next?

Something shifted atop a nearby china cabinet, a slinking blur. I looked up. Two small dots hovered in the black—eyes: one a cold blue, the other a dark brown.

Brownie.

The cat, perched atop the china cabinet, tilted its head, looked down at me, and offered a slow blink. Completely indifferent to my plight. Upstairs, yet another door creaked open, followed by the sound of methodical scouring. Brownie blinked again, once, twice, then . . . she crouched, and dropped down from the cabinet like a spill of liquid. Her front paws hit the hardwood first, followed by her hind legs:

Du-dum.

The rummaging on the second floor stopped. The Visitor's footsteps began making their way toward the staircase. *Fuck hell.* Brownie trod off into the shadows, totally oblivious to how much she'd just screwed me over. I hurtled into the back hallway, tried the first door: locked.

The next: locked.

I kept going, trying each handle as I went, but all were locked, even the study, even the storage closet.

I looked to my right, and . . .

The basement door was half-open, a column of warm glow casting out, beaming across the wall, up onto the ceiling. Thump, thump, thump, the Visitor's footsteps shambled through the kitchen.

With nowhere else to hide, I descended into the basement, one hand sliding over drywall for balance, the other gripping the switchblade. I stepped onto the glossy concrete. Only a single light was on, down at the end of the narrow hall: an incandescent bulb directly above the old TV pushcart.

I took a few steps forward, my footfalls silent—no broken glass down here. Again I searched for a place to hide. To my right was a cramped utility room and a cluttered closet. To my left, a spare bedroom. And straight ahead, at the end of that long hallway, behind the TV pushcart, a solitary bone-white door.

Upstairs, those plodding footsteps thudded ever closer, closer, until they slowed at the top of the stairs.

t-t-t-t-tink.

The light above the TV snapped OFF, and everything plunged into blinding dark. A rail-spike of adrenaline stabbed into my brainstem: *HIDE.*

My limbs jolted into action. Arms outstretched, knife pointing, I shuffled forward, trying to remember where the nearest room had been. I kept moving, uncertainty clouding every step, as if the floor beneath me might suddenly vanish, and—

t-t-t-t-tick-mmmmmm—

The TV snapped to life—a blue square hovering in the black, all the way at the end of that narrow hall. Its screen, warped by white scan lines, pitched a pale wedge over the yellow walls, the concrete floor. I froze like a deer in headlights . . .

The jittery scan lines disappeared and a video began to play: from the bottom of the solid blue frame, a dark shape slowly rose, circular and black—the silhouette of a head, held aloft by a withered neck. The shape came to a stop in the frame's dead center, and a horrible realization finally struck me: this figure wasn't *on* the screen, it was standing in front of it.

I tried to back away, but I couldn't even move my eyes. Couldn't blink. Couldn't breathe.

Then, a strained and wheezing gasp rang out, underlined by a guttural rattle, like an empty can of spray paint being shaken. The head was enveloped by a plastic bag, glossy and black. As the figure exhaled, the bag swelled like an exposed lung, nearly blotting out the entire screen behind it. A ragged inhale—the bag collapsed, wrapping tightly around the shape of a gaunt and hairless skull. Exhale—the bag swelled. Inhale—the bag shrank.

Terror, pure and liquid, pulsed through my veins like cold water, soaked into my extremities and began to freeze. Then, in perfect unison: the door at the top of the basement stairs slammed SHUT, the TV snapped OFF, and everything fell back into blinding dark.

2
GOOD THOUGHTS

Hide. Survive until sunrise.

I pushed through the crushing darkness. My breath came in sputtering bursts. And my heartbeat couldn't decide on a tempo: one moment thumping so fast it might just shatter my ribs, the next seeming to stop altogether. Panic crawled across my skin like a swarm of sightless bugs, goose bumps rising.

HIDE.

I kept moving through the dark, knife raised, arms sweeping back and forth. Left foot forward, right foot forward, left foot, right—

The quivering blade scraped into drywall. I pressed my shoulder against the wall and slid forward. All the while, those ragged exhales, now accompanied by shuffling footsteps, drew near.

I kept moving. Kept groping through the dark, sliding along the wall. My splayed fingers met the edge of a doorframe and clutched a cold brass knob. My wrist turned. I slipped into the spare bedroom, yanked the door shut, and locked it. I pressed my back to the door and tried to get my breathing under control: *In through the nose, out through the mouth.*

In the room's far corner was a high window, compact and thin, too small for escape. *In through the nose, out through the mouth.* The faintest spill of moonlight invaded the dark, lending the shadows a murky definition. Beneath the window sat the blurry outline of a twin bed. *In through the nose, out through the mouth.*

Those shuffling footsteps, muffled by the closed door, continued to draw closer.

I lunged forward, dropped to my stomach, and pulled myself under the bed. The rusty spring mattress scraped against my back, the cold concrete below stroked my face—

The doorknob began jostling.

It can hear your thoughts.

I slammed my eyelids shut, tried to think of quiet things again, gentle memories. I thought back to a time Dad took us to a shelter for old cats. I was sitting in a plastic chair when a gray tabby with a crooked tail crawled onto my lap and purred so loud Dad and Jemma could hear it from across the room.

The jostling at the door grew quieter.

Then, the cat's purring turned to the sound of a roaring engine. The room from my memories began to shrink, contort itself into a pickup truck, walls becoming car doors, the floor becoming a windshield. Everything nose-diving toward the Willamette River. The windshield caved in with a deafening crash and a torrent of water slammed into me—

The jostling at the door turned to violent bangs. The frame cracked, wood splintered, and—the door swung wide, its brass knob punching a hole into drywall. Silence. Ragged breathing, slow and steady, spilled into the room.

Don't look.

Again, I clenched my eyes shut. More ragged breaths—Inhale . . .

Exhale . . . Inhale . . . Exhale . . . Then, footsteps, bare and scraping, shambled forward. A closet door slid open with a low scrape. Clumsy rifling through hanging clothes. I cracked one eye. The bedroom door was still ajar. I braced my arms, readied myself to make a run for it, when—

Withered legs shuffled directly into my line of sight. So close, I could see maggots writhing beneath pale skin, thousands, all mashed together—like squirming hamburger meat beneath vacuum-sealed Saran Wrap. The mattress above creaked, and the figure began to lower itself, inch by inch.

Never look.

I shut my eyes, held my breath, gritted my teeth, and . . . swung the knife.

Time slowed. My clenched hand grazed over concrete, then came to a sudden halt, punctuated by a wet and fleshy SQUELCH. My eyes opened. The blade was lodged, right up to its chrome handle, directly into the figure's ankle. The Achilles' heel.

I tensed. Pulling sideways with all my strength. The wiry tendon, strained and twitching, kept the blade in place. I gripped the knife with both hands, heaved and wrenched until, with a nauseating POP—the tendon SNAPPED, recoiling up the leg like a snake with its head cut off. The calf muscle turned to quivering jelly, the ragged breaths to high-pitched wheezing.

In one quick motion, I pulled myself out from under the bed, shot to my feet, and bounded across the room.

I yanked the door shut in my wake, then toppled a wooden shelf to block it. Those wheezing breaths shrieked out from the other side.

I needed to get the FUCK out of here.

Still wielding the knife, I flailed through the all-consuming dark, waving my arms until they found the drywall. I slid forward, stumbled onto the staircase, and scrambled up, half-crawling. A thin line of gray moonlight was cutting through the darkness above. The door. I rose to my feet, turned the knob, and pushed, pulled, but it wouldn't budge. Somebody was holding it in place. From the other side, soft whimpers—or was it laughter?—leaked out. *How many Visitors made it in?* Behind me, a hollow THWUMP, followed by ragged breathing, scraping sounds—that maggot-filled atrocity was dragging itself over concrete. I tried the door one last time, shoved and pulled and rammed against it with my shoulder. Futile.

HIDE.

I bolted down the stairs, and made it halfway across the room, when a cold hand snagged me by the ankle and brought me to a vicious halt. A weightless free fall that ended when my chin met the concrete. My jaw snapped shut—blood burst over my tongue—the switchblade flew from my grasp. I whirled onto my back, kicking and twisting, but the cold hand only clamped down harder—cutting into my ankle like a noose, pulling me closer, closer.

A malignant force seeped out from the ever-constricting grip, invaded my body like needles through skin. A rising sting that slid up my leg, snaked up my spine, filled my head with intrusive horrors beyond reason. The thin ropes holding my sanity in place *snap, snap, snapped*, and I spiraled into a claustrophobic paralysis that felt more real than my entire life. Like I'd only been dreaming until now and had finally awakened.

My head split open and my skin peeled away like a thousand zippers all rushing down, down, down—reality molding into an ever-narrowing pit, an endless funnel pulling, *crushing* me deeper and deeper. I couldn't move my arms, couldn't turn my head. And every swell of my lungs was cut short, compressed by solid rock on all sides. Yet still I fell, breathless, skinless, shrieking, squeezing—my eyes bulged, my bones splintered and snapped, my very existence crushing down to the width of a rusty pipe, then a metal straw, and—

My fingers found the knife's chrome handle and hoisted me out of the hallucinatory hell-pit. I curled forward and started slashing—slashing and stabbing into the pitch dark. Cold blood splashed out with every swing, spattered onto my face, my arms. I stabbed and slashed, until the figure's grip turned limp, until its wheezing fell quiet, until it stopped moving altogether . . .

Still I kept stabbing. Stabbing the dead body until the switchblade, slick with blood, slipped from my grasp. I fumbled around, my fingers finding purchase on the chrome-plated handle. I tried to pull it out, but the blade was stuck between jutting ribs.

Finally, I crab-shuffled away, crawling as far as my exhausted limbs would carry me. I fell onto my back. Heart pounding, breath scraping. I lay there, eyes closed, staring into a black void.

Cold blood spread over the concrete, soaking my legs, my torso, but I barely even noticed. All I could do was breathe: *in through the nose, out through the mouth, in through the nose, out through the mouth.*

A thin line of light hit the side of my face. I opened my eyes, turned my head. The morning sun was beaming in through that compact window. Rays of swaying light cutting between the towering pines outside. The sun rising over Brooksview Heights was not a terrible shade of red—it was a familiar golden white.

I shut my eyes again, and let it warm my blood-stained skin.

3
DEVIL'S PLAYGROUND

It's important that one keeps the house generally tidy. The messier the house, the more likely you run into trouble.

◆

I don't remember leaving the basement, barely remember showering to wash off the blood. Reality was distant, like I was watching myself on a screen, suspended in a state of sleep-deprived shell shock. And the horrors of last night were stowed away in the same folder as half-forgotten nightmares: Slashing. Stabbing. Cold blood spilling.

I'd won. That's all that mattered. I'd prevented a devastating setback, stopped a red sun from rising. I had saved humanity, and protected Jemma. Macy Mullins, savior of the world. If I weren't so exhausted, so traumatized, I might've felt proud.

Post-shower, I stepped out of the bathroom, clad in baggy sweatpants and an oversized T-shirt. As I walked, broken glass clinked beneath a pair of hard-soled slippers I'd found in Grace's bedroom. My hair still wet, I descended into the foyer and slowed at the edge of the living room.

My phone buzzed—call from Jemma. I pressed ACCEPT.

"Hey," said Jemma, her voice tired and groggy. "How's it goin'?"

I surveyed the disaster of a house: broken glass, fallen picture frames, smeared and muddy shoeprints, spattered dots of blood.

"It's going . . ." I said. "How are you?"

"Just woke up. Getting ready for my interview."

"Interview?"

"Target. Thought I told you?"

"Right . . ."

Loaded silence. "You uh . . ." Jemma paused. "You sure everything's good there?"

"Yeah." I chewed on a fingernail. "Just . . . saving the world."

"Ha. What time you home tomorrow?"

I almost replied with a mirthless laugh. "Not sure yet," I said. Earlier that morning, I'd called Grace a few more times, only to get her voicemail with each attempt. The chance of her ever coming back was getting close to zero. It seemed Jemma was right from the start: Grace had passed her "curse" on to me. I'd likely be stuck watching this house until the day I died. A fact I wasn't even remotely prepared to process, let alone divulge to my sister. "Anyways," I said, "gotta go, but good luck with Walmart."

"Target."

"Right. Good luck with that."

"Thanks—"

Again, I ended the call before Jemma could question me further. I tucked away my phone, and trudged forward, slippers crunching broken glass. Time to get to work.

♦

THE CARETAKER

I started with the fallen picture frames. Had no clue where each one went, but I tried my best. My only guide was a vague template of discolored squares and rectangles on the wood-paneled walls—a vertical jigsaw puzzle. As I worked, Brownie watched, perched high atop the china cabinet like a little gargoyle.

I hung the pictures, mentally piecing together a rough narrative of the Carnswels' pasts. Anything to distract myself. Anything to maintain whatever crumbs remained of my sanity. It seemed David's wealth had come from an inherited lumber empire. In one photo, he stood cross-armed in front of a sixteen-wheeler semitruck, flanked by men in fancy suits and white hardhats. I faintly recognized the logo—a dark green, twin-peaked mountain: "CARNSWEL TIMBER." Another photo showed him touring a lumber mill, blue collar employees regarding him with reverence and a hint of fear.

I hung photo after photo, stringing together more elements of David's character. He played violin. Loved cats, and dogs. He used to be into downhill skiing, and was an MVP in college lacrosse. It seemed he'd been married at least once before Grace, and had a son. I didn't see a single photo of his son looking older than twenty—and he looked sad in most of his pictures, even when he was smiling.

Again, memories from last night started to surface: slashing, stabbing, cold blood spilling—I pushed them back down, kept working. Kept putting up pictures, piecing together the Carnswels' backstory to distract myself.

Grace appeared to be something of a hippie back in the day. In one image she sat cross-legged on a floral-patterned blanket at an outdoor music festival. She was in her mid-twenties here, wearing a green shawl and playing an acoustic guitar. A man with long hair and a crown of flowers had his arm wrapped around her shoulders. An old family photo showed Grace with that same man, both in their thirties. They had three children. It was only two photos, but she looked happier with him than with David. I wondered if he had passed away too.

After I finished with the picture frames, I grabbed the vacuum from the storage closet. As I stepped back into the hall, the basement door caught the corner of my eye—open, just a crack. Another jolt of vivid memory flared into my thoughts: squirming maggots, wheezing breaths, snapping tendons. I shook it all off with a jittery shudder. I went over to the basement door and pushed it shut. I didn't know if the dead body was still down there, or if it had vanished like all the other Visitors. And I wasn't sure which option was worse. Maybe I'd have to drag that withered corpse out into the woods, bury it in the clearing.

That was another problem for the Macy of tomorrow.

I started on vacuuming the main and second floor. It took three passes through the house for the crackling sound of shattered glass to stop. Next, I replaced every single broken bulb. Then, I mopped the floors and scrubbed the carpets. I couldn't get the spatters of blood out entirely, but like I'd already concluded: Grace probably wasn't coming back anyways.

That all-knowing voice in the depths of my head whispered: *You're going to be trapped here forever, Macy. Turning off lights, chasing rabbits, and following footprints into the pitch-dark woods.*

Somehow, I almost didn't mind.

Yes, I still felt miserable, but for the first time in my life, it felt like I had direction, like I was actually contributing to something. Protecting humanity, protecting my little sister. I continued bargaining with my plight, continued trying to "look at the positives." I had a roof over my head. A roof without the ever-looming threat of eviction. And maybe, when I got a handle on these Rites, maybe I could convince Jemma to live here too?

I imagined my sister scoffing, repeating her earlier refrain: *I wouldn't take a million bucks to step within a fifteen-mile radius of that house.*

Still, I kept trying to look at the glass half full. Kept telling myself things really weren't that bad, even though everything was completely and totally fucked. I'd likely go back to feeling horrified and hopeless when the shock wore off, but for now . . .

I finished cleaning around half past five. My stomach grumbled. I hadn't eaten anything all day. Come to think of it, I'd barely eaten anything the day before too. In times of crisis, basic self-care often fell to the wayside. In the months after Dad went, I constantly had to remind myself to shower, to sleep, to eat. I cracked open the fridge—still empty. I popped open the freezer above—a few ice trays, frozen blueberries, and, wedged into the back corner: a box of Eggo waffles.

Grace didn't have any syrup. The waffles were freezer burnt and tasted like cardboard, but that was all just fine.

Around the time I finished my waffles, the rotary phone started ringing. I rose from my chair, crossed the living room, and stepped into the foyer. I brought the phone to my ear. "Hello?" I said, holding the pen over a notepad I'd found while cleaning.

"It's Macy, right?" This time it was the voice of an old woman. A soft-spoken voice with a hint of Southern drawl that reminded me a little bit of my late grandma. In the background, the sound of children playing rang out, laughter, a barking dog. "How're you holding up?" the old woman asked.

"Been better . . ."

"Sorry to hear that," she said, seemingly sincere. "You're doing important work though, Macy."

"Who are you?" I asked. "Why do you call here?"

The old woman exhaled a long sigh, "Because it's the only thing we—"

A flurry of tiny stomping footsteps rushed by, children laughing as the dog continued barking. The old woman turned from the phone, yelling something about the dog not being allowed in the kitchen. She chuckled to herself and turned back. "Sorry, the grandkids are over."

"What do I do now?"

"Today? You just need to fix the mower and mow the lawn, that's it. There's no rush, just get it done by tomorrow—"

Another flurry of stomping footprints rippled by, more barking. The old woman gave an exasperated groan. "I have to go," she said, "but thanks for everything you're doing."

CLICK.

I kept the phone to my ear for a few good seconds, then set it back down on its base. I started over to the patio door, and stared out across the unkempt lawn. I released a tired sigh, feeling little more than nothing. "All right."

4
MAINTENANCE LANDSCAPING

The lawn mower repair was simple enough, broken drive belt and a dirty spark plug. They had spares for both, stowed away in a steel cabinet. As I worked, the smell of stale grass clippings and motor oil stirred up old memories, memories I normally would've tried to ignore, but I let them stay and soon enough didn't even mind their company all that much.

With the mower ready to go, I flipped it over and hoisted it off the workbench. I grabbed a yellow jerry can from the backyard shed, gave it a sniff to make sure it was actually diesel, and filled the tank. I pushed the mower onto the unkempt lawn. I pressed the prime bulb five times and pulled back on the cord. The DeWalt roared to life, vibrations humming against my palms. I set to mowing the lawn.

The blades were dull, and the grass was so overgrown it took four passes at different wheel heights to get it all done. As I worked, more old memories surfaced, but again, I didn't mind so much. Despite everything, I still felt oddly calm.

Don't you worry, Macy, the shock will wear off soon, just you wait.

I finished mowing the lawn a little before sunset. I stowed the mower back in the garage and wandered inside. I lay on the beige couch, using the armrest as a pillow, staring into blank space. I don't know how long I lay there before I pulled out my phone and started scrolling through old photos. Photos of Jemma, myself, and Dad. The same photos I'd almost deleted years ago.

I scrolled through album after album, photos from the Enchanted Forest, photos from soccer practice, camping trips, photos of Dad teaching us how to make a campfire, Dad mowing lawns and pruning hedges, Dad building us a backyard swing set. Dad pasting the Mullins Mowing logo to the side of his truck . . .

I put away my phone and continued staring blankly into empty space. I looked to the wall, the crooked picture frames. I looked to a green rug below, spatters of blood still faintly visible even after all the scrubbing. I rolled onto my back and stared at the ceiling. A knot welled up in my throat—I shoved it down. I shut my eyes, and . . . saw Dad with younger Jemma up on his shoulders. Saw Dad catching a spider with a cup and letting it outside. Saw Dad laughing and smiling. The imagery dissolved into darkness. Into nothing. The knot in my throat welled up again, and this time I finally just let myself cry. Not tears of rage, not tears of bitter self-hatred, just sadness. Painful, but cathartic—disinfectant to a wound that had been open for the last three years.

♦

It was dark out by the time I finished crying. I opened my eyes, staring up at the ceiling. Bluish-gray moonlight and tree branch shadows. Something shifted in the corner of my vision. I turned my head. Across the living room, sitting atop the green rug, was a white rabbit with pale blue eyes. I breathed out my nose. I'd almost expected it. *Walk in the rain.* Slowly, I sat up, swung my feet off the couch, and readied myself for another chase, but . . .

The rabbit hop, hop, hopped toward me. It nuzzled between my feet, looked up, and blinked, as if asking me to reach down and scratch it behind the ears. I took a deep breath. Exhaled. I leaned forward, scooped up the rabbit with both hands, and held it close. It was docile in my cradling grip, soft and warm against my arms. I rose from the couch, scratching the rabbit gently behind the ears, whispering sweet little nothings as I walked through the living room, across the kitchen, and toward the fireplace.

5
COMPANY

If you fail to burn the first rabbit: You can no longer catch rabbits and let them outside, you must burn each and every one within five minutes of sighting.

◆

I kneeled at the fireplace, working steady but quick. My phone lay face up on the hardwood, a timer counting down on its screen:

Four minutes seven seconds left.

I'd started with the kindling, balling up sheets of newspaper beneath a crooked pyramid of dry sticks. The white rabbit was watching me from a wire cage I'd dug out of the storage closet. Its pale blue eyes were filled with mild curiosity: What is this human up to?

It's not real, I told myself. *It's not real.*

I grabbed the lime-green wand lighter from the wooden tray. I toggled the safety switch and pulled the trigger, *click*—a dim splash of sparks sputtered from the nozzle, but the flame didn't catch. *Click*—nothing. *Breathe, Macy. Breathe. Click*—nothing. *Click*—nothing. *Stay calm. Focus. Click, click, click*—nothing, nothing, nothing. "Mother. FUCKER." I hurled it across the room. *Breathe, focus, think.* I flew into the foyer, dug into the pocket of my Dad's parachute jacket, and fished out the Uber Driver's "Live Free or Die Trying" lighter. I marched back into the living room, and kneeled at the fire. *Two minutes and thirty-three seconds left.*

I lit the paper and blew on the flames, coaxing the fire to life.

The white rabbit tilted its head, and blinked. It seemed to sense something was wrong, but it couldn't quite figure out what. I looked away, and felt the rabbit's stare, drilling into the back of my skull. The kindling crackled as the swelling fire licked against the black steel above. I set the logs in next, one on either side of the pyramid. The flames spread slow, hissing cracks growing louder.

I held the door open a sliver, letting air gust in to fuel the blaze. Soon enough, the fire was roaring.

One minute and twelve seconds left.

I looked back to the rabbit. Now, its eyes were wide with a terribly expressive fear.

It's not real, Macy. It's not real.

I unlocked the cage and snagged up the rabbit. It trembled beneath my grip. I stroked its ears, whispering more sweet nothings. "It's okay, we're okay." The rabbit calmed, its trembling turned to slow breathing.

Forty seconds left.

I used my elbow to angle the door fully open. A blast of heat spilled out, fanning against my arms, my legs. As I brought the rabbit closer to the billowing flames, it started to kick and squirm. Its overgrown claws sliced my skin, left behind burning cuts—I tightened my grip, raising the rabbit to the fire, closer, when—

BZZ . . .

My phone buzzed angrily against the hardwood:

JEMMA CALLING

The rabbit twisted free, leapt from my arms, blurred across the living room, careened through the kitchen, and vanished into the back hall. Unthinking, I scooped up my phone and dashed after the rabbit. My legs carried me with determined speed. At the end of the hallway, I slid around the corner—the basement door was half-ajar, the rabbit's claws click-clacking against the vinyl stairs. I strode forward, swung the door fully open, and froze. Another rush of flashbacks from last night shuddered through me: more stabbing, slashing, splattering blood . . .

My phone buzzed again.

TIMER COMPLETE

My hand slipped from the doorknob and dangled at my side. I took a slow backward step, that sickening sense of failure falling over me yet again, like I'd done something morally abhorrent, something vile and contaminated. But this time, the feeling was quickly dethroned by an even worse realization: If last night was the result of failing to catch a *brown* rabbit, what would be in store for me now—

My phone started buzzing once more.

JEMMA CALLING

I turned from the basement, carried myself down the hall, and, barely able to think, pressed ACCEPT.

"Yo," said Jemma.

"Hey . . . how's it going?" I asked. *Keep up appearances Macy, make sure your sister doesn't come up here.*

"I got the job!" Jemma said.

"Y-yeah?" My voice was shaky, the crushing sense of impending doom only growing heavier—horrific visions rattling around my head like a dead rat in a plastic bottle. And I didn't even know what my sister was talking about—got the job? What job?

"Interview went surprisingly well," Jemma continued, her words blurring into a warbled mess. She was saying something about the first shift being tomorrow. I must have replied, because Jemma said, "What? What does that even mean? Are you okay?"

I stumbled into the kitchen, grabbing the counter for balance. My stomach dropped, like a trapdoor had opened beneath it. *A devastating setback. A devastating setback. A devastating*—"I'm good," I said, "I'm g-good. I'm just tired, I just—" My own stammering voice echoed back at me through the speaker, blathering gibberish. My stomach lurched, half-digested Eggos threatening to lunge up my throat. I barely kept them down.

"Macy," said Jemma, "did you even hear what—" Her words muddied into another warbled mess.

I slowed my breathing. *In through the nose, out through the mouth.* "I just, stomachache," I said. "Bad waffles."

"Bad waffles?" Jemma paused. "Do I . . . do I need to come up there, or like, call somebody?" Jemma sounded scared now. She could tell I was lying. "Macy?"

"No, no, it's okay." The prospect of my sister getting pulled into this clusterfuck snapped me out of the doom spiral. I stood up straight, cleared my throat. "Everything's good, don't worry about—"

Behind me, across the living room, around the foyer corner, three hollow knocks echoed at the front door. I lowered the phone and peered back over my shoulder. Silence. A silence so long, it made me question if I'd even heard anything to begin with. I brought the phone back to my ear—

"Macy?" said Jemma. "Can you hear me?"

"Yeah, I j-just—"

Three more knocks rang out, louder, more insistent, this time followed by a muffled voice. "Hello?"

Hide.

Phone still in hand, I started for the back hallway. The voice spoke out again, louder, clearer. It sounded like a middle-aged man. "Anybody home?" More knocking. "Hello?"

I froze.

A swarm of grim dread scaled up my back. It wasn't *him*. It couldn't be *him*.

"MACY." Jemma's voice crackled through the speaker. I brought the phone to my ear. "Who's there?" she asked.

"I . . . I don't know . . ." I whispered.

More hollow knocks echoed. Knuckles against glass. I swallowed a lump in my throat and took one mindless step toward the foyer.

"Macy," Jemma spoke through her teeth, "if somebody's there, you need to hide—"

"It sounded like—"

"I know, but it's not him, even if it is, it's not. You need to hide."

More knocking at the front door. "Hello? My truck broke down, need to borrow a phone." Every syllable made the knot between my lungs swell, made that corkscrew twist wrench tighter, tighter, tighter and—before I realized it, my legs were carrying me across the living room, toward the foyer. A slow but inevitable stride.

"Macy," Jemma hissed, "HIDE. Don't let him see you—"

Stuck in a horrible trance, I ended the call and slipped away my phone. My legs kept moving without my brain's permission, kept bringing me closer and closer to the foyer. *Macy*, I thought, *what are you doing? You're walking the wrong way. Don't be fucking stupid, HIDE. HIDE. HIDE—*

At the last second, just before I was about to step around the corner, I came to my senses and lurched to a stop. I pressed my back up against the wall, clenched my eyes shut, and exhaled a painful, stuttering breath.

What was I doing? Every part of my being wanted to glance around that corner, and I didn't even know why. Just follow the Rites. Hide. Wait it out. I drew in another breath, exhaled, and—with renewed determination, started to push off the wall, but—

The photo of the Windfall Inlet. From this vantage point, reflected in its glass, I could see the Visitor at the door, transposed over the stormy clouds: a hazy, almost black-and-white silhouette. Tall and broad. I focused my vision, only to confirm what I already feared, already knew:

The Visitor at the door was the spitting image of my father, down to every last detail. He looked the exact same as the night he'd stood up in the middle of watching *Back to the Future*, strode to the front door, and said, "I'll be back in an hour, maybe two." He even wore the same clothes: grass-stained work boots, worn-out jeans, and a Fleetwood Mac T-shirt.

Not only was he the spitting image, but he moved, and breathed, and somehow existed just like Dad did. As he peered through the door's floor-to-ceiling glass panel, he smiled patiently through his thick beard. His expression was filled with the exact same spark of gentle kindness it always had. A spark that used to make me feel so safe, but now, seeing it here, filled me with unimaginable terror. Like a bloated cyst had burst inside my stomach, unleashing a mass of wriggling maggots, eating me from the inside out.

The Visitor who looked exactly like Dad tried knocking again, squinting through the glass, and then . . .

He looked right at me.

PART V

REDUNDANCY

BLUE

I used to think everyone else felt as miserable as I did—that it was normal to wake up each morning and think: Shit, again? *I was fourteen years old when I first considered that maybe, just maybe, I was "depressed."*

Depressed.

The word made me feel pathetic, like a party animal balloon eternally leaking air, hssssss. Soon I would be little more than a shred of rubbery plastic, wrinkly and deflated on the ground. Sweep me up and throw me in the trash.

I was "depressed" long before Dad went. Sometimes I forget that. Sometimes I tell myself everything was perfect and happy when Dad was still alive. Tell myself that everything would be perfect again if only he were back.

But that's not true.

Yes, things would be better, but Dad or no Dad, negativity lives in my bones. Sits perched on my shoulders like two deadbeat angels, dreary and day-drunk, mumbling into my ears: Just stay in bed, Macy. Stay in bed because what's the point of doing anything anymore. Stay in bed until you fall back asleep and the sun sets all over again.

Dad's death only gave those voices more ammo. Made those voices angry and bitter. Made those voices tell me the world might just be a better place without me in it.

Get yourself together, *I used to think,* just stop being sad. Stop being weak. You can fight this off.

I tried lots of things. Running. Journaling. Positive thinking. None of it worked. I couldn't afford counseling or prescriptions, so I'd scour online forums for advice, and come across dull mottos like:

"Everything happens for a reason."

"God never gives you more than you can handle."

"Suicide is just a permanent solution to a temporary problem."

I always sensed a hint of smugness behind these little platitudes, like the person typing them had it all figured out. "Just try to look at the good in life. After all, things could always be worse." Gee thanks, that sure cheers me up.

I never went to Dad for help with my depression, and I couldn't even say why. He was always a good listener. Maybe I worried about adding to his stress. He had so much on his plate as it was, lost clients, ever-rising bills, and all the other banal necessities of life.

I've thought a lot about the things I would've said had I known that I'd never see him again.

"I just wish I could've said one more thing."

I'd heard that line so many times before in books and movies. And I always assumed it was one of those clichés that existed for good reason. But until I lost Dad, it never truly resonated with me. Sure, I always understood the sentiment. Of course I'd want to have one last moment with somebody before they left forever. But it's one thing to understand something, and it's another thing to feel that empty pit in your gut, that screaming wall of nothing, nothing, nothing. That irreversible stab wound of permanent loss, like a physical part of you, a vital organ, was ripped away and burnt to ash and hurled into the sea. A complete and total annihilation of someone so close, you knew the exact sound of their footsteps, knew exactly what kind of goofy little jokes made them laugh, knew what made them smile, what made them proud.

"I just wish I could've said one more thing. Sat down and talked with him one last time."

I've run that scenario in my head again and again and again. I've pretended Dad didn't drown in a river, pretended he got sick instead. I've envisioned sitting next to him at his deathbed, holding his hand close against the side of my face, listening to his breath. But the funny thing is, every time I've met Dad in my thoughts or in my dreams—every time I've had the chance to tell him one last thing before he fades off into nothing . . .

I never know what to say.

1
HAZEL

Only open the "IN CASE OF EMERGENCY" envelope when you feel like there's no other choice. Listen to your gut. If the time comes, you will know.

◆

"M-Macy," the Visitor who looked exactly like Dad stammered. "W-what are you doing here?" He sounded even more bewildered than I felt. His hands shot to the doorknob—a strange, spasmodic movement, so sudden it almost looked involuntary. He pushed, pulled, but the door held strong. Again, he looked at me in the picture frame's reflection. "Macy," his voice cracked, on the verge of tears, "you have to run."

My hands clasped over my mouth, holding back a stuttering sob. The Visitor, jostling the door, kept pleading, "Macy, this isn't me—you have to hide." But despite his pleas, he kept trying to break inside—his words begging me to leave, but his hands trying to force their way through the door.

I pried myself away from the foyer and stumbled into the living room. My vision tunneled, the entire house seeming to shrink. I steadied myself against a wall. *Breathe, Macy, breathe.* I wanted to scream, to puke my guts out, to stop existing altogether, when—outside, muffled footsteps trudged.

The Visitor was searching for another way in.

My eyes darted to the patio door: unlocked.

He, *it*, was already on the way there, determined, brisk. *It* marched parallel to the windows, but its head was turned at a sharp angle, unblinking eyes locked onto mine as it strode forward. I scrambled over, and just as the Visitor grasped the handle—I leapt, shot out an arm, twisted the lock shut.

Our gaze met, and I finally processed the color of its eyes. They weren't hazel like Dad's, like Jemma's—they were that cold blue, so pale they were almost white. As we stared at each other, my breathing stopped—a strange, soundless moment filled the room. "Macy, I . . ." Fear creased in the lines of its face. Its eyes started to water. "Macy, I don't . . . I don't know how I got here . . ."

What if this really was Dad? What if he had been revived from the dead, brought here against his will?

His eyes kept watering, but his grip on the door handle tightened. A tendon in his neck twitched.

It's not him.

I snapped out of my stupor and took a backward step.

It's not Dad.

Hide.

Follow the Rites.

Without conscious thought, I turned, snatched the third and final envelope from the wooden tray, tore it open. It said only one word:

BASEMENT

THWUMP.

The Visitor rammed its shoulder against the patio door, tears trailing down its face.

THWUMP.

The glass wobbled in its frame, a brittle, rattling sound. The Visitor backed up and threw all its weight forward—thin cracks splintered around the edges. "Macy," it wept, "RUN."

I stuffed the letter into my pocket, fled into the back hallway—past the study, past the storage room. I slid around the last corner, pushed off the wall, and heaved straight toward the basement. I slammed the door shut behind me, bracing my back against it.

My heart raced. I inhaled, exhaled. In through the nose, out through the mouth. I couldn't stop shaking—an uncontrollable, jittery quiver. All the while, the Visitor, distant and muffled, rammed into the patio door, again and again.

THWUMP. THWUMP. THWUMP.

I tried the nearest light switch—nothing. I fumbled out my phone, only for it to slip from my trembling hands, and clatter down into the darkness below. *Stupid fucking idiot.* I descended, too fast, my foot met thin air where it should've met a step. I tumbled forward, the world spinning until I slammed into cold concrete, a crumpled heap. My bones ached. I pushed up to my hands and knees.

Off in the distant black: a thin red line hovered. I narrowed my eyes—it was the crack of a closed door, red light glowing from beneath.

Upstairs, a thundering crash—heavy footsteps boomed. The Visitor was inside, opening doors, overturning furniture—searching. Hunting.

That thin red line started glowing brighter, reflecting off the concrete like the moon over a frozen lake. A spreading glare that exposed the emaciated body, still lying where I'd left it the night before—a contorted silhouette surrounded by a black circle of dried blood and dead maggots.

I rose to my feet, caught in a trance. I carried myself forward, step by step, toward the thin red line. A dreadful magnetism possessed my every movement, as if some unseen force was pulling me closer. Moth to a flame. The Visitor continued hunting upstairs, stomping around, rummaging, but that all sounded so far away now, so meaningless. I reached a bone-white door, wrapped my hand around a cold brass knob, and—

With my sanity teetering on the edge of a cliff, I turned the knob, pushed open the door, and stepped into a windowless room. Red light drenched every surface here, casting over the concrete floor, the concrete walls, the exposed insulation of the ceiling. In the room's dead center, sitting atop a metallic pushcart—the VCR and the old TV. Its screen was solid red, flooding the space with its hellish glow.

I shut the door behind me and locked it. I turned to face the TV, and shakily pulled the letter from my pocket—now it was covered, front to back, in the same word, again and again:

WATCH WATCH WATCH WATCH WATCH

The VCR whirred to life with a dull CLICK—and an ominous tone began to rise. The tape had begun playing on its own. I stood rigid, transfixed.

I had no choice but to watch.

2
IN CASE OF EMERGENCY

The ominous tone continued to rise.

The red screen turned solid blue. Then back to red. Then blue. Red. Blue. Red. Blue. Faster, faster, the colors blurring into a pinkish-purple smear—the tone rising higher and higher without resolve.

Darkness. Silence. And then, the black screen cut to—

Rocky cliffs, crooked hemlocks, gray skies: the Windfall Inlet. Rumbling waves crashed against jagged rock, wind howled, seagulls cawed. The image held for about five seconds, and just as a golden-white sun began to crest over a distant horizon, the screen cut to black.

Silence.

Then, a camcorder shot of the foyer. The camera lay on the side table, a slanted angle. David Carnswel stood hunched over the table, eyes wide with fear. He wore an olive-green rain poncho, spattered with mud, and the glossy white phone was tucked between his ear and collarbone. He listened to someone on the other end, wildly scribbling away into a leather-bound notebook.

The footage cut to a jittery close-up of David hiding in a dark room. He was holding the camera, shaking. "If you're watching this," he spoke in hushed tones, voice quivering, on the verge of tears, "it m-means a Visitor has taken the form of someone you l-lost." He looked down, reading something off-camera. "This is a consequence of your failure to burn the white rabbit alive . . ." He clenched his eyes shut, a tear trailed down his face and slipped into the corner of his mouth. He opened his eyes, continued reading, "You can try to hide, but if the Visitor finds you, you have to . . ." He breathed in deep, exhaled a stuttering sob. "You have to kill it."

He kept reading, "If you survive until the morning, the light, the foyer light will turn on—switch it off within three minutes to prevent a r-red sun from rising—"

David lowered the camera—an upside-down view of metal shelves, cleaning supplies, spare light bulbs. The storage room. The camera swished back up to David's face. He whispered, "The Visitor w-will do everything it can to make you hesitate, don't let it fool—"

"Dad?" the muffled voice of a young man called out. "Where are you?"

Dread flooded into every corner of David's face. He shut his eyes and started whispering a strange and desperate prayer: "For you protect those who cannot protect themselves. And you were there when they buried the sun, you drowned the deserts, and led us to the—"

He fell silent, clasping a hand over his mouth. And then, beyond all explanation, all reason, the footage cut to—

A shot of younger me, my sister, and Dad. Our childhood garage. It was dark, the only source of light a workbench lamp. Overhead glow, soft and warm. Our backs were turned, silhouetted. Dad was hunched over the workbench, tinkering with a detached lawn mower engine. To his left stood Jemma, who looked to be about seven or eight, and to his right stood me, around twelve years old.

The scene was oddly cinematic, well composed. And the frame pushed ever forward, so slow the movement was almost imperceptible. It felt less like camera footage, and more like peering through the eyes of some timeless being. Peering into something forged from bygone memories and half-forgotten dreams.

Jemma pointed to the lawn mower engine. "What's that part?" she asked.

"The muffler," said Dad.

"What's it do?"

"Helps reduce the sound," he replied.

Jemma considered this, then said, "It *muffles* the sound."

"Yep."

"But." She tilted her head. "It's still pretty loud."

Dad nodded. "Just imagine how loud it'd be without it." He looked to his right, down at twelve-year-old me. "Macy," he said, "can you grab me the uh"—he glanced back at the engine—"quarter-inch socket head."

Young Macy, with a dutiful nod, turned away and began rifling through a toolbox. She retrieved the quarter-inch piece. Dad took it, and went back to fixing the motor. My younger sister and I both stepped closer, watching him work, fascinated. As the frame pushed ever near, Jemma rested her head against Dad's arm, and another high-pitched tone started to rise. The footage cut to—

An underwater space, murky and gray. A vicious current whipped dirt and debris from left to right. All the while, like nails on a chalkboard, that dissonant tone continued to rise, growing louder, louder. The frame kept slowly pushing forward. In the distance, a hazy and familiar shape began to form.

A pickup truck . . . white Ford Ranger. Or at least, it used to be white—now, most of the paint was rusted away. Despite the years of corrosion, the Mullins Mowing logo was still visible. Dad's cartoon face—peeling and flecking like cracked mud in a desert—still smiling that lopsided smile, still giving that signature thumbs-up. And then, the screen cut back to solid RED.

3
REUNION

I stared blankly at the red screen, paralyzed by what I'd just watched. The tone continued rising, so loud I could barely think—

A heavy THWUMP filled the room.

I spun around.

THWUMP.

The white door rattled in its frame, the Visitor ramming against it from the other side, over and over. It wouldn't hold long.

Survive.

Follow the Rites.

I scanned the room, searching for something to defend myself with, but aside from the TV and the VCR—

The VCR.

I bolted over, and yanked it off the cart. The power cord ripped out with a burst of sparks, but the TV screen remained solid red, and the tone continued growing louder, louder, drowning out all other sound. I backed into a corner next to the door and raised the VCR, ready to strike.

It's not Dad, it's not Dad, it's not Dad—

The Visitor kept ramming into the door, each impact heavier than the last, until—everything happened at once: the door burst open—a shadowy figure staggered in—I leapt, swung—a brittle THUNK echoed through the room—the figure stumbled forward, caught its balance on the cart, turned to look at me, but it wasn't Dad . . .

Jemma faced me. Her jaw lowered, and she tried to say something, only for a short breath to escape. She lifted an arm and pressed a trembling palm against her temple. A thin line of crimson red trailed out from beneath her palm, dripping onto the floor.

I looked to my hands, the VCR, its metal frame warped and smeared with red. I looked at her eyes, expecting to see that same pale blue, but the TV glow reflected off her glasses—solid red circles concealing her eyes from view. *The Visitor will do everything it can to make you hesitate.* I gritted my teeth, stepped forward, readying to strike again, but . . .

The *Visitor* staggered backward and, in a single timeless second, fell. A stiff, teetering lurch. The base of its skull met the concrete with a sickening CRACK.

Silence.

Even the rising tone had stopped.

I stepped closer, peering down. Jemma, no, not Jemma, the *Visitor* lay on its back, neck turned at a strange angle, fingers curled and twitching. Its chest rose and fell with shuddery breaths. Beneath its head, a pool of blood formed, spreading quick, claiming the concrete in all directions. I still couldn't see the color of her eyes.

It's not her.

The Visitor's chest rose once more, fell, rose, then stopped moving altogether. Motionless. I waited for the breathing to continue, but the Visitor only lay there, stiller than a porcelain doll, framed by the ever-growing circle of blood. Blood that pooled around the toes of my sneakers.

It's not her, it's not Jemma, it's not—

My protective instinct took over—I tossed the VCR, rushed to her side, dropped to my knees, and tore away the glasses . . .

Pinprick beads of sweat popped onto my brow, cold and biting. Blood pounded into my temples, a booming thrum, thrum, thrum. Growing louder, louder.

The Visitor's eyes were not a pale blue.

They were hazel.

Just like Dad's.

Just like—

It's not Jemma.

I grabbed her by the shoulders and squeezed. "Jem?" Nothing. I checked her breath. Nothing. "Jem." Her pulse. Nothing. Nothing. Nothing. I shook her. "Jemma, it's not . . . Jem . . . this isn't . . ."

It's NOT Jemma. It's NOT Jemma. It's NOT Jemma—

Her hazel eyes stared blankly up at the ceiling, unblinking and lifeless.

A devastating setback . . .

That ever-present tightness between my lungs rose with a vengeance, twisting and bloating like a carnival balloon. My rib cage swelled, threatened to snap, shatter into a thousand pieces. It's just another trick, another fucked-up twist of the knife. It's only—

A devastating setback. A devastating setback. A devastating—

I disassociated. Abandoned my body, drifted back from the scene as if it were happening to someone else. Happening to a carbon copy Macy.

I watched myself try CPR. Chest compressions. Watched myself try again and again. Even when my sister's blood reached the walls and her skin turned cold, I kept trying to save her, again and again and again and again and . . .

It's not Jemma.

I pushed off my knees to stand, repeating the mantra over and over. *It's not Jemma . . . It's not Jemma . . . It's not Jemma . . .* I stepped out into the basement hall, and pulled the door shut behind—as if somehow that thin, fragile barrier might separate me from the horrors within. Then, with the distant glow of the light upstairs to guide me, I made my way forward. One foot after the other.

It's not Jemma . . . It's not Jemma . . . It's not Jemma . . .

But as I reached the bottom of the stairs, my foot crunched against something. The brittle sound pulled me back into my body.

I looked down. A rectangle of light. My phone. Slowly, I leaned forward, and picked it up. Seventeen missed calls. Nine voicemails. All from Jemma. My hand shaking, I held the phone to my ear, and listened. "Macy?" the first message began. "Are you all right? Traffic's fucked, but I'm on my way." The next message, "MACY! Whatever you heard at the door, I heard it too. You need to get out of there, NOW!"

It's not Jemma.

I looked over my shoulder. That thin red line was still glowing in the distant dark. My fingers tapped the screen, called Jemma's number. In my ear, a single tone and then . . .

At the end of the narrow hallway, behind the bone-white door, Jemma's ringtone chimed. It rang out until . . . her prerecorded voice played in my ear: "Hey hey, it's Jem, can't get to the phone right now, too busy doing something cool. Don't leave a message, just text me like a normal person."

It's not Jemma.

This was all the house, it was breaking its own rules, tormenting me, driving me into unimaginable misery. I tucked away my phone, and wandered upstairs.

It wasn't Jemma . . . It wasn't Jemma . . . It wasn't Jemma . . .

4
GOOD WEATHER

If you survive until the morning, the foyer light will turn on—switch it off within three minutes to prevent a red sun from rising.

◆

It was still dark out when I stepped into the kitchen. But the early morning sky, bluish-black and murky, whispered the faintest hint of sunrise. A whisper too quiet to determine what color that sun might be. I stood there, one hand propped against the kitchen island, the other pressed against my aching forehead. My stream of thoughts was a distant drip feed, sluggish and vague. I turned my head, and looked to the foyer. All the lights were off . . .

I looked to the patio door. Still firmly shut. The glass was cracked, fractured around the edges, but the door had held, confirming what I already knew. *The Visitor never made it inside.* The ache in my forehead turned numb, and a slow wash of empty nothing crawled down my limbs, and bled through the floor, and seeped into the earth.

My gaze flitted to the fridge. The white rabbit was sitting at its base, pink nose twitching. It hopped over to the patio door, then looked at me, tilted its head, and blinked. It seemed to have forgiven my earlier betrayal. I drifted over, and slowed at the door. Out on the patio, my Dad's bootprints, no, the *Visitor's* bootprints led away. Grass-stained bootprints that trailed down the wooden staircase, across the freshly mowed lawn, and off into the shadowy trees. *The Visitor never made it inside.*

A cold draft brushed against the side of my face. I turned to see an open window, white curtains fluttering in a gentle breeze. The bittersweet scent of rotting trees and the Pacific Ocean. My sister's handprint smears were still visible on the glass, and her wet shoeprints led from the window, off toward the back hallway, toward the basement.

t-t-t-t-t-tick-bzzzzzzz.

Behind me, a light stammered on—I looked over my shoulder—the foyer light. My left eye twitched. A tired sigh exhaled out my nostrils. I stayed rooted to the spot, far longer than I should have. Unfeeling, I finally carried myself across the living room, and slowed at the foyer's threshold.

Follow the Rites . . .

My eyes found the light switch—right beside the photo of the Windfall Inlet. I shuffled over, reached out, and . . . with the tips of my fingers grazing the plastic switch, I froze . . .

That voice somewhere deep within my head pleaded—*Just turn off the light, Macy. Just follow the Rites . . . Follow the Rites . . . Follow the Rites . . .*

With each utterance the knot in my chest wrenched tighter, tighter, tighter. My breath grew shallow and—

No.

I was done.

Done with all of this.

I stepped back from the switch. Lowered my arm. And stood there. I looked up to the glowing bulb, incandescent and buzzing. I shut my eyes. Jemma was gone, and I was done. Done with the house, done with Brooksview, done with the Visitors, the Rites, the entire fucking world. Done with everything.

I breathed deep, in through the nose. I exhaled, out through the mouth.

I pulled Dad's parachute jacket off the coatrack, and trudged back through the living room, toward the patio door. For the last time, Jemma's movie night commentary played in my head, but now, instead of sounding angry, she only sounded confused: *Why wouldn't you just turn off the light?*

I put Dad's jacket on, and pushed through the patio door, and walked down the wooden steps. The white rabbit shot past me, hopping alongside the Visitor's grass-stained bootprints. With nothing better to do, I followed. The prints led across the lawn, past the shed, and off into the dark woods.

I kept moving, down the winding trail—left foot forward, right foot forward, left foot, right—until I reached that pale thin rope. The Visitor's bootprints vanished at its boundary, as if he had just snapped out of existence. And the rabbit only made it three hops farther before collapsing onto its side.

I lingered there, the pale thin rope stretched taut before my shins. The rabbit's cold blue eyes remained open, unblinking. Its ears twitched, its back leg convulsed, then it stopped moving. Stopped breathing.

I stepped over the rope. Kept walking, kept placing one foot in front of the other. Soon, the baritone rumble of the ocean hummed in the dirt, hummed in my aching bones. The lookout wasn't much farther. Keep moving.

The trees ahead gave way to that early-morning sky, bluish-black and cloudy. I still couldn't tell what color the rising sun would be, but I didn't need to—I knew exactly what was to come. Humanity was doomed, and I didn't even care.

The path spewed me out onto jagged rock. That semicircular clearing where nothing but lichen and moss could grow. The cliff. The Windfall Bluff. I ventured my way to its edge, and slowed to a standstill, my feet mere inches from the void.

Again, I breathed deep, in through the nose. I exhaled, out through the mouth. In through the nose. Out through the mouth. A salty breeze swept upward, cold spray spitting onto my chin. I stared at the crashing waves and jagged rocks far below. Then, for the first time in years, that ever-present tightness between my lungs dissolved, melted down to a warm, gentle nothing. And just before I was about to shut my eyes, and finally stop teetering—the morning sun crested over the distant horizon, its raw shine beaming through a gap in the dark clouds, but . . .

It wasn't red . . .

My brow furrowed, eyes squinting into the golden-white glare.

My phone started to buzz.

The sun continued rising, those golden-white rays cutting through ragged hemlocks on the far shore.

Why wasn't it red?

My phone kept buzzing, ever insistent.

My hand reached down, and brought it to my ear.

On the other end . . . my sister.

"Macy?" she said.

A swell of wary relief bloomed in my gut. "Jem?"

"Oh my God," she said, "I thought you were—are you okay?" In the background, I could hear the staticky hum of a car engine, or maybe the bus . . .

Jemma was alive.

She'd never made it to the house, and . . .

"Macy?" she prodded.

But I couldn't even think now, let alone speak.

"Are you okay?" Jemma repeated. "Is the Visitor still there?"

I tried to respond, only for a strained voice crack to escape.

"I'm just coming up the last hill," said Jemma. "I called 9-1-1 too, real help is on the way. Just, just hang in there, a little bit longer, stay on the phone, all right—?"

Jemma kept talking, kept trying to comfort me, kept telling me everything was going to be okay, but I was barely listening anymore. Not because of anything my sister had said. Not because that miserable tightness between my lungs had come back. No, I'd stopped listening because the white sun rising over Brooksview Heights had suddenly turned a terrible shade of red.

ACKNOWLEDGMENTS

The Caretaker would not be in your hands without the feedback, hard work, insight, and contributions of so many people. From its earliest inception as an unpublished short, to the novel you just finished reading, countless individuals have been a part of this story's creation.

To start, I want to thank the incredible folks at Simon & Schuster, Atria, and 12:01 Books. I am so fortunate to be working with people who care about these stories as much as I do. Editor Emily Bestler has been a champion of my work from day one. Whether it's catching a major plot hole or splicing in the perfect word, implementing her suggestions is always a no-brainer. And to everyone on the editing and publishing side, I could not be in better hands: Hydia Scott-Riley, Paige Lytle, Shelby Pumphrey, Libby McGuire, Rick Willett, Liz Byer, Wren Watkins, and many more. For the marketing/publicity side, many of whom also worked on my debut novel, I am still in awe at the sheer number of hands you've gotten these books into. Thank you to Maudee Genao, Debbie Norflus, Natasha Kempnich, and everyone else.

The art department—Jimmy Iacobelli, Amanda Hudson, Claire Sullivan, Alexis Minieri, and more—once again knocked it out of the park, from interior design to that beautifully ominous cover. I often find myself flipping through these books and admiring the attention to detail you put into every page.

I am so proud to be represented by Verve. I'm still in shock at the career they've launched me into. A huge thank-you to David Boxerbaum, Adam Levine, Ora Damelin, Ashley Filipek, Kristen Prue, Emma Kapson, Noah Ballard, and the entirety of the Verve family.

And to my manager, Scott Glassgold, the best sounding board and collaborator a new author could hope for. Whether helping me crack a character's arc or pushing me to overcome a writer's-block wall with a single note, you consistently take these stories to the next level. And it is such an honor to be the inaugural title of 12:01 Books. Here's to many more.

A massive, resounding THANK-YOU is owed to everyone who read, gave notes, helped with research, and/or provided edits to this book (either in its novel or short story rendition). Including, but certainly not limited to: Kat Pölkki, Jon Gravelle, Melissa Gross, Nick Bottyan, Charlie Kliewer, Liz Parker. Your input and work goes so far beyond mere feedback. Whether it was physically typing for me after I pinched a nerve in my neck, answering depraved medical questions about Achilles tendons, encouraging me to show instead of tell whenever I could, and/or suggesting ideas and chapter titles far better than anything I had in mind (some of my favorite visuals and character moments in this novel were contributed by these folks). Needless to say, this story would be a shell of itself without the support, collaboration, and guidance from each and every one of you.

And I am so grateful for all my friends and family. My parents, siblings, cousins, aunts, uncles, and grandparents. Thank you for your unconditional love and support, even when you may find the subject matter of these books to be understandably questionable. A special thank-you to my older sister Jessika, who brought the cryptic symbols to life.

ACKNOWLEDGMENTS

Much gratitude to the township of Salem, and the state of Oregon as a whole. I wasn't able to fully crack this story until I found a home for its main character—and Salem became something of a second home to me as I researched and crafted this world. I felt so welcomed by everyone I met there—whether at an impromptu book event organized by the bookstore with a cat (The Book Bin) or a peaceful walk through Minto-Brown Island Park.

To the staff, both past and present, of Denny's on Ryan Drive in Salem: Bobbi, Tina, Phillip, Sheron, Roberto, Javier, Leo, Jeremey, Camilia, Luisa, Julia, Sheryl, Marelyn, Elijah, Dolly, Eliza, Kacie B, Valerie, Shyann, Robert, Adrian, Monica, and everyone else. Thank you for welcoming this reclusive Canadian into your midst, enabling my excessive decaf intake, and preparing my strangely specific food orders.

To the r/NoSleep and r/OldHouseArchive communities of Reddit. Your early support and enthusiasm for these worlds is a constant wind in my sails. I will be thanking you in every book I ever write. (Bonus shoutout to Sandy & Skye's podcast: Inside Old House.)

Thank you to my counselors, Cassandra and Jaime. They have been a steadfast anchor and support through these last few whirlwind years. And I must acknowledge the social safety nets and mental health resources in my country of Canada. Yes, our healthcare system is far from perfect, but I likely would not be here without it. A society that doesn't help those in crisis, is a society doomed to fail.

Last, but not least, thank you, dear reader. To everyone that buys a book, shares it with a friend, leaves a review, posts a YouTube video, and/or DMs me "WHAT THE HELL DID I JUST READ?" It truly means the world.

ABOUT THE AUTHOR

Marcus Kliewer is a writer and stop-motion animator. His debut novel *We Used to Live Here* began life as a serialized short story on Reddit, where it won the Scariest Story of 2021 Award on the NoSleep forum (eighteen million members). Film rights were snapped up by Netflix, and it was acquired for publication even before it had been extended into a full-length novel. *The Caretaker* is his second novel. Marcus Kliewer lives in Vancouver, Canada.